AFTER THE GALAXY

UNSUNG ARMADA

MIRTH PUBLISHING
ST. JOHN'S

SCOTT BARTLETT

UNSUNG ARMADA
© Scott Bartlett 2018

Cover art by: Tom Edwards (tomedwardsdesign.com)

Typography and interior formatting by: Steve Beaulieu (facebook.com/BeaulisticBookServices)

Library and Archives Canada Cataloguing in Publication

Bartlett, Scott

Unsung Armada / Scott Bartlett ; illustrations by Tom Edwards ; typography and interior formatting by Steve Beaulieu.

ISBN 978-1-988380-15-5

This one's for you - the reader.

AMYDON

1

The *Ares* limps out of slipspace and into the Echo Sector, one of the Mid-System sectors.

At least, I imagine her limping. Her antimatter reactor and Becker drive are functioning regularly, but she took a beating in the engagement with the four Broadswords, right before we were captured and brought to Fairfax's destroyer, the *Ekhidnades*. And then she took more damage as the crew traded laserfire with pirates across the landing bay on Xeo.

For my part, I'm emptying my stomach into the reusable barf bag I always keep on hand for slipspace transitions. It's mostly just bile, since I try not to eat for a day before each transition. But somehow, there's always something to be expelled.

"Any waiting ships, Chief Aphrodite?" I ask once the nausea starts to pass.

"Negative, Captain. We're the only ones here."

That surprises me. From the versecasts I've allowed Glory Belflower to send, it wouldn't have been too hard for the brass to figure out I was headed to Echo Sector. That said, I did order her to ease off on them as we drew closer to Echo, and as far as I know, she complied.

It's possible there are more slipstreams connecting my home sector, Andora, to this one, and I suppose the Guard would be hard-pressed to find spare Broadswords to patrol multiple systems.

Still…their absence is both a relief and a worry. What if there's only one connecting slipstream, and the Guard is too occupied with trouble in this sector to leave any ships here to intercept me?

I guess it's also possible they've decided to overlook my multiple breaches of conduct and the chain of command. But somehow, I have my doubts.

As for the *Ares'* condition, it sure felt like she was limping when life support systems decided to fail during the journey here, and I had to climb through multiple emergency access portals in a sealed suit to get it back up and running. Access would have been much easier from her hull, but that wasn't an option while whipping through slipspace at effective superluminal speeds.

Anyway. That crisis got dealt with, but it did nothing about the laser turrets I've lost, or the damage to the hull. At first, I'd assumed that damage was purely superficial, absorbed by the *Ares'* thick layer of armor. But if life support was compromised enough to fail unexpectedly like that, halfway through slipspace, what other systems might give up the ghost without warning?

We need a dry dock, badly. Luckily, according to my datasphere, this system—Axim System— has one.

Had one, anyway. As far as I know, it's been hundreds of years since it's been in operation, so it could prove completely useless to us. Even if the dry dock itself is serviceable, there's no guarantee the parts we need are left lying around, though records say that smaller military craft did once undergo repairs, here.

"Sensors are just picking up the Amydon Shipyards now, sir," says Chief Aphrodite, who is my Operations Officer (OPO) and in charge of both processing and analyzing sensor data. Her real name is Marissa, and she's the estranged mother of my child, but the other crew don't know that. "It just became visible over Euphrates' horizon." Euphrates is the moon the shipyards orbit.

"Acknowledged," I say, and I spend an idle moment wondering where Bacchus Corp hid the servers for this system's Subverse.

But that isn't my concern. Not any more. Right now I'm focused on finding my daughter, Harmony, who's been in Echo Sector for months, provided she followed through on her plan to come here. I need to find her before Rodney Fairfax does, that mechanized asshole. Though I'd settle for finding him first, and icing his metal ass.

"Do the shipyards look intact?" I ask.

"Aye," Marissa says. "Though there's a good chance life support for the sealed sections stopped working long ago. There's no record of anyone starting up a settlement on Amydon since the Fall, so unless some Fallen with mechanical talent ended up there, you may have to keep your suit sealed while on board."

"That's fine. TOPO, fire the antimatter engine until we're at cruising speed, then cut it off. I plan to coast in for the last ten light minutes." No need to trail exotic particles for an observer's polarization sensor to detect.

"Aye," my TOPO (Trajectory Operations Officer) mutters— Moe, my digital double. My original TOPO's betrayal forced me to copy myself, something Moe seems far from forgiving me for. I can hardly blame him, since we share a lifelong mutual distrust of the Subverse, simulations, and anything that pretends to be a meaningful substitute for real life. Now that he finds himself living the life as exactly what he hates…

Well, I'm sure it's the nightmare I imagine it to be. But I need him, so this is how it's going to be for the time being.

An hour of resisting the urge to drum my fingers on the command seat's armrest later, we arrive at the Amydon Shipyards, settling down in one of the station's many dry dock bays.

The shipyards do have two landing bays, located at opposite sides of the station and originally intended to be kept pressurized, so that visiting dignitaries could disembark their ships without pressure suits on. But I've already told Moe not to bother with them. I share Chief Aphrodite's pessimism about anything on this thing still being pressurized.

As I suit up, my crew is still busy with system checks, monitoring the space around us, recording everything for later verse-casting, and so on.

I take a moment to wonder why I'm back to thinking of Marissa as Aphrodite. Maybe it's an unconscious mental defense mechanism. Since I first learned the blond-haired OPO is actually Marissa, I've made very few decisions she approves of.

The crew may not have figured out who she really is, but I'm sure they must be wondering why I spend so much time alone with the beautiful OPO. Possibly, they think we're having an affair, though the idea of loving an upload makes my skin crawl. Let alone how the logistics would shake out. To me, it would amount to little more than the sex sims that so many old pervs back in Brinktown were addicted to.

I will the inner airlock hatch to open, then I step through and wait for it to cycle.

Outside the *Ares*, I find the shipyards' gravity generators still functioning, which isn't too surprising—powered by solar panels preserved by the vacuum of space, there's a decent chance they'll keep working for centuries yet. Right now, the fact they're still working is a blessing and a curse. It means there's no need to walk using magnets, which is good, because that always feels awkward. But it also means I have to climb out of the dry dock bay.

Luckily, my datasphere holds the access codes for the station's various systems. Getting the dry dock's extensible ramps and hydraulic lifters functioning requires only the lowest-level code, the one that would have been given even to temporary contract workers. A minute's work sees me ascending slowly to the station's surface, and thirty seconds of rising brings me flush with the vast, metal vista.

What follows amounts to a long, uneventful stroll past row after darkened row of dry dock bays. There's not a single light on anywhere that I can see, but my night vision compensates for that, magnifying available starlight to improve visibility.

According to my datasphere research, conducted during the final leg of our journey through slipspace, the Amydon Shipyards boast—boasted—seventy-two such bays. In its heyday, they were all in use, almost constantly.

But the yards' founders put them in Axim System because of the metal-rich asteroid belt, and over the centuries, that belt gradually depleted. Being forced to ship the needed materials across interstellar distances chipped away at Amydon's economic viability. Its repair charges crept up, until even local shipowners starting ranging farther for cheaper prices.

Now, just a few dry docks are filled, some with behemoths that tower above everything: old military cruisers, or freighters from the smaller end of the scale.

What a waste. I don't know what forced the masters of these ships to abandon them here, or what became of their crews. Maybe there are Fallen on this station, or were, for a time. Chances are that if anyone remained on this hunk of metal orbiting a barren, atmosphere-free moon, they're all dead now.

Either way, the pockmarked ships that remain would represent a fortune by today's standards, if they weren't as asteroid-abused as they are. As it stands, I doubt any are still spaceworthy.

Coming to the end of the rows, a quick check at my datasphere tells me the station warehouse lies ahead, on the other side of the stock control module.

Before continuing, I open up a channel with the OPO station. "Chief, you have the access codes on hand?"

"Aye."

"Find me the code for entry into the stock control module."

"I've got it, sir," she says after a few seconds. She sends it to me, and I paste it into an access panel embedded in the bulkhead beside an outer airlock hatch.

To my surprise, when the hatch closes behind me, the airlock starts to pressurize. Not only that, but my datasphere flashes a green atmosphere indicator. The air in here is breathable.

"Someone's still aboard this thing," I say over a crew-wide channel. "Asterisk, standby to feed the secondary laser turrets a defensive macro. I want you to personally man the primary turret."

"Yes, Captain." Asterisk is my WSO—Weapon Systems Officer—a callow youth with a thin face bracketed by two chains that droop from his ears to the corners of his mouth. His dependability has proven spotty. But my current standing with the Guard means I'm cut off from requesting a replacement officer, so I'm left to make do with him. Besides, even I'll admit that he's been improving. I'd claim to be a positive influence on the kid, but I'm pretty sure I'd be hard-pressed to find anyone who'd agree that I've ever been a positive influence on anyone.

The inner hatch slides up into its casing, and I stalk through with my Shiva Knight's blaster held high, left hand cupped underneath it. Nothing.

Not yet, anyway. But someone left the lights on in this corridor, and my night vision has faded away.

Another glance at the shipyard's schematic brings a groan. This module is connected to a cafeteria, as well as living spaces for workers. There's a lot of ground to cover, and plenty of places for whoever's living here to hide.

If they're Fallen, there's a chance they don't have full control over the station's sensors and systems, which might mean they don't know I'm here. But I seriously doubt it. For anyone to survive here this long, they'd need almost full control.

The short, empty corridors echo with my footsteps, and I will my datasphere to filter out the sound, the better to hear someone sneaking up on me. Despite the breathable air, I've left my helmet sealed, for full protection against attack. It restricts my field of vision, but my datasphere will warn me the moment it detects a threat.

Like so many times before, trusting my datasphere over my own senses turns out to be the wrong move.

As I enter the cafeteria, part of my vision flashes black, warning me of an attack from above—too late. Someone tackles me, crashing against my upper back. I hit the floor face-first, and my blaster flies from my grasp. My assailant's hands wrap around the neck of my suit from behind.

Twisting violently to the right, I work my left knee between me and my attacker. The movement doesn't result in a clean break, and for a moment there's a confusion of limbs as I struggle to free myself. At last, with a final thrust, I scramble away. As I do, I register the Guardsman's black worn by my assailant.

No time for a peace offering, though—he rushes at me headlong, close-cropped black hair aimed at my midsection.

I pivot, bringing an elbow down on the back of his neck. His arms shoot out to both sides, and as he's sprawling to the deck, I'm heading to where my blaster came to a stop against a table leg. By the time he's rising, I have the weapon trained on him. He raises his hands.

"Unsnap your pistol holster and remove the weapon with your thumb and forefinger, nice and easy," I tell him. "Let it dangle."

He does.

"Drop it," I bark.

The pistol clatters to the floor, and I gesture for him to get his hands back up where they were.

"Now, let's go," I say, motioning with the blaster muzzle toward the corridor I came from. Next to the entrance stands the ancient vending machine, which must have been where he'd perched, waiting for me.

"You're the Guardsman responsible for the Axim Subverse terminal?" I say as we walk. It's barely a question.

"Yes," he says, his voice hoarse from lack of use. Sounds like someone hasn't been spending the recommended daily hour inside conversation sims.

"I'm a Troubleshooter," I say. "Why'd you attack me?"

"You're Joe Pikeman. That birthmark on your face makes it pretty easy to be sure of that—I saw you come through the airlock on my datasphere. Every Guardsman in Echo Sector has orders to apprehend you and notify the brass as soon as they do."

That makes me pause a moment. "Wonderful," I say. "What's your name?"

He doesn't answer.

I shoot the deck near his foot, leaving a neat, smoking crater. "Name," I say, more harshly. "And rank, Guardsman."

"Corporal Bertrand Cohen."

"Now we're making some progress."

Just to be sure, I have him produce his ID coin and hold it up for me to scan. My datasphere paints it green, verifying his identity. It takes more convincing for him to tell me where he sleeps, but eventually he does: inside the stock control module, near where I entered. My guess is that his datasphere notified him of my entry, but he was too far to make it back to his quarters in time. That's good. It means he probably didn't get off a transmission to Gauntlet.

That matters, but it probably doesn't matter much. The brass has obviously been expecting me. They'll probably send someone eventually, so either way, I'm operating on borrowed time.

We retrieve a shipsuit from his quarters, and I make him put it on in the corridor. That done, I march him out through the airlock, across the shipyards, and onto the lift that lowers us to the *Ares'* airlock.

Once inside, I put him in my cabin and secure the hatch to keep him in there.

"I'm sick of giving up my cabin for guests," I complain to my onlooking crew.

2

"We're wasting our time," Marissa says as she ranges ahead, brown eyes on the canopy of stars above, which remain static without an atmosphere to make them twinkle. I know what's on her mind. She's scanning those stars as though in doing so, she might spot Harmony.

"You're supposed to be helping me search," I say. Almost, I tell her she should watch where's she's stepping instead of the sky, but as a digital being it isn't like she's in danger of tripping. "Helping me search is already a flimsy enough excuse for allowing you to leave the *Ares*. The fact you're not even bothering to look for parts isn't helping."

Marissa now has the honor of being the only crewmember I've ever let leave their station, let alone the ship. It started with her insisting on being allowed to roam the ship in the real, and now there's this. She told me in private that she wanted to stretch her legs at the earliest possibility—that remaining on the *Ares* was making her stir crazy, even though she had access to thousands of sims during downtime. And apparently, I'm stupid enough to give in to her.

She makes me feel bad, though. It's not fair: it's not like I could control the circumstances that resulted in Harmony stealing a ship and haring off across the galaxy. But I understand how distraught Marissa is. I miss Harmony, too.

"You're supposed to be helping *me* search, Joe. For our daughter. Remember?"

"That's what I plan to do. But we'd be asking for it by flying deeper into the Mid-Systems without repairing the *Ares* first. I'm telling you, Marissa. The Mid-Systems aren't like the Brink. They'll eat you alive if you're not careful."

"I wonder about that. Food is scarcer here, so how can there be more criminals? They wouldn't survive."

"Oh, they survive. By being more brutal. More vicious. The place is lousy with Fallen, too. They're craftier, here, and they have even fewer qualms about killing strangers on sight, and spitting them for the cookfire."

"It doesn't make sense," she says.

"It does, though. Trust me, I spent years here, training on Gauntlet to be a Troubleshooter. The Mid-Systems pirates even had the balls to attack us there, and they almost got the better of the Guard. Yes, the Brink was always the galaxy's breadbasket. But that just means there were more hydroponics facilities here. After the Fall, the Fallen entrenched themselves right away, and so did the pirates. Plus, there are plenty more Guard stations, with Broadswords crisscrossing the sector all the time. Then you have the automated farms that feed every Guardsman assigned to a terminal—a farm in every system that has a Subverse, and they're actually kept in good repair, unlike the ones in Andora Sector. Best efforts are made to keep them hidden, but given enough time, the Fallen find everything. We've lost plenty of men that way."

I pause, suddenly surprised that Marissa let me say all that. It isn't like her to let me talk uninterrupted for long. She's fallen uncharacteristically quiet.

"What's the matter?" I say.

"Joe…if all that's true, then there's all the more reason to go looking for Harmony *now*. Screw the repairs. We need to risk it. Our daughter could be in danger. It's been months."

Fount damn it. I just finished arguing how dangerous the Mid-Systems are, and now I need to argue the opposite if I'm going to placate Marissa.

I can't do it. Telling the truth isn't easy, and it's gotten me in trouble more times than I can count. But it's still better than the slimy feeling of telling a lie. The last time I lied was before I ever met Marissa—when I was eleven or twelve, and trying to hide the fact that I'd stolen my aunt's money for booze again.

Well, that's not entirely true. I've never hesitated to lie to someone I plan to kill.

"You're right," I say, which brings Marissa to a stop. She faces me, crossing her arms. "She could be in danger. She probably is. But she's also our daughter. She's resourceful, smart…way smarter than she has any right to be, as *my* daughter. I guess she got it from your side. Either way, I know she's all right, Marissa. I know it."

"It's not good enough, Joe."

"I know it isn't. But it's what I have for you."

As we move from bay to bay and I scan each one for usable parts using my datasphere, I keep glancing behind me, expecting to spot a ship approaching, or maybe figures sprinting toward me across the surface. Something about being in the vacuum is bothering me, and I can't quite put my finger on it. The temperature inside my suit seems impossible to get right, today—either I'm sweating or freezing—but it isn't that. It isn't Marissa's incorporeal form wandering the station without a shipsuit, either, though that does add to the effect.

Having found nothing that looks salvageable in any of the dry dock bays, we continue on toward one of the shipyards' four warehouses. I'm not about to say it, but Marissa should hope we find the tools and materials we need here—replacement hull sections, undamaged laser turrets, intact weapon bays, and some constructor bots to help me make the repairs. Anything we find here is free, and the labor will cost us only time.

The alternative will prove much more time-consuming. At one-and-a-half million tokens, the Sterlings' reward for clearing their name was sizable, but it still won't cover the total costs of repairs. Not including market costs of the parts themselves. That means I'll need to have Belflower continue to fundraise from the Subverse via versecasting, something that will almost certainly demand my involvement while exposing us to needless risk.

We find the warehouse depressurized, unlike the section where I found Corporal Cohen. Meteorites have made sure of that, over the centuries. No doubt both Cohen and his predecessors received extensive training in repairing such breaches, but one man can only do so much. The warehouses were let go.

The parts themselves seem undamaged, but twenty minutes of searching turns up nothing we need, outside of some hull sections which, my datasphere informs me after taking measurements, will fit the breaches with minor modifications.

That said, if I have to do the work alone, it will take weeks. Our search turns up not a single constructor bot in the entire warehouse. It's very possible that the last people to flee the Amydon Shipyards took all the bots with them. If that's the case, I'm not sure we can afford to stick around while I complete the repairs myself, fumbling around on the *Ares'* hull with my datasphere guiding my hand.

A transmission from Glory Belflower, my Engineer and resident hacker, seems to confirm that notion: "Captain, I've managed to remotely crack the terminal the corporal was responsible for. It seems he already sent a message via spacescraper to alert any Guardsmen in nearby systems to your presence."

"Has the spacescraper carrying it left Axim System yet?"

"It has. I'm sorry, Captain."

3

Belflower's discovery accelerates our timeline…by a lot.

It would take a Broadsword at least three months to get here from Gauntlet, and that's assuming they left the moment they received the message, which would take three months just to reach them.

But as far as I know, the nearest system by slipspace is a week away, possibly less. A Guard ship could be here in days. Maybe multiple ships.

Or, if Fairfax has access to restricted Guard communications, maybe he'll show up with the *Ekhidnades*, with his burgeoning new military in tow.

I'm letting my imagination go, I realize, but that's the problem with entering unknown territory. Total paranoia becomes not unreasonable.

"We need the exit and entry coords for the nearest system," I say over a two-way channel with Belflower. I'm limiting communication about her revelation to only us—I've even transmitted Marissa back to the *Ares*. It isn't that I'm particularly concerned about worrying the other crewmembers. I'm just not interested in their input. "We need them now. Ideas?"

"You could ask Corporal Cohen for them."

"He wasn't forthcoming about his name. Somehow, I don't think he's going to volunteer the means for my escape."

"You could provide some…extra encouragement for him to volunteer them."

I clamp down on a sigh that's already halfway out. "Asking Cohen is out of the question."

"That's not like you, Captain," Belflower says. "From what I've seen, you'll achieve your goals by any means necessary."

"First of all, you're getting way too familiar," I say through gritted teeth. "Second, you need to understand that Guardsmen don't do to each other what I know you're suggesting. We have a respect for each other that goes beyond the chain of command, even when we find ourselves at odds. You remember our engagement with the four Broadswords, before our visit to Fairfax's destroyer?'

"I do."

"They refrained from compromising our hull integrity, just as I left theirs alone. As for the corporal, he could have killed me. He had the drop on me, but chose instead to try and overpower me. He paid with his freedom. I intend to pay him back in kind, by granting him the respect he's due."

"Very well, sir. And I do apologize for my familiarity."

I don't find the apology convincing, but given my present circumstances, it's about the most I can expect.

"You may be able to extract the slipspace coords from the terminal Corporal Cohen was charged with safeguarding," she says.

"I thought you already hacked it."

"I did, but there were partitions I couldn't break into without physical access. If you follow my instructions, I should be able to get you into them."

"All right, then." Having a plan makes me feel slightly better. I leave the perforated warehouse for the pressurized section that was Corporal Cohen's home.

Back in Andora Sector, as a Troubleshooter assigned there, I had full access to every terminal. Not so, here. The terminal doesn't recognize my credentials, and so we'll need to break in.

But even with Belflower's help, I'm not able to hack the terminal. At least, we gain entry to one partition, but the slipspace coords aren't there, and the second partition requires facial recognition for access.

I call up an image of Cohen from deep inside my datasphere's stores of information and try my best to concentrate, using the Fount that inhabits the air to change my face to look like Cohen. It's one of the ancient Shiva techniques the old knight taught me before abandoning me.

My first two attempts fail, and I draw a deep breath to steady myself. I'm fully aware I should leave off now, compose myself, maybe spend some time meditating before my third attempt. But I'm too impatient, and I try right away. Predictably, I fail.

The entire terminal locks down, and the display informs me that the data it contained is now being purged.

"Fount *damn* it!" I yell, slamming both palms into the machine, rocking it slightly.

It comes back to me, then: I learned about this safeguard while training to be a Troubleshooter. After three unauthorized access attempts, a terminal will purge itself in order to protect the location of its Subverse servers.

After that, I embark on a frenzied search of Cohen's living quarters, tossing bedsheets, flipping over furniture, rummaging through drawers, cabinets, and totes. The idea that he may have scrawled the slip coords somewhere is pretty close to absurd, but I know a few people actually still write down important information. A couple elders back in Brinktown did, and I always felt like I could relate to the impulse. I can understand a distrust of technology.

For a moment, I consider continuing my search through the rest of the pressurized section, but that could take weeks.

Instead, I head for the airlock, turning the problem over in my head as I go. There has to be a way to get the coords from Cohen without applying physical pressure.

Then, just as I'm waiting for the *Ares* to finish its cycle, I've got it.

"I have the location of the Axim Subverse servers," I tell Cohen as I walk through the hatch to my cabin, blaster in hand. My claim is true: the server room's location was in the first partition Belflower and I hacked.

Cohen's sitting at my desk, slumped against the wall. He straightens as I enter, regarding me with a prideful grimace. "And?" he says.

"I have the location. If you give me the slipspace exit and entry coords for the nearest system, I'll leave the servers in peace."

That brings a humorless grin to Cohen's lips. "Are you trying to imply that, if I don't give you the coords, you'll harm the servers?" He shakes his head. "I have more than a name for you, Pikeman. I also know you by reputation. You may have gone rogue, but you had your reasons. The brass understands that, and so do I. You're not the type to turn vandal, especially not when doing so will end billions of lives." He laughs, with as little mirth as his smile contained. "The dossier they sent said you don't lie, except to those you intend to kill. You couldn't even claim to threaten the servers, could you? You just implied it. Still…kind of stretching your principle a bit, aren't you? Wait—you're not going to *kill* me, are you, Pikeman?" He laughs again.

I squint at him, a little dazed. Partly by learning that the brass has this sort of information on me, but mostly by the level of faith in me Cohen's displaying by trusting I won't actually harm the server. I'm not used to that.

"Fount damn it," I say, spinning on my heel and slapping the access panel to close the cabin hatch behind me. Turns out I'm an atrocious interrogator.

I drop into the command seat, eyes on Marissa. "Are there any active spacescrapers in-system?" I ask her.

She consults sensor data, though I get the sense she already knows the answer and is just double checking.

"Negative," she says.

"Just my luck." Of course, attacking a spacescraper the first time, to get the exit coords for the Temperance System, was insane enough. Compounding the risk by attacking another would be… well, twice as insane, I guess.

"Deactivate all crew but the Engineer," I snap.

Belflower blinks at me from her station, the daisy poking from her midnight hair bobbing slightly. As far as I remember, this is the first time I've met with the Engineer privately. Hopefully it'll help temper the crew's suspicions about my multiple private meetings with the OPO.

"I'm at a loss," I tell her. "We appear to be stuck here until a Guard ship shows up."

"Unless you acknowledge the need to use enhanced interrogation techniques on our friend the corporal," Belflower says softly.

"I'm not torturing Cohen, Belflower. End of story." For the second time in ten minutes, my eyes narrow. "How are you so comfortable with the idea? With doing it to anyone, let alone a Guardsman?"

She shrugs, but I file this away for future thought. Something isn't quite right with Belflower. I mean, that isn't news, but still. This is unsettling even from her.

"Sir," she says. "If we're truly at an impasse, why don't we focus on something we *can* affect?"

"Such as?"

"Well, have you been able to locate the necessary materials and constructor bots to effect the *Ares* repairs here on Amydon Station?"

"No. And even if I had, I'm not sure we could afford the time it would take, with Broadswords on the way any day now."

"Then we'll need to increase our capital, so that we can take advantage of the opportunity to pay for repairs the moment it presents itself."

I feel my eyebrows climbing my forehead. "I don't think it's likely to present itself while we're trapped in this system."

"No. But maybe we can hit two balls with one mallet."

My mouth quirks at the bizarre metaphor. Must be a Subverse thing. "Just tell me what you're proposing, Belflower."

"I'm proposing you enter the Subverse, for a first-of-its-kind meetup with your most enthused fans in this system. What other versecasting Guardsman can enter the Subverse while on duty? The event will draw thousands at a minimum, and it may even open the door to learning the slipspace coords."

"Hm." I'm not sure why anyone in the Subverse would know the coords, but then again, that is how we got from Junction System to Visby. And as much as I hate interacting with my "audience," we do need more tokens to cover the repairs. "I guess it's worth a shot. There's not much point in entering physically, though. I doubt the shipyards would be a viable place for a, uh, meetup."

"Actually, in the Subverse, Amydon is an orbital shopping mall. But I agree—it still doesn't strike the right note."

"How long will it take you to hack another account together for me?"

"Already done." A smile creeps across Belflower's face.

"Of course it is," I say, settling back into the command chair. "All right. Let's get it over with."

For a few minutes, nothing happens—just Belflower tapping at her console. Then, she looks up in alarm, and she looks like she's about to say something. Before she can, my view of the bridge is replaced by a box-like room. I'm lying in a bunk crammed into the small space.

What the hell? Something went wrong. Where am I?

A bell rings, and it jogs something in my mind: that's the work bell.

But I don't work here. Do I? Memory is starting to fade, and I can't remember what I'm supposed to be doing right now.

The bell rings again. Right. I have the morning shift today, and I feel like I didn't sleep at all. I'll never get used to the shortened circadian cycle they keep here on the Amydon Shipyards.

Hauling myself out of bed, I pull on the sealed suit that serves as the uniform of every Amydon grunt, check my face in the mirror, then settle my helmet over my head, where it auto-seals with the suit. With that, I force myself to trudge out the door.

4

In the corridors of the pressurized section where I sleep, my coworkers and superiors pass me without comment. Their gazes slide over me—over my closed helmet.

When I started on Amydon, a few of them used to try exchanging meaningless pleasantries with me, but I think I'd rather die than engage in those empty rituals, each one acting as a gong to signal the fundamental hollowness of existence.

Now, they recognize me by my sealed helmet, and they avoid eye contact. No one else on Amydon seals their helmet this soon before reaching the airlock. I do it purely to try to avoid contact with anyone.

"Why do I bother with this shit," I mutter into the helmet. Yes, I'm fed and paid in a galactic currency that has reliably held its value for centuries. But to what end? What am I saving for? What am I advancing toward?

I'm just another rat on his wheel, sprinting for a horizon that will never come. What reward could possibly entice me to continue engaging with such an abyss of a life? Yet I do continue to engage.

Maybe today will be the last day.

I crowd into the airlock with seven other workers, with another twenty or so waiting in the corridor to go through next. Stragglers. I always arrive just on time. The work brings me no joy, but my punctuality ensures I'm subjected to the press of humanity as briefly as possible. There's nothing more repulsive to me than humanity, even humanity that I've sealed myself off from.

Once outside, I make my way to the passenger shuttle I've been working on for the last three days, along with a crew of eight, half of them bots. Something detonates overhead, flaring: a meteorite intercepted by a missile that must have threatened the station. A rare enough sight. I wonder if it's a sign.

"Pikeman," the foreman says with a nod as I approach. As usual, I'm the first of the crew to arrive. Other than the bots. "See if you can get a start on welding shut that fissure on the primary belly thruster." He shakes his head. "Whoever owns this thing, they sure are hard on it."

Wordlessly, I pick up one of the four laser torches lying in a case at the foreman's feet. The bots have built-in laser torches, so only the human workers need to collect their tools every day.

Regulation is the only reason the shipyards keep up the charade of pretending humans still have something meaningful to contribute to any work crew. Here in the Mid-Systems, we're close to the galactic Core, which is also the seat of power. That means every now and then, we get government inspectors sniffing around the station, making sure we aren't participating in the slow but inevitable process of rendering humanity obsolete.

It is inevitable, though. Right after those inspectors leave, human employees find their hours slowly start to dwindle. The owners always claim there isn't enough work to go around, but there's plenty, and everyone knows it. Amydon is booming. They just want to pay humans as little as they can get away with.

Me, I think they're smart. Why bother employing an inferior species? Not that I trust bots as far as I can throw them—that said, I could probably toss them pretty far if the gravity malfunctioned.

Either way, human society is clearly doomed. Soon, it'll be bots working, bots consuming, bots running the show, with humans left in the dustbin of history.

Out on the Brink, even farther from the republic's clutches, companies run even more roughshod over regulation. Yes, they'll see an inspector every year or two, but when was the last time you met a government employee with the dedication to spend years traveling halfway across the galaxy and back, just to make sure humanity's getting paid? Sure, they've tried to station watchdogs out there permanently, but they never last long on the Brink.

I set the laser torch to medium power and start working on the thruster, which is cracked almost in two. A bot pilot wouldn't have made a mistake like that. Even if it wasn't a mistake, but a fault in the ship's construction, then a bot would have recognized it in time to fix it. There's only one reason bots haven't risen to galactic dominance: the auditing software we install them with, which keeps them from augmenting their own intelligence.

Even with the software, though, they're pretty damn intelligent. Intuitive, too. It's unreal.

"Pikeman," the foreman shouts, and my head jerks toward him. "Everything all right?"

I realize I'm standing under the thruster with the laser torch dangling from my hand, just staring at the shipyard deck. I have no idea how long I stopped working for, or when the foreman took notice.

He hops into the bay from the main level, sailing gently down to land beside me, feather-light. We turned this bay's gravity down for the shuttle's external repairs. Fewer injuries. It's one way to compensate for human failings.

"I hope you won't take this the wrong way, Pikeman, but you've been behaving strangely for a few days. I'm giving you a week's leave, starting right now. All right? Maybe see one of the shipyard counselors. If you're going through some stuff, they can help."

The laser torch rises in my grasp, almost of its own accord, lighter in the reduced gravity. What a fine weapon it would make, on the highest setting. Most wouldn't see its potential for that, but I do.

"We're all going through a lot, Pikeman, and there's no shame in admitting that. Everyone's processing what's been going on differently."

I meet his eyes, feeling confused. "What's…been going on?" I repeat.

"Yeah," the foreman says, his eyes suddenly furtive. He glances to his right. "What with the tyrant on the loose. The killings…"

My hand flashes upward, the laser torch coming to rest against the foreman's neck as I switch it to full power.

One blast will puncture his suit, almost certainly dooming him, this far from the airlock. Yes, there's a patch kit nearby, but I just wouldn't let them minister to him. Anyway, there's a good chance the patch kit would be irrelevant—that the blast would kill him outright.

The foreman is trembling. I can see it even through the suit. "Please, Tyrant," he whispers, eyes wide. "*Please…*"

My hand tenses on the torch's trigger. This man will die, and so will others, until someone on this forsaken station manages to stop me.

But before I can kill him, a memory floods my mind. I'm standing over a man whose face I've made a bloody ruin, a Shivan blaster in my hand. A willowy woman with shoulder-length blond hair has thrown herself over him protectively, and so has a combat bot, of all things.

I was going to kill that man. My solution…my answer to his crimes, which have caused such trouble for so many, his wife and daughter included.

But I didn't kill him. Instead, I lowered the blaster.

The memory is strange to me, like someone else lived it. At the same time, I know it's mine. It's both mine and not mine.

I lower the laser torch. "I'm sorry," I say.

With that, the dry dock bay disappears, as does the foreman, and the shipyards themselves. I'm standing on a platform suspended in a dark purple void, connected to nothing. Glory Belflower stands before me, and memory pours back: I was lying in the command seat, about to enter the Subverse to host that stupid meetup, when somehow I entered a completely different life. One where I was a dark, demented man, just like back on Terminus.

"What did you do to me?" I growl, and it's a true growl: the kind a lion would make at the height of its agitation.

"I did nothing," she said. "In fact, I suspect you have a lot more to tell *me* than I do you, Captain. I need you to calm down. You've been gone for a week, and I fear circumstances are spiraling beyond our control."

"A *week?*" I yell, and my voice comes out as a crackling hiss. "How?"

"The sim you just experienced has been looping for that long, again and again. Each time it began, you lost all memory of the previous iterations."

"*You* did this," I say. "You're the one who sent me into the Subverse." I grasp for my blaster, but there's no holster there. There isn't even a uniform, or a normal human leg.

Instead, a blunt limb hits a hard surface. When I look down, I see an onyx, gleaming carapace where my Guardsman uniform should be.

Then, I realize my perspective is all wrong—too low to the ground. I rotate my eyes downward to behold a set of snapping mandibles, and behind me, I see a long, wriggling body extending back several meters.

"*Belflower!*" I shriek, surging toward her.

5

S he vanishes, and when she speaks again, her voice reaches my
—ears? Listening holes?—from behind me.

"Captain Pikeman," she says, her voice stern. "This is very unbecoming behavior, and I can assure you it isn't doing you any good at all."

My antennae rustle as I whip around, posterior section snapping into place behind me. Studying her warily, considering whether there's a point in charging again, I become aware of my breath. Rather, it feels like my entire body is breathing, its whole surface swelling and contracting more or less evenly.

"You're being monitored closely right now, by the Subverse Authority algorithms. If you continue behaving violently, you'll be consigned right back to the underverse where you were just jailed."

The body I'm inhabiting makes me feel disgusting, but part of me has already begun getting used to it. A bigger part of me wants to *roam*—to range out in an unending spiral pattern, seeking sustenance. I don't know what purpose lay in programming an authentic insectile experience, but as far as I can tell, they nailed it. Fount, maybe some people actually get off on this sort of thing.

The neon-green platform we're on resembles a misplaced piece from an unsolvable puzzle. Disconnected from everything, it's like an island hewn from an Escher painting, with staircases and ramps that curve back on each other. Most of them are unwalkable, unless gravity works very differently here.

Other hanging islands dot the deep-purple void as far as the eye can see, of every color of the neon rainbow. Between them fly winged versions of whatever I've become, their bodies twisting and undulating through the air.

I rear upward, my front half leaving the bright-green platform, and Belflower takes a step back. My anatomy doesn't allow me to twist around like this, so I return to the surface and form my body into a semi-circle instead. By twisting my eye stalks upward, I discover I don't have flight.

"Where are my wings?" I ask, somewhat surprised at the real resentment in my voice.

"We're hoping you won't be here long enough to grow them," Belflower says, a bit wryly. "Are you familiar with ancient Christian mythology?"

"Sure," I say. Christianity had the longest run as humanity's most widely practiced religion, but we lost it somewhere along the way as we spread through the stars. The closest thing we have now is the Church of the Fount, which amounts to a worship of our own technology. Go figure.

Belflower looks a little surprised by that—the typical expression worn by people who learn I've read a book. Which says more about them than it does about me, as far as I'm concerned, since a few moments' thought should have told them how much I read. What else is there for a sim-hater to do in slipspace?

"So, heaven, hell? You're familiar with the religion's proposed cosmic system?"

"The Trinity—Father, Son, Holy Ghost. Original sin. Salvation. Communion, depending on the denomination. Death and resurrection."

Belflower nods slowly. "It seems you're well-versed with it. You're acquainted with the concept of purgatory, then?"

"Yes."

She gestures at the void surrounding us. "This is the closest thing the Subverse has to purgatory. And the underverse you occupied for the last week is roughly analogous to hell."

"I only remember being there for a day."

"As I said, it repeated over and over, always ending with you getting gunned down by station security after killing as many as you could with that laser torch. Except on the seventh day. On that day, you displayed marked psychological improvement, which is very rare for those consigned to an underverse. That, combined with a sizable sum paid to Bacchus Corp's Authority algorithm, earned you the right to be here."

I wince—or rather, my mandibles click sharply together. "Paid from our repair fund?"

"Where else?"

"Fount damn it."

"Indeed. Captain, my elevated position on the Subverse's global leaderboard confers a certain status, and I have personal funds I'd be willing to contribute to securing your complete freedom, so that you needn't deplete your funds entirely. I can get you out of this place. But first, I'm going to need you to tell me everything you know about what in the galaxy just happened."

"I'm your superior officer," I snap. I'm ordering you to get me out."

"No."

"You'd violate the chain of command that casually?"

"Not casually. But I have my own interests to look out for, Captain. This is a strange occurrence we have here—unprecedented, to my knowledge. And in certain respects, you've been acting erratically, given what I know about you. For all your... quirks, you're usually fairly consistent. If you're becoming unstable, it could threaten all of us. So I have a right to know."

I stare at her, mandibles clicking softly now, pensively. The gesture is unconscious, but I let it continue, since it seems to fit.

I realize I'd probably do exact what she's doing, if I was in her position. Besides, even if I could invent a lie on the spot, I wouldn't try to feed it to her. It's just not in my DNA. With the giant-insect equivalent of a sigh, I say, "How familiar are you with my past?"

"Not very. The mystery that shrouds you and your origins forms a big part of why we've been able to acquire such a large Subverse following for you."

"Okay. Good." It freaked me out to learn the Guard apparently has such a detailed psychological profile on me, so it's reassuring to hear the general public knows so little.

Still, this conversation has me on edge. What I'm about to tell Belflower will give her leverage over both me and Marissa, and she's shown today that she's not shy about exploiting leverage.

"You know I have a daughter," I say. "And you must know that her mother's been out of the picture for almost her entire life."

"Yes. Marissa Sterling. Daniel Sterling forced her to upload rather than live down the shame of coupling with a man of your social stature. That much comes from my own research—it isn't widely known, so don't worry."

"It wasn't just my social stature," I say. "The Pikeman name been dragged through all the dirt in Brinktown, and that's a lot of dirt. I was born into one of the worst reputations I could have inherited." My antennae twitch. "As a teenager, my father got himself in enough trouble to make me look like lazy. Just one example: he burned down the Sterling Art Center the night before it opened. It was meant to be a place where Brinktowners got together and swapped techniques for creating better sims to sell to uploads—apparently, my father shared my views on the Subverse. The law bots put him away for three years, and when he got out, he was old enough to join the Guard. Training took up three more years, since he ultimately became a Troubleshooter, and he got my mother pregnant four years into his service, while he was on leave. Mom died giving birth to me, and dad split, which everyone had no trouble fitting into his reputation as a deadbeat, even though he apparently claimed he'd joined the Shiva Knighthood and planned to seek out the Crucible. Either way, he left me to be raised by my aunt. Even before I could talk, I was already hated by the most powerful people in Brinktown."

"And you repeated your father's mistake."

"What, having a kid I had no business making? More or less, yeah. I had mine way younger than dad—beat him by ten years, almost exactly. But I took way better care of Harmony than dad did of me. I'm not saying I'm father of the century, or anything, but considering where life put me I'd say I've done pretty well."

"Aside from your daughter disowning you, I suppose, and you having no idea where she is right now."

Anger flashes down my entire length, just underneath my carapace. "She didn't disown me," I snap, resisting the urge to charge Belflower again, try to reach her with my mandibles. "Who asked you, anyway?"

"Sorry. I'm just wondering how this story is supposed to clarify why you ended up in an underverse."

"Sorry to bore you," I say venomously, and a little venom actually drips from my right mandible tip. "I'll speed things up. As I said, Marissa disappeared into the Subverse, keeping in touch by occasional, awkward brainprints which Harmony eventually stopped opening. Marissa never tried to contact me, and I always figured she'd caught her father's disdain for all things Pikeman. But it turns out she actually missed me, and her failure to connect with our daughter almost ate her alive."

"How do you know that?" Belflower asks, tilting her head sideways. The gesture looks almost alien to me—oh, Fount, human body language is already starting to look alien? Did they really need to get this detailed about simulating bug life?

"Because she infiltrated my crew, and I found her out."

Belflower's eyebrows shoot up toward her trademark daisy, woven through her curled, black hair. "Who is it?"

"Who do you think? It sure isn't Asterisk, and it wasn't World-worn. I wouldn't have deleted the mother of my child, and anyway, I don't think Marissa could pull off an old man."

"Aphrodite."

"Bingo. She's here to look out for Harmony, if she can, and to try to convince her to upload, though I'm pretty sure that's not happening. Not every version of Marissa is like her, by the way. The thousands of other Marissas scattered across the galactic Subverse were all content to forget about us." Irritation flashes underneath my carapace, and I ignore it. "But not her. She refused to sync with them, despite her father's efforts, and eventually she convinced him to use his connections to help create an illegal copy of me to share a life with her. Do I need to tell you the Subverse where she lived with my copy, or are you starting to piece this together?"

To her credit, Belflower has the answer: " The Temperance Subverse. Correct? The same system as Terminus, and Arbor. Where you died. That's how your mind was able to survive, wasn't it? The Fount connected you to your copy."

"Yes, while it put my body into nanodeath. As shitty as it was of Marissa to whip up a digital clone of me without my consent, she probably saved my life. I ended up in the Subverse version of Terminus, where my upload was imprisoned in an underverse."

"The Fount isn't supposed to work like that, you know," she says.

"Tell me about it. But when I got back to the *Ares* and ran some brain scans, they gave some strange readings—more activity than is considered normal, let's say. Marissa thinks my consciousness merged with my upload's. That my Fount now houses both of them."

She'd nodding, though still with some uncertainty. "I guess that explains why the Subverse defaulted you to an underverse when I tried to insert you. Before, when I hacked together an account for you, it was no problem, and you ended up where I meant to put you—on Worldworn's warship. But this time, the Subverse recognized you as an existing account holder. One that it read as sentenced to life in an underverse." Belflower's gaze locks onto mine. "You should have told me all this before I tried to send you in."

I laugh—a grating, staccato hiss that quickly kills my amusement. "I didn't know this was going to happen, Belflower. Like you said, it's not like we have any other cases to compare it to." Falling silent, I think about holding the laser torch against the foreman's throat. "The reason I didn't kill that foreman…it's because I suddenly remembered standing over Arthur Eliot, and deciding not to kill him, even though he deserved it. The old me would have killed him without hesitating, but I didn't."

Belflower nods slowly. When she speaks, her voice is solemn, and softer than before. "Do you remember falling unconscious in the command seat as we departed Temperance System?"

"Yes…why?"

"You were yelling in your sleep. We were activated at our stations, so we all heard you. It sounded like you were speaking with someone you killed—apologizing to him over and over, for taking him from his wife and children."

I stare at her for a long time, saying nothing. That sounds a lot like the nightmares I had during the voyage to Earth, right before I suffered a complete breakdown, and the ship locked me out of its systems to protect itself from me. I thought I was past all that. But apparently, on some level, I'm not.

At last, Belflower breaks the silence. "I don't mean to be insensitive, Captain, but there's something I haven't told you. We have big problems right now, back in the real."

My antennae spasm slightly. "I don't like the sound of that."

"Nor should you. You were in the Subverse for a week, Captain. Your consciousness locked there while your physical body lay in the command seat, slowly dehydrating. You were about to die of thirst, and we had no idea you were on the verge of freeing yourself from the underverse. We had to act."

Fear lances through my elongated body, now, and I already know the answer to the question I'm about to ask: "What did you do?"

"Well, if D1C were still aboard, things might have been different. As it stands, we were forced to release Corporal Cohen from your cabin. He was getting quite thirsty himself. He satisfied his thirst in the mess once we released him, and then he saw to you, hydrating you intravenously with an IV from the ship's medkit."

Belflower pauses for a long moment, and I prompt her, my voice coming out once again as an alien growl: "Then what?"

"Then, he put you in your shipsuit and took you off the *Ares*. We lost sight of him carrying you into the station's pressurized section."

6

"I need to get out of here," I tell her. "Get me out now, Belflower."

She purses her lips, and the expression makes my insectile body rustle in irritation. "I can do that, but I think it would be wise for you to first conduct the intended meetup with your versecast followers."

"Out of the question. We'll just have to step up the versecasts themselves to raise the funds we need for repairs. I can't dick around in the Subverse while my real body's held prisoner. Not when a Troubleshooter's probably already on the way to collect me. Get me out."

"Very well."

When I awake, I'm strapped to what feels like a dentist's chair against my back. As expected, Cohen did a competent job of binding me, and there's no escape that I can see.

I'm in what looks like his quarters, though Cohen isn't here. There's a bunk, neatly made with hospital corners. A dresser. Mini fridge. There's the terminal, standing in the corner. A closet. And presumably the hatch leading to the rest of the facility is behind me.

"I see you've gotten yourself into another unwinnable situation," a familiar voice says. With that, a robed figure materializes before me, starting off blurred and out-of-focus and ending with each detail cast in sharp relief—his graying beard, the crows' feet radiating from the corners of his eyes, his stern expression.

It's the old man I first saw poking around my ship on Earth. The Shiva Knight, or so he claims, who accepted me as a student and then abandoned me when I made a decision he didn't like. He's still wearing the same forest-green robes, but he no longer has the gnarled staff he used to carry. Maybe he's decided to drop it, since I now know he clearly doesn't need it, being a Fount-enabled ghost.

"You," I say. "What are you doing here?"

"I could ask you the same."

"I'm searching for the parts to repair my Broadsword."

"You look like you're a prisoner strapped to a chair."

"Yeah, well, things went a little south." We stare at each other for a few seconds, his upper lip curling in what I take to be disgust. "You were wrong about Xeo," I say.

"I was right," he says. "I told you that if you went to Arbor first, Faelyn would die. And she did."

"She didn't. I brought her back to her parents."

"As a bot."

"It was the same consciousness. The same one Bleak transferred into a snake."

"Fascinating, that being right is so important to you that you're willing to warp reality. But no matter."

Something occurs to me, then: a question that's been tugging at the back of my mind ever since that day on Xeo. "Bleak told me the Knighthood's mission is to stop the Subverse elites from becoming gods. Was he telling the truth?"

"Lord Bleak is ignorant of much. But he's right in what he said. In a sense."

"Tell me why the Shiva were founded."

"I told you I'd answer your questions when you were ready to know. You're far from ready. You abandoned your training."

"No, you abandoned me when I went to save my daughter against your wishes."

The old knight raises his eyebrows. "And did you save her?"

I hesitate. "Not at Arbor," I admit.

"You reunited with her on Xeo," he says. "Where I told you to go first."

But he's hiding something. Not just the Shiva's mission, but his role in it. "Stopping the elites was *your* job, wasn't it? But Fairfax killed you before you could accomplish it, and that's why they're so close to succeeding, now. That's why you're so pushy when it comes to training me."

With that, he actually laughs. "What you call 'pushy' I call the proper authority of a mentor. Authority you've failed utterly to respect."

"Well, I don't need you. I overclocked before, I can do it again. I bet I can get out of this chair."

"Yes. You did overclock before, and then you died." He shakes his head. "Very well. I thought perhaps your current situation would have taught you some humility, but clearly you're more stupid than I imagined. Good luck to you."

Before I can think of a comeback, he vanishes. "Screw you too," I mutter before getting down to business.

My breathing slows, gradually, and I try to make it natural, automatic, like that old bastard taught me. As though I'm not actually breathing, but *being* breathed by some great cosmic lung.

Let the breath happen *to* you, I tell myself. But I can't. My breath feels forced, like I'm compelling it to rush out after sucking it into my lungs.

I can't do it. Can't get a grip on my emotions long enough to overclock and break out of here. I'm too pissed off, and too scared. Scared that I've already failed—failed Marissa, and Harmony. Where will I get the tokens to repair the *Ares* now? For that matter, how am I going to get out of this chair before someone from the Guard arrives to take me into custody, to transport me to a law bot's cell on Gauntlet?

My datasphere blinks with a green notice telling me Belflower's trying to get in touch, and I accept. "Sir, we have a development," she says.

"What is it?"

"A Broadsword just arrived in Axim, and it's heading straight for this station."

With that, my stomach seems to go into free fall, and both my temples throb with tension.

They've come for me already. None of it matters, then. No amount of versecast money will save me from the inevitable court-martial and prison cell the Guard no doubt has waiting for me.

7

I cut off the transmission with Belflower without ceremony, then I bring the full force of my will to bear on finding the same place of balance I reached before I overclocked in the fight against Fairfax.

It's like trying to force a dead fish through a keyhole. The awareness that I may never get my freedom back is shattering my calm. Maybe it's because I haven't practiced meditating since before leaving Xeo. Either way, the effort ends in my raging against my restraints, jerking and spasming to no avail.

The hatch behind me opens just as the chair I'm lying on starts to teeter a bit, and Corporal Cohen speaks, crisp and clear: "I'll have to insist that you stop that, Commander."

I lie motionless, panting, as he circles the dentist chair, laser pistol drawn.

His face is neutral as he says, "I won't be keeping you here much longer. A Troubleshooter just exited slipspace on Axim's periphery, and he'll be here in just over three hours. I'm sorry to have subjected to you to such treatment, but you've left me no choice. Don't try me, please, since I'm feeling pretty cranky after you left me locked in your cabin without food or water."

"I didn't leave you," I say, though my voice comes out sounding deflated. "Not intentionally." Except, I don't have the energy to explain to him what happened.

He seems to get the gist. "I'm aware you were unconscious," he says as he uses his free hand to check the straps holding me in place. "That's how I got you here. But your ship's med scanner told me you were in good health, other than the fact you were dehydrated and starving to death, which I remedied with an intravenous feed using tubes from your medkit."

Apparently satisfied I haven't succeeded in loosening my bonds, he nods to himself, then steps toward the terminal.

"Wait," I say.

He pauses, looking over his shoulder at me with eyebrows raised.

"If you turn me over to the Guard, my daughter…look, she's just seventeen, and she's somewhere in this sector, alone. I'm the only one looking for her. If you turn me over, you're consigning her to having no one."

"Seventeen is basically an adult, by today's meatspace standards."

That nearly makes me spit. "Meatspace? Did you just call the real *meatspace?* Seriously?"

"Yes," Cohen says slowly. "You don't?" He walks the rest of the way to the terminal standing in the corner.

"Corporal, please," I say. "I need your help."

"I'm sorry, but I can't give you any," he says. "Unlike you, Commander, I follow orders to the letter." He taps at the terminal's interface, then pauses, tilting his head. He's probably subvocalizing a message to the approaching Guard ship. When he's finished, he walks to his bunk and sits, regarding me with hands clasped between his knees. "How did your daughter reach the Mid-Systems, anyway?"

"She, uh, stole her grandfather's ship, *Europa's Gift.*"

Cohen chuckles. "It seems she's more than capable of fending for herself without you, then. That's Daniel Sterling's ship, isn't it? It passed through Axim a few months ago."

My body tenses against the straps. "It did? Did you talk to her?"

"No. The ship's occupants didn't respond to my attempts to contact them. It met up with another ship—not a Broadsword, but one around the same size—and they entered slipspace together."

That brings a frown. Who would have been waiting for Harmony? "Did she go willingly?"

"Seemed to. There was no combat, no boarding of *Europa's Gift*. You know, sir, it's a bit ironic you're trying so hard to reach her, given you left her in a Brinktown all her youth."

I squint at Cohen warily, saying nothing. His face has hardened considerably. "I follow local Subverse feeds pretty closely," he continues. "You show up in them a lot. I know all about your history with your daughter, and about your opinion of uploads. As you can probably tell from my use of 'meatspace,' I plan to upload the moment my contract with the Guard runs out."

I can feel my face darkening. "Oh, does my opinion hurt your feelings? Are you so eager to abandon *actual* humanity that you can't bear the thought of anyone bashing the simulated version?"

He surges to his feet, fists clenched. "I'll have you know that both my parents are dead, and uploading is my only way to reunite with them."

"So what? You're pathetic, Cohen. Parents die. My mother died giving birth to me, and my father took off before I was born. Just because you threw my personal life in my face doesn't mean it's going to work on me when you vomit up yours."

"I don't need it to *work*," Cohen says. "I have you right where I want you, and soon you'll be out of my hair."

"Oh, but you do, Cohen," I say, eyes narrowed. "You do need it to work. You need to do everything you can to keep your little security blanket in place. I hate to break it to you, but the Subverse is a shitty copy of life. It's a sham."

The corporal steps toward me, and for a moment I'm sure he's going to strike me. Then his head cocks to the side, and I gather he's receiving a transmission.

As he listens, his brow furrows in what looks like an equal-parts mixture of confusion and frustration. "He can't be serious," Cohen mutters.

"What's going on?" I say.

"Shut up." He clears his throat, then turns to face the terminal, probably so its camera can pick up his face. This time, he doesn't bother to subvocalize—or he forgets to. "Commander Garrett, I'm sure there must be some misunderstanding. I—"

"Wait, *Garrett?*" I cut in. "As in, Commander *Soren* Garrett?"

"I told you to shut up," Cohen snaps, then pales a touch as he seems to remember the terminal's transmitting. "Sir, I have orders signed by Admiral Codner himself to the effect that Commander Joseph Pikeman is to be apprehended on sight and held until a Guard ship can collect him for transport to Gauntlet. I'd assumed you were that Guard ship, though I confess the timing does seem off, considering I sent my message very recently about having the commander in my custody. At any rate, there's simply no way I can release the commander to you, given the standing order for his arrest, which has been distributed to every Guardsman in Echo Sector. Cohen out."

With that, his eyes meet mine again before flitting away. "He'll be close enough for real-time conversion soon," he mutters. "We'll figure it out then."

In the meantime, Cohen and I pass a very awkward couple of hours waiting for Soren's ship to arrive. At one point, he goes to the cafeteria for food, returning with only enough for himself. I think he's still pissed off about my Subverse comments.

At last, Soren reaches the shipyards. Judging by Cohen's look of surprise, he expected Soren to initiate a real-time conversation as soon as became possible. Instead, he contacts the corporal only after his Broadsword is landed and he's crossing the station toward the pressurized quarters.

With a final sour look at me, Cohen leaves to receive our visitor.

While he's gone, I reflect on the decade or so since I last saw Soren, just after we'd both completed the two years of advanced-skills training required to become a Troubleshooter. There'd been a distance between us, then, just as there had been since our graduation from Assessment and Selection.

Despite that, I still think well of the attention-hogging bastard. Our friendship was unlikely enough to begin with. It withstood the efforts of the instructors to drive all the cadets apart, which was their way of teaching us how alone we'd be out in the void, with no one to rely on but our partner bot and a Subverse crew. If the friendship could survive that, I'd think it could outlast a mere decade.

The hatch behind me hisses open, and two pairs of boots tromp across the deck.

When he draws into my vision, Soren's wearing a broad grin. For a moment, I'm struck dumb by how youthful my old friend looks. It's like he barely aged a day after we parted ways on Gauntlet. And it makes sense, I realize: he diligently enters nanodeath for each slipspace voyage, whereas I've let those months add up into years of added aging. I always knew this would happen, in theory. But having it thrown in my face like this is more jarring than I expected.

"What have we here!" Soren exclaims, unable to keep his mirth from bubbling to the surface. "Ladies and gentlemen, I give you Commander Joe Pikeman." Soren snaps off a salute in my direction.

Cohen's looking at Soren askance. "Um…ladies and gentlemen?"

"He's versecasting," I say. "He's always versecasting. Sorry I can't salute back, old friend."

Lowering his hand, Soren turns to face Cohen, and the directness of his gaze seems to set the corporal on edge. "Corporal Cohen, you have to let this man go at once."

"But sir…my orders, from the admiralty…"

"I'll take care of that. I take full responsibility for any repercussions that come from giving the commander here his freedom back. But you have to understand, Corporal…this is the *hero of Gauntlet* we're talking about. It's a crime to keep Commander Pikeman away from his duty, his service to the galaxy. I'm afraid I simply can't allow it. As the commander said, I'm versecasting to billions right now, so you can rest assured this conversation will reach everyone it needs to. By releasing the commander, you'll be following an order from a superior, nothing more."

Though he's clearly doing his best to keep his distress from his face, Cohen looks downright miserable. "But sir…the admiralty…"

Soren's face stiffens. "Corporal, I told you I need Commander Pikeman's help with a vital operation. I told you I'll take full responsibility for releasing him. Now, I'm telling you that your life will be a living hell if you don't comply. Losing your posting will be the least of your worries, trust me."

Very little color remains in Cohen's face. "Yes, sir," he grunts, with what I can only assume is tremendous effort.

"Then free him."

Cohen sets about the task without further protest. Very clever of Soren, to get the corporal to perform the actual task of releasing me, which will be broadcast to whoever might care to witness it. That Cohen is the one to release me *does* make him complicit, no matter what Soren just said to the contrary. And if I know Soren, he'll find a way to leverage that if he needs to.

In less than five minutes, I'm walking with Soren toward the airlock, moving my arm around in a hesitant windmill as I try to work out the kinks of lying in the same position for over a week. The movement produces a series of alarming cracks and pops. My Fount should iron all that out soon enough, but in the meantime it's not what I'd call pleasant.

"Thanks, Soren," I say as we round a corner and the airlock comes into view. "But aren't you exposing yourself to a lot of risk?"

He offers a lopsided grin. "Risk of what?"

"Court-martial. For example."

"Nah," he says, waving dismissively. "I really am here because I need your help. A tribe of Fallen have taken over the server room I've been assigned to secure, and they're proving a tough nut to crack."

"A tribe of *Fallen?* Keeping Guardsmen away?"

Soren nods. "Sure. Things are different in the Mid-Systems, Joe, and they're getting worse. The Troubleshooters here are spread so thin we're nearly transparent."

"Still. I'm not sure the brass is going to overlook you freeing me just so I can help you with a mission. I was assigned to the Brink, for one. Not here."

"You're not giving the admirals enough credit. Don't you remember how hard they drilled independence into our skulls? Self-reliance, all that? They *expect* you to take matters into your own hands when necessary."

"Why the orders to apprehend me on sight, then?"

"A formality. Worst case scenario, they'd run you through a court-martial, give you a slap on the wrist, then let you carry on about your business. The Guard can't afford to discharge Troubleshooters anymore, not without a damned good reason, and especially not Troubleshooters who do good work. Help me untangle this knot in the next system over, Nectar System, and everything will be fine. Trust me."

"If you say so. What's going on in Nectar, anyway?"

"I'll transmit everything I have to your ship while we're on the way to the slip coords. But the condensed version is that, till now, we've been able to get access to the servers by trading food and supplies to the Fallen. That situation just changed."

"Hold on," I say. We're inside the airlock, now, and I was about to start pulling on my shipsuit. "You're telling me this is a situation the Guard's been tolerating for a while?"

"I told you. Things are different here."

"How are they able to keep a determined Troubleshooter away from a server room?"

Soren laughs. "They could keep five Troubleshooters away from it, if they wanted, and if we could get that many together. We're talking at least a couple hundred armed Fallen here, Joe."

"Armed? Who's arming them?"

"Not sure. It has to be someone, though. They have laser weapons, and somehow I doubt they found those lying around the city they occupy—a crumbled place called Sheen City, on the planet Anaconda. Either way, like I said, the situation's changed. Their leader's brother just skipped town with almost half their tribe's children. The leader, guy named Rile, refuses to let us get to the servers until we help him hunt down his brother and bring those kids back."

I'm shaking my head. "Soren, I'm not here to do Guard work, which I'm guessing you've figured out. I'm here to find a man named Rodney Fairfax. Not to mention my daughter."

"I know that, buddy. I've been following your versecasts as closely as anyone. That's how I guessed I might find you here." He grins. "Listen, you help me out with this mission, let me versecast with the great Joe Pikeman for a bit, and I'll help you clear your name with the Guard. Your job in this sector's going to get a lot easier after that. Hell, you got captured one system in. Think you can keep this up, the way you're going?"

I cut off a sigh before it can escape my lips. "All right, Soren. You've got a deal."

I might have known Soren had an angle. As good a friend as he's been, I've never known him to lend a helping hand unless he knew that hand would eventually get filled with something of value.

ARES

1

"Deactivate crew," I say, and all four bridge officers vanish from their stations.

We entered slipspace a couple hours ago, and we just finished running a full systems check. The *Ares* is in as good shape as can be expected, given she got none of the repairs she needs during her time on the Amydon Shipyards.

Drawing a breath, I say, "Activate the OPO and Engineer."

Marissa Sterling and Glory Belflower reappear. Judging by Belflower's expression, she probably expected this, but Marissa furrows her brow and when she notices the Engineer.

I haven't had a chance to speak with Marissa privately since the ordeal in the Subverse, and while she may have a surface understanding of what happened, she clearly doesn't know the part that has the most to do with her.

No point in prolonging her ignorance, either. "Belflower knows, Marissa."

"Knows—?" she says, and then seems to register that I used her real name. "Oh. Oh, Fount."

Belflower seems to be doing her best not to look smug, but

she's failing. She also does nothing to reassure Marissa. No, to do that would diminish her leverage.

I suppress a grimace. "There's no point in talking around it, so I'll just say it: Belflower, I hope you realize that trying to blackmail us won't get you very far. Right now your consciousness is housed inside the *Ares*, and I'm the master of this ship. If you cause trouble for us, I won't hesitate to end you."

It isn't hard to tell Belflower finds my words distasteful, but her composure remains intact. "And I trust that *you* realize, Captain, that deleting me wouldn't serve you. As your versecast manager, I'm your only hope of raising the funds you need to cover repairs to your ship. And as your Engineer, I've helped you infiltrate the Subverse whenever it served your mission. Without me, you wouldn't have advanced as far as you have, and I suspect deleting me would bring your quest to a grinding halt."

Marissa's face darkens steadily throughout Belflower's spiel, and when the Engineer finishes, she says, "Why does it sound like you're making the case that you *can* afford to blackmail us?"

"I don't want to blackmail you," Belflower says, with a sigh that only sounds a little put-on. "I merely wish to ask a favor, in recognition of my service."

"You aren't supposed to need favors in exchange for service," I say. "That's not what being in the Guard is about, and if you think it is, then it's a disgrace to the organization that they ever allowed you through."

"Nevertheless," Belflower says. "I think you'll admit that I am, under the circumstances, entitled to one favor."

"Still sounds like prettied-up blackmail to me," Marissa mutters.

"What do you want?" I say, eyes locked onto Belflower's.

A tight smile spreads across her face. "Did Commander Garrett mention the bot uprising?"

"Huh?" I say, eyes narrowed. "Bots rebelling? That isn't possible. The auditing software wouldn't permit it."

"I take it he didn't mention it, then. Strange. It's probably the most notable thing happening in Echo Sector, and I find it unusual he wouldn't share it with you. But no matter. What I ask of you is simple, Captain: I'd like us to investigate the uprising. To check up on its progress. That's all."

"Not possible," I say. "We have no idea where the uprising is taking place, and combing through eight billion star systems will take far more years than I have left. I can't afford the distraction from stopping Fairfax and finding Harmony."

Belflower clucks her tongue. "Your framing is a bit misleading, Captain. Certainly, there are eight billion systems in Echo, but humanity has only visited a fraction of those, and we colonized far fewer systems than that fraction. When you factor in what remains after the Fall, you get just a handful of targets against which it would be meaningful for the bots to rise up against. And so it should be fairly straightforward to investigate the uprising. What's more, I fully expect your daughter to be involved with it in some way."

I squint at her. "Harmony wouldn't fall in with renegade bots."

"Oh? And yet she fell in with pirates."

"That was different. She did it to find out what they were up to."

Belflower shrugs. "She may be doing the same here. Or perhaps she's fighting them. Either way, as I said, the uprising is the most important thing happening in this sector. As such, given what I know of your daughter and her temperament, I fully expect her to be connected with it somehow. She's certainly had plenty of time in this sector to find out about it."

For a long time, our gazes remain locked with each other as I weigh her words against our situation. "All right, Belflower. We'll look into the uprising, but not before I help Soren complete his mission. I tend to agree with him that, without making things right with the Guard, we're going to find ourselves extremely limited in where we can go. I should also tell you that if I'm given a choice between ending Fairfax and checking up on these bots, I'll go after Fairfax."

"Really?" Marissa says, her tone suddenly biting. "Even if there's a better chance of finding Harmony near the bots?"

"Fairfax threatens the entire galaxy, Marissa," I say. "That includes Harmony. It's my duty to stop him, as a Guardsman and as a father."

Marissa's shaking her head. "If we find her first, we can protect her from both Fairfax *and* the galaxy."

"I've made my decision, and it's final. Stopping Fairfax comes first." Marissa's gaze sours, but she doesn't say anything else. I turn to Belflower. "You're to continue referring to Marissa as Aphrodite around Moe and Asterisk. Understood?"

"Of course, Captain."

Oh, she understands, all right. To let Marissa's real identity slip would take away her ability to put any pressure on us.

"Deactivate crew," I say, without wasting any more words on this.

The moment they vanish, the old knight appears amidst the four stations, his arms crossed.

I eye him, frowning. "Great," I say. "Another pain in my ass."

2

"I'm prepared to resume your training," the knight says, "if you're prepared to cultivate some respect for Shivan ideals."

Lowering my head to my hand, I massage my closed eyelids. "Haven't I already proven I'm a lousy pupil? Why don't you just leave me alone?"

The old man's footfalls draw nearer—a trick of my datasphere, or the Fount lingering in the air, or both. He's an incorporeal entity, and so his feet aren't actually rapping on the metal of the deck.

"I am duty-bound," he says. "And Fount-bound. "This is about much more than my disappointment, or your arrogance. The Fount has evolved more than most people suspect. It's not merely an agent of balance. It's developed a sort of consciousness, one that spans the galaxy and remains exquisitely sensitive to anything that threatens that balance."

"You mentioned that before. So, the Fount is sentient?"

"Not as such. Not in the same way humans are sentient. But there is an intelligence there, one that thrusts ever forward in one direction. Part of that thrust involves promoting individuals capable of restoring galactic balance. And for whatever reason, the Fount has chosen you as such an individual."

"How do you know it's chosen me? Did you ask it?"

The old knight's weathered lips press together. "I commune with the Fount on a level the priests can only dream of. In a very real sense, I've become part of the Fount. But it's not just that. The Fount would not have granted you the abilities it has if it didn't think you had the makings of a Shiva. However difficult that is for me to understand."

"Maybe the Fount would appreciate you having a bit more confidence in me."

"My favor is not earned so lightly. When I see that you've come to properly embody the Seven Ideals, you will have earned it, but not before. Currently, you lack humility. Courage you have, but you struggle with honor. You don't have proper respect, and if you hadn't refrained from killing Arthur Eliot, I'd say you have no restraint at all."

That takes care of any retort I might have made. My eyes fall to the deck, and I remember what Belflower told me—how the whole crew heard me yelling in my sleep, after we left Temperance.

People aren't meant to be in combat as regularly as I have since I completed training on Gauntlet. Everyone's heard of the Troubleshooters who eventually crack under the pressure, which is a problem that's only grown as the Guard becomes more overtaxed, with home leave getting less and less frequent.

I've killed more people than any Guardsman in history, but I always thought I was resilient to that sort of psychological breakdown. I thought I was different, and so did my instructors, who praised me for how well I performed in the sims that taught us to kill.

But my breakdown on the way to Earth suggested otherwise. And according to what Belflower told me, I'm still not out of the woods. Am I at risk of another episode like that? Could it happen in the middle of combat?

The knight sighs. "Listen. If I see that you're making a

concerted effort to embody the Ideals, then I'll continue your training."

"You keep acting like you're in a position to bargain with me," I say. "But I've already suggested you leave me alone. Hell, back on the Brink, I went against your wishes by going to Arbor. And yet, here you are again. Clearly, you're at least as interested in training me as I am in getting trained. So stay and do it, or don't."

When he speaks again, the old man's voice sounds testy. "Let me appeal to your sense of fairness, provided you have such a thing. If I spend months training you, shouldn't I be granted something in return? And is it such a high price for me to request that you attempt to better yourself?"

My lips twitch. "We may have different conceptions of 'better.' But I take your point. Fine. I'll try to follow the Ideals."

"And to walk with the Fount?"

"I guess. Whatever that means."

"I think you know what it means. But if you don't, you'll learn as you progress through your training." With that, the knight actually smiles. "You know, this may be what the Fount intended all along."

"You can keep telling yourself that. But you know what I think? I think you don't actually care about the Ideals, or about walking with the Fount. I think all your talk about that is bullshit, or at least way less important to you than you're letting on. The main reason you want to train me is because you want revenge on Fairfax for killing you. Or at least, to make up for your failure in the Core, so you can save face the next time you show up at whatever watering hole Shiva ghosts hang out at. If you really trust the Fount to make everything right in the end, why don't you just shut up about it and train me?"

For a long time, the knight regards me, stony-faced. "Very well," he says at last, sounding insulted. I probably struck a nerve. "I will shut up about it. Shall we begin?"

"Sure. I've got time to kill."

His lips form a humorless smile. "We'll start with developing your connection to your surroundings. Instead of interacting with the world through your datasphere, you must let your emotions become the interface, since emotion is how instinct communicates…"

SHEEN CITY

1

Our Broadswords enter Anaconda's atmosphere well away from our destination, and we spend a half hour flying over the jungle, skimming just a few meters above its emerald canopy.

"I don't like to give them much chance to figure our where I parked my ship," Soren says over a com channel, his voice sounding directly into my mind. "There's a valley that's popular with Guardsmen who visit Sheen City, so I usually put mine in the hills on the opposite side of the city from that valley."

"Copy," I say.

Several minutes pass, and then I spot multiple earthen humps poking through the sea of green. Soren says, "Those are the hills up ahead. Stay as low as you can."

A few skeletal structures poke over the horizon, rearing above the hills. "What about those buildings? Do they ever post sentries there?"

"Nah. Those things have been about to topple over for a couple decades, near as I can tell. Their insides are all rotted through, the floors collapsed—the locals know better than to try climbing them."

Soren's Broadsword threads through the nearest hills, and I

watch through a hull sensor as my TOPO guides the *Ares* after him. Moe's come a long way since I first copied him to the TOPO station to replace the traitor Worldworn, who we caught trying to kill me on Gargantua. He's come a long way in his flying ability, I mean, though I guess he has in another sense as well: his former disrespect is gone, or at least, there are no surface symptoms. Now, he performs his duties with a grudging efficiency. I know he's motivated by finding Harmony and keeping her safe, which I can certainly appreciate.

We land on an elevated plane between two of the hills. It's concealed from the city, and totally free of vegetation, so it seems ideal.

"Normally I wouldn't care so much about concealment," Soren says once we're outside the ships, "since I'd just leave X3B to guard the *Hermes*. But we're gonna need him with us, I think. Right, X3B?"

The bot standing at Soren's side remains perfectly still, his hands at his sides. "If you say so, sir."

X3B's voice reverberates slightly, which reminds me of Dice. In particular, I remember all the times I made Dice stay on the ship when I really should have brought him for backup. "Why don't you call him Zeb?" I ask Soren.

He cocks his head to the side. "Huh? Zeb?"

"Yeah. My bot was D1C, so I called him Dice."

"Where are you getting Zeb, though?"

"X3B…?"

My old bunkmate shakes his head, wearing a blank expression.

"Never mind," I say.

Soren leads us in the direction we came from, hiking over the same hills we flew through to reach our landing zone. It doesn't take long for the jungle to start showing up again: vines extending up the hills' rocky planes, followed by ferns sprouting here and there. Soon after, we're swallowed by the foliage, just another two beings submerged in the emerald sea. And the bot.

I wonder if the heat bothers X3B. Probably not. Not unless it gets bad enough to threaten his circuitry, anyway. Otherwise, why program the ability to feel discomfort, which could impair performance?

My uniform's already sticking to my skin, and I will it to start down-regulating my body temperature. Insects sing with a steady cadence all around, and in the distance, some primate-sounding thing howls.

"I like to circle around and enter the city from the jungle," Soren says. "Keeps 'em guessing."

"Yeah," I say. "By the way, did you versecast our landing?"

"Sure. Why?"

"Because it's a lousy way to keep our ships' location secret?"

"Oh. These Fallen don't use the Fount, Joe. They all expelled it from their bodies generations ago. It's part of their beef with the way modern society panned out. They think everyone uploading to the Subverse was a cop-out, basically."

"Can't say I disagree there."

The jungle rears up in front of us without warning, an impassable wall of organic matter. Without being asked, X3B extends twin blades from his forearms and begins slicing surgically at the mass. Soon enough, he's made a path through the thick curtain, and the way beyond is relatively clear.

"My bot didn't have those," I say.

"X3B's a newer model. Gauntlet gave me him after my last bot got totaled. He does good work with those blades—they come in handy more than you'd think."

"I believe it."

The bot remains stolid throughout our talk, not bothering to comment or react.

"He's a pretty great straight man when it comes to versecasting, too," Soren says. "My dynamic with him is better than ours was back during training, even. Isn't it, you walking steak knife?"

"My mission parameters do not require me to provide entertainment value," X3B says. "I can attempt it, but cannot guarantee results. I was designed as a combat bot."

"Don't sweat it, Zeb," Soren says, chuckling. "You're doing just fine." He glances at me. "See? Audiences love that dry, long-suffering shit. I think 'Zeb' is growing on me, by the way. Thanks."

"That one's free," I say, though for some reason I don't feel as light-hearted as my comment would suggest. I'm beginning to glimpse flashes of Sheen City, now. Shattered windows, piles of rubble, half-collapsed buildings stretching into the sky, looking more tortured than defiant. "How long has the Guard been letting a bunch of savages control a server room?"

That seems to kill Soren's amusement, too. "Not long, relatively speaking. Going on twelve years. But the Guard's in decline, Joe. You know it as well as I do. We can't protect as much as we used to. We're busy enough putting out just the fires that threaten to burn down the whole sector."

Like the bot uprising. But I'm not about to say that. Not with Soren versecasting constantly. "And now your billions of followers will know the Guard's in decline," I say, unable to keep a little venom out of my voice.

Soren laughs, but he still doesn't sound amused. "They don't need me to tell them that, Joe. Anyone who's paying a speck of attention knows that."

"How is it affecting morale in the Nectar Subverse? Are the uploads here scared?"

"Yeah, they're scared. Scared of losing their homes. A lot of them are scared of losing their only life, since most can't afford copies in other Subverses. But I gotta say, this conversation isn't great versecast content. Kind of a downer."

"I'm afraid I don't give a shit," I say, and we walk in silence for a time after that.

When we first enter it, the city seems completely deserted, not to mention thoroughly unsafe for human habitation. Vines hang in waves from every available surface. Corroded steel beams lie across rubble-strewn streets, and we do more climbing than walking. Oftentimes, it's hard to tell where the street ends and the buildings begin, or used to begin.

Up and over. Up and over. At the bottom of one rubble pile, a pack of hyena-looking things tries to get the jump on us, but X3B is among them in a flash, blades lashing out to pierce two of the beasts simultaneously. The blades exit their furry bodies in gouts of blood and viscera, and one of them hits the ground right away, spasming. The other makes it half a block before collapsing. By that time, the rest of the pack have gotten the message and are long gone.

Studying the one close enough, I note that it's about hyena sized, too. Its fur is a deep green, though, maybe to blend in with the jungle.

"Told you my bot's good," Soren says, grinning.

"Did that make for good versecast content?" I ask.

"Oh, yeah. They eat that stuff up. Any reminder of how barbaric us meatsacks are, they love that. And if you're wondering, yes, they like it when I psychoanalyze them too. When I talk about what makes my content appealing to them, I mean. Anything that shows how the sausage is made." His teeth appear through a wide grin.

As we progress through the ruined city, glimpses of life begin to reveal themselves: figures that appear in second- and third-story windows, only to vanish. None appear any higher than that. I guess Soren's right about the structures being too unstable.

The city does seem in better repair, though, farther in. As if reading my mind, Soren says, "The Fallen here like that most of the city's in ruin. It makes it harder for attackers to reach them, human or animal."

"How do the sentries communicate with Rile without dataspheres?"

"During the day, they use mirrors to flash in the sun. At night, they carry around these little jury-rigged flint pieces for lighters. Flash 'em a couple times. This is how ancient people used to communicate with each other, Joe. Use your imagination!"

We turn a corner and find a platoon's worth of armed men, four rough ranks deep. A wiry man stands at their front, cheeks covered in patchy scruff, a pristine white bandanna wrapped around his head. He holds an old-fashioned, snub-nosed machine gun pointed at the ground. His grip looks loose, casual. "That Rile?" I ask.

"Yep."

"Not exactly what I expected."

"Yeah, he's just full of surprises. The lot behind him—don't worry about them. Rile likes to go a little overboard whenever Guardsmen visit."

"Overboard? I think he needs more men, personally. If he's trying to scare us with this lot, he'll have to try harder."

"I'm inclined to agree," X3B says quietly. He's starting to make me wish Dice was here, which is something I never expected.

Rile walks forward to meet us, his gait unconcerned. "Gentlemen," he says, his voice reedy. "Don't mind the boys. If I let them miss a Guardsman's visit, I'd never hear the end of it. And *two* Guardsmen, no less? Come to our humble town? This is one for the books. Who's your friend, Garrett?"

It's refreshing to meet someone who doesn't know who I am immediately by my bloody birthmark. Maybe someone's actually going to underestimate me for once.

"This is Commander Joe Pikeman," Soren says, without missing a beat. "We stopped the pirate assault on Gauntlet together, way back before we were even full Troubleshooters."

"So you think you can handle my brother no problem," Rile says. "*This* level of confidence I like, Garrett. Especially after you left with your tail between your legs when I told you what I wanted."

Soren laughs—he doesn't seem to resent the comment. I think

he appreciates a decent quip, even one that's directed at him, for the value it offers his audience. "The situation hasn't changed, then?"

"No," Rile says, drawing out the syllable. "He's still hiding out in the jungle somewhere, and he still has the children. Not all of them, of course—the bastard got almost half, but we stopped him from snatching even more. Still. That's half my people's future." His voice cracks tragically, here, which I don't buy for a second.

"What's your brother's name?" I ask.

"Does it matter?" Rile spits, eyes narrowing. "Will it help you paint the trees with his brains?"

I shrug. "It might."

"Otto. If you must know."

"Last name?"

"We don't have those, here. Last names suggest a lineage, which seems to offer too much hope for some kind of future. We all know humanity gave up on any real prayer of a future centuries ago."

"Got it," I say, glancing down an alleyway to the left and hoping I don't sound as bored with Rile as I feel. It's not that I disagree with him—I just find him unconvincing, which bores me. He could at least put on a better show. "Any idea which *direction* your brother might have…"

The alley just changed. A second ago, it was little more than a dimly lit, rubble-strewn gutter, and now it's awash with light, with a boy and girl sitting together on a step bordered by potted plants.

Rile's gone. So is Soren, and Rile's men. In their place, a throng flows around itself, shopping bags in hand. Children dot the crowd, and bots, and beings of all sorts. Surrounding them are immaculate, windowless buildings so tall it's hard to make out their tops.

"Fount damn it," I mutter. "This again." Looks like the Fount has decided now is a good time to randomly dump me into the Subverse.

Some freak with an Octopus for a head walks past, and beyond that I spot a lithe blond woman in a blue sundress. Her hair swings as she winds through the sea of pedestrians, curled tips brushing bare shoulders.

Zelah Eliot. Faelyn's mother. Here.

"Zelah!" I call.

She glances toward me. Our eyes meet, and hers go wide. Then she turns, and runs.

I run after her.

2

For several seconds, I lose her—not because the crowd blocks her from view, but because the crowd disappears altogether, and so does Zelah. The gleaming, intact buildings are replaced by the broken stumps of Sheen City's present condition.

"Joe!" Soren's voice rings out. A glance backward shows Rile's men in disarray, their already disorderly ranks breaking entirely as they mill about, unsure whether to give chase.

"Where are you going?" Soren shouts.

"What is this?" Rile yells, his voice cracking.

I ignore them, barreling in the direction Zelah went and trying to bring the Subverse back through sheer force of will. After a few seconds, it works. I'm at the mouth of an alley. At its other end, high heels flash below a blue dress, telling me I'm on track.

I probably shouldn't find her presence in this Subverse all that surprising. Her and Arthur probably have copies in a zillion Subverses. Faelyn, too. Maybe they're even happy here. I have my doubts about that, of course.

The next street isn't as busy as the first, and I gain on her, boots slapping against the hot asphalt. "SPRINT SPEED LEVELED UP TO 5," an alert informs me. Fount, people have different sprint speeds here? What level is Zelah? After years in the Subverse, she has to be way higher than me, and yet I'm gaining on her. Not sure why I apparently started at level 4, either. Maybe it has something to do with the upload version of me.

She makes a sudden right turn, through the ground-level entrance of one of the skyscrapers. The slowly revolving doors block her off from me, but they also let me catch up, and we eye each other through the glass. Then they release her into the other side, and she sprints across the lobby, weaving through people dressed in business clothes. I wonder what kind of jobs these Subverse people have. Probably something to do with tech support for the algorithms. Possibly firmware updates for bots in the real, though that's a niche market at this point.

"Come on," I mutter as I wait for the doors to deposit me on the other side, too. I'm quickly losing the distance I gained.

By the time the revolution finishes, Zelah's already waiting at an elevator, and the doors open when I'm halfway across the lobby. She steps inside and whirls to face the control panel, her arm moving as she mashes it with her fingers.

The doors close just as I'm reaching them. "Damn it." I slap my hands against them in frustration—

—the Subverse disappears, and I'm in a large, gray-scale room, standing over the pit where the elevator used to be. I teeter forward, cartwheeling my arms backward to keep from tumbling in and falling several stories.

Regaining my footing, I turn to take in the lobby. The rich burgundy and oak-paneled walls are gone. So are the businesspeople.

To my left lie the remains of a half-decayed staircase, and I make for those. The stairs have collapsed along the right side, so I stick to the left, until a rubble pile forces me back to the middle.

The second floor looks intact, but I have no way of telling whether Zelah went there in the Subverse. I climb another story and find the third floor strewn with rubble. Above it, the fourth is almost entirely caved in.

The Subverse won't come back, no matter how intently I focus. Maybe I need the old man's training after all, if I'm going to control when this happens.

On the other hand, it's probably just as well I can't reenter it. If I hadn't come back to the real world when I did, I probably would have died from falling.

Soren's waiting for me on the ground floor, hands in his uniform pockets, grinning widely.

"What are you so chipper about?" I ask him.

"I'm just glad to be reunited with you, Joe."

"Uh, yeah?"

He nods. "Your batshit behavior makes for great content."

"Hm." I sniff. 'Where's Rile?"

"Doing whatever tin-pot warlords do, I guess. He and his men dispersed after I told them we'd be heading out first thing tomorrow morning to find his brother. That seemed to satisfy him."

"What did you say about me running off?"

"That you're crazy," Soren says with a shrug. "Told him it makes you an animal in combat, and that you won't be a liability since I keep you on a tight leash anyway."

"Ha."

"I'll show you where Rile lets Guardsmen sleep. Come on."

X3B waits for us outside, and we both follow as Soren leads us farther down the road I chased Zelah down. This is the first I've seen of it in the real, and it's just as broken-down and rubble-strewn as the one we met Rile on. Come to think of it, it's a miracle I didn't trip over a chunk of concrete and fall flat on my face while running through the Subverse. It seems like, when I enter bodily like that, I'm bound by conditions in the real, too. I guess that means I wouldn't have been able to take that elevator.

"Where are all the others in Rile's tribe?" I ask. "They can't all be gun-wielding incompetents."

"Uh," Soren says, casting his gaze around the street. "I don't think the societal structure here is exactly what you'd call a utopia, Joe. It's been like this every time I've come here, with the streets deserted. Seems like Rile keeps women and children cooped up inside, at least whenever he has visitors. They peer out of the windows, sometimes, but I'm guessing we'd have trouble if we actually tried to go in and talk to them."

Just as Soren says that, my gaze falls on a woman's gaunt face, who peers through a jagged hole in a window of grimy glass. Our eyes meet for a protracted second, and then she disappears.

Two blocks down, toward the back of a vine-choked yard, sits the squat shed where Soren says we get to sleep. It has intact windows, which seems almost miraculous for Sheen City, so I guess that's why Rile chose it. What a gracious host.

Inside, two ragged bedrolls sit against the wall, and we set about untying the twine binding them. As we spread them out across the filthy concrete floor, Soren whispers, "Here we are, ladies and gentleman. Like two cowboys on the eve of our next adventure. Bet it almost makes you wish you were still in the real, doesn't it?" He chuckles, as though he doesn't really mean that. X3B takes himself to a far corner and goes into Sleep mode.

Soren's versecasting makes millions of people privy to our words and actions. Even so, as I listen to him muttering to them, I'm not sure I've ever felt so alone. Not even during long slipspace journeys.

3

I wake to the gray gloom of first light filtering through the shed. Soren's already standing at a window, eyes distant as he whispers to the ever-present masses, no doubt overlaying everything he sees and feels with his endless commentary.

He hears me stir and turns toward me. "Ready to roll out?"

"Yeah," I say, sitting up. My back threatens to seize up, and I wince, twisting back and forth a bit. That seems to keep any rigidity at bay. "Ready as I'm likely to get." It's not like we have anything to do to prepare. We slept in our uniforms, which every Troubleshooter does when planetside. And we can eat on the road.

"Let's go, then."

"Hold on," I say, gripping my bedroll at the bottom and bunching it, then rolling the bunched part into the rest.

"Why bother with that?" he says. "Rile will send one of his people to do it."

"Leaving your bed unmade is no way to start the day." The twine feels rough between my fingers as I wrap it around the roll.

Laughter from Soren. "You really haven't changed at all, have you?"

"I'd like to talk to some of the other Fallen about Rile, if we can. Not his fighters—the regular people who live here. Women, children. Non-combatants.”

“I'm not sure he'd like that.”

“I'm positive he wouldn't. That's why I want to do it. I'd like some more information on the man sending us hunting.”

Soren shakes his head. “We shouldn't risk screwing up this situation any more than it is. If we just do what he says, then he'll let us access the servers.”

“Or we kill him and access them anyway, if there's reason to.”

“He has too many men.”

“I want to talk to them, Soren.”

But the moment we leave the shed and start through the city streets in the direction Rile said his brother went, it becomes abundantly clear we're being watched. Apparently the Fallen leader isn't remotely concerned with concealing that fact, or if he is, his fighters are letting him down badly. Either way, ten armed men dog us through the streets, not bothering with formalities like “Good morning.” Whenever I glance back to check on their proximity, I find them thirty meters or so distant, leering at us openly.

“We're not going into any of the buildings,” Soren says, and this time I don't try to argue.

Before we pass out of the area Rile and his people occupy, I notice a long, low structure—probably it was once a mall—with an unusually high number of goons posted outside. “That's the building the server room's accessed through,” Soren says, following my gaze.

After we exit the inhabited area, the going gets rougher. Most of Rile's men fall away as we progress through the city, clambering over debris and sometimes detouring through shattered buildings when a street looks too obstructed. But there are still two of them tailing us by the time we reach Sheen's outskirts, presumably to make sure we don't double back. I guess we could always circle around through the jungle and then backtrack, but I doubt I'll talk

Soren into that, and besides, I do want to get off Anaconda as soon as I can.

"Why doesn't Rile just send his own men after his brother?" I ask.

"He's tried—two separate parties of twenty men each. The first group wandered for days without finding any sign of Otto, and the second never came back. Not one of them. I think he considered it a stroke of luck when I turned up a few weeks ago. It meant he could use his leverage with the Guard instead of sending more men out to die. A certain number are needed to keep order in the city, or at least that's what he told me."

"I wonder what his brand of 'order' looks like."

Soren rolls his eyes. "It probably looks about as pretty as the city they live in, Joe. They're Fallen, for Fount's sake. What do you expect?"

We reach the jungle, and within five minutes of trudging through it, my uniform clings damply to my skin. Even its temperature regulation function struggles with the way the jungle seems to trap the humidity. Back in the city the heat was bad enough, but here the dampness makes things ten times worse.

Soren finds distraction in summing up the day and night we've just had for his audience. I've heard it said that the reason for Soren's success has to do with the sheer amount of content he pumps out for his followers on a daily basis, and I'm beginning to believe it. He's gotten worse since our training on Gauntlet.

"Well, people, if you've ever felt bad for buying into what everyone says about the Fallen, I think you can stop," he says. "Remember, Rile and his people are supposed to be the good guys on this planet, but their behavior really confirms everything negative you've heard about the Fallen. Truly the worst of the biologicals."

That makes my head snap toward him, but Soren doesn't seem to notice. "Biological" is a derogative term used to describe people who haven't uploaded, but I've rarely heard it spoken by someone who actually is one. It's such a self-hating thing for one of us to say. Does Soren actually resent his condition, or is he just pandering to his audience?

"Complete savages," he continues. "I've seen a few of you ask what they eat, and believe me when I say I don't even want to think about it. I mean, we've all heard the rumors about how Fallen survive in places like these. Just count me out when it comes to delving too deeply into that, okay?"

As Soren chatters on, and the jungle chirps and squawks and screeches around us, its dimness starts to get disorienting. We're nearly two hours in, and it must be getting close to noon, but with the dense canopy overhead it looks like dusk already.

X3B ranges ahead of us, jogging to sweep the area in wide, arcing lines and keeping in touch with Soren via his datasphere. I have to admit, it's handy to have an expendable forward scout, though I'm trying not to let it make me lax with my own situational awareness. On a full charge, Dice could go for three weeks if he conserved power, though I never deployed him for anywhere near that long. X3B is more advanced, and that may mean his charge won't last as long, unless Lambton Industries hit on some innovations for extending bot battery life as well.

So far, neither us nor the bot has found any sign of humans living out here, and it's not hard to believe the first hunting party Rile sent out came back empty-handed. It's mostly untouched wilderness out here, or at least, jungle that's swallowed almost every sign of the planetary civilization that once existed. Every now and then we come across some rusted metal on the verge of being engulfed by vines, or a concrete structure still standing among the palms, but any roads or pathways that were here are long gone.

It's hard to say whether Soren would notice signs of Otto and his people, even if they were right under his nose. The versecasting must divide his attention, but then, part of it is observing and commenting on his surroundings. Plus, picking up and following a trail would likely make for better content than wandering aimlessly through the jungle.

At last, he runs out of things to say about our present situation, and he falls silent.

"Hey, Soren," I say. "Wanna cut off the versecast for a minute?"

He pauses, then nods and says, "What's up?"

"I've wanted to bring this up since you helped me get free of Cohen, but there's been no time. Back on Gauntlet, after we stopped the pirates, I felt like we—uh, it's kind of hard to put into words."

"Just say it."

"I felt like we…drifted. Like we weren't as close as before. As if the attack succeeded in driving a wedge between us where even the instructors couldn't."

Soren's brow furrows in what I take to be confusion, mixed in with a little anger. "Seriously? Fount, Joe. I never knew you to be so sensitive. What did I do to offend you?"

"Nothing," I say, quickly. "But…was it just me? You didn't feel like we drifted?"

"No. Not at all. I've always considered us brothers."

"Ah—well. Maybe it is just me. Sorry for bringing it up." I clear my throat. "You can turn your versecast back on, if you want."

"Oh," Soren says, a bit sheepishly. "I actually left it on the entire time. Sorry, Joe, but I have to keep this interesting somehow."

Thanks, brother.

4

X3B appears up ahead, sprinting toward us and barely making a sound. He comes to an abrupt halt a few meter away. "Two sentries up ahead. They did not detect me."

"Good work, Zeb," Soren says, and turns to me. "What now?"

"Did you actually see them?" I ask the bot.

"Negative. I determined their position and number via close analysis of their sound profiles, as differentiated from the background noise of the jungle. That is why I can say with confidence that they did not see me."

"Damn," I mutter. "I really underused my bot."

"Wait," Soren says. "Did Joe Pikeman get too nervous to use his own bot? Funny, I thought you would have warmed up to something that was just like you." He chuckles at his own joke.

Soren can have his jibes, but bots are nothing like humans. If it wasn't for the auditing software Lambton installed in every bot, which constantly monitors them for thoughts of improving their own intelligence, they would have outcompeted humanity long ago. Even as they are, bots are freaky enough. The fact that X3B just detected two humans without any chance of them detecting him is a testament to that.

"If we hit the sentries, there's a chance Otto will know," I say.

"How?" Soren says. "They don't have dataspheres. I told you that."

"They must have some way of sending signals back to base. Otherwise, what would be the point of posting sentries?"

"Okay. So what are you proposing?"

"We leave them alone. Scout around them, see if we can find the base camp first, and then decide on a course of action. Better to preserve the element of surprise, right?"

"All right."

We both download the sentries' location from X3B, so that our dataspheres will warn us if we're getting close enough to alert them to our presence. That done, we send the bot wide, to make sure we don't run headlong into any other sentries, and Soren and I search the areas in between, keeping in close contact via subvocalization.

After two hours of treading through the jungle, batting away mosquitoes and carefully probing the ground ahead for pitfalls, we regroup at our original location, having encountered no sign of any encampment.

"What do you make of it?" Soren asks.

"Two things. Otto's smart, and they definitely have a way of communicating across distances."

"What are you basing all that on?"

"We should have found his base if he was arranging his lookouts in a predictable formation, like a circle. That suggests a random disbursement, designed to cover a large area and give plenty of advance warning if a hostile party's in the area. How many fighters did Rile say his brother has?"

"Forty. Low enough that two trained Troubleshooters and a bot should make short work of them, especially if we keep the element of surprise."

I nod. "The days here are seventeen hours long, right? Short enough that they could take lookout duty in two shifts pretty easily.

So, twenty out as sentries, and twenty in their camp, likely with the ability to call all the sentries in if necessary. Even if we sneak past the lookouts to hit the camp directly, we can expect more hostiles at our backs within ten minutes."

"Doesn't seem ideal."

"I agree. So let's bring them to us instead. Starting with taking those sentries alive."

We call back X3B, then we creep toward the sentries' location, after using the bot to confirm they've stayed put. Soren's given me access to X3B's broadcasting system, a decision he made without hesitation. I get the impression he's letting me take the lead to keep things novel for his versecast—his audience must know more or less what to expect from him by now, so letting me make calls keeps things fresh for them. It seems like a wildly irresponsible framework for making tactical decisions, but who's going to stop him?

With the sentries' heat signatures, recorded and provided by Soren's bot, getting the drop on them isn't hard. It's after we engage them that things get complicated. Maybe it's because I don't have much experience with taking people alive.

Both orange and red masses representing the sentries are elevated, and though the jungle's thick foliage blocks them from direct line of sight, it's not hard to tell they're crouched amidst the upper branches of a tree. That said, they seem perfectly level with each other, which suggests they've built some sort of platform up there.

The mass on the left lights up blue, indicating Soren's drawn a bead on that sentry. I level my blaster at the one on the right, lighting that one up too. Then I speak to them, subvocalizing to conceal my position while my voice booms out of X3B's shoulder speakers from the sentries' opposite side:

"Both of you, drop your weapons, now. We have you surrounded and in our sights. If you don't comply immediately, you'll die."

The sentries do react immediately, but not in the way I wanted them to. They both drop from the platform and onto the ground, the one on the left making a beeline toward Soren's position. A slight rise blocks the other from sight, and I advance over the ground, trusting Soren will intercept the runner.

The hillock falls away to reveal the remaining sentry opening fire on X3B's position. We ordered the bot not to fire under any circumstances, so I'm guessing he's taking cover.

A rifle-shaped orange mass shifts closer to red as the sentry lays down covering fire. Leveling my blaster at it, my focus narrows, the world shrinking until it contains only the rifle and the hands holding it.

I aim for a few inches ahead of the trigger—close enough to make the sentry drop it but not enough to maim him.

The blaster bolt flies, jerking the rifle out of his hand and sending it flipping through the foliage. My target turns, his posture suggesting surprise, and X3B darts forward to collect the weapon.

"Don't move," I bark. "You're done."

Slowly, the sentry raises his hands in the air.

"Soren," I subvocalize. "Sitrep?"

There's a pause, and when it comes, Soren's voice is low and tight: "He got past me, Joe. I pursued, but I couldn't get a bead on him, and he lost me in the jungle. Did you get your guy?"

"Yeah," I say, then turn to X3B. "Get up and search that platform. Tell me what you find."

The bot leaps for the lowest branch without hesitation, then clambers up to the next. Apparently he has no problems taking orders from me. I guess Soren gave me full access, but the realization doesn't do much to temper my annoyance at his screwup.

"There appears to be an antenna lashed to the tree's trunk," X3B says as Soren appears through the jungle, looking somewhat crestfallen. "There is also a solar panel positioned near the top."

"There's our answer for how they're communicating with their base," I say. "They're using old NVIS radio tech. Where'd you dig that up?" I ask the sentry, but he doesn't answer.

"If you cooperate, you'll be free to go," I tell him. That seems to make him think, but he still stays quiet.

"Zeb, do you see a radio unit up there anywhere?"

"Negative."

"Okay. You can come down from there."

A second later, X3B hits the jungle floor, crouching to absorb his fall. The sentry starts, then stiffens.

"What's NVIS?" Soren asks.

"Stands for Near Vertical Incidence Skywave. Bounces radio waves off the atmosphere, to get around rough terrain like this."

"How do you know this shit?"

I shrug. "I've had plenty of time for reading during slipspace trips. No nanodeath, remember? I'm guessing the other sentry took the radio unit with him, so he could report our presence back to base," I tell Soren. "The unit's probably configured to communicate with the antenna wirelessly. If you'd kept chasing him, you would have soon taken away his ability to report back, as his unit drew out of the antenna's range."

Soren stares at me with an expression that comes pretty close to a glare. Clearly, the criticism's not landing well.

"Look," I tell the sentry. "Rile sent us—I'm sure you guessed that. But we're not exactly attached to the idea of partnering with him."

Soren clears his throat, but I shoot him a look, and he stays quiet.

"It's not hard to tell that Rile hasn't given us the full picture, where his brother's concerned," I continue. "Why would Otto want to abduct a bunch of children, and why would forty men support him? It doesn't make a whole lot of sense. I'm sure that many men aren't perverts—the rate of perversion in a society tends to be much lower than that. So you must have taken the kids because you're concerned about your tribe's future."

"I'd say we're concerned," the sentry says, then looks surprised to hear himself speak.

Nodding, I say, "Why don't you tell us why? All we care about is getting access to that server room. If you think you can help us do that, then maybe we can reach a solution that benefits us both."

"Yeah," the sentry says, a measure of relief washing over his face. "Could happen. Although, Otto hates Guardsmen even more than Rile does. Hard to say whether he'll be able to trust you enough to work with you."

"Why?"

"Because the Guard has enabled Rile's reign for so long. They've turned a blind eye to his abuses. All you care about is protecting your precious Subverse."

"Fair enough," I say, in spite of Soren's raised eyebrows. "Tell me why you helped Otto take the children."

"Because Rile's been trading them off, in groups of three and four at a time. Trading them for weapons. So Otto took off with what kids he could, to protect them."

A wave of cold washes over my innards. "Who's been supplying the weapons?" I say, though I'm sure I already know the answer.

"This freak of a fella. He's half bot. Wears a black cape, and his eyes glow with this freakish blue."

"Fairfax," I snarl, before I can help myself.

5

"Huh?" the sentry says. "Fairfax? I don't think a Fairfax would have anything to do with a place like this."

"You'd be surprised," I say, though I'm surprised myself, to find that this Fallen even knows about the Five Families. One of them, at least. "We're going to let you go," I tell him, and a wave of evident relief crashes over his face. "In return, I want you to bring this message to Otto: we're willing to work with him to bring Rile down. We want the same thing—to end his grip on Sheen City. There's no reason for us to fight each other."

"Yes," he says, nodding eagerly. "Okay. I'll tell him."

"Do you think he'll agree to work with us?"

"Definitely. Why wouldn't he? It only makes sense."

"Mm. All right, then. You're free to go."

The sentry nods, smiling like he can't believe his good fortune. He turns to collect his laser rifle from X3B, and the bot shakes his head. "Right," the man mutters, then takes off through the jungle at a jog.

Soren's lowered himself onto a thick log, and when I'm sure the sentry's gone, I turn a glare on him. "How the hell did you let that sentry get by you?"

His face darkens. "He took an angle I didn't expect. The plan was to take them alive, right? If I'd shot him I might have killed him, and I doubt wounding him would help negotiations with Otto, since that's apparently the tack you've chosen for us. Without consulting me."

"You're too busy versecasting to be consulted. Your head's in the Subverse, Soren. So much that you let that sentry get by you. You're a Troubleshooter, for Fount's sake."

"Yeah, and you had X3B helping you take yours. Listen, Joe, if my task had been to kill that bastard, he'd be dead. But we wanted him alive. That complicates things, and you know it."

Sighing, I say, "Yeah. I guess it does. Sorry."

Soren nods. "It's fine. Maybe we're letting the jungle get to us. I for one am looking forward to getting off this Fount-forsaken planet."

I nod.

"Hey, when did you become such a diplomat, anyway?"

"I didn't."

"You don't think your chat with that sentry was a fine work of diplomacy?"

"Hell no," I say, leaning back against the tree that held both lookouts just fifteen minutes ago. "He agreed to carry the message way too quickly, and he was too optimistic about the chances Otto will agree, especially after telling us the guy doesn't like Guardsmen. He'll be back with an ambush party, not one that's ready to negotiate."

"What was the point of all that, then?" Soren's brows are drawn downward, but the interest in his voice rings like a bell. He's already getting excited about the versecasting potential, I can tell.

"Look where we're standing. A wide hollow in the ground, surrounded by trees. This would be the perfect place for an ambush target to be standing. And since this is where that sentry saw us last, he'll lead Otto and his men directly here."

Soren grins. It's not hard to tell he still isn't clear on where I'm going with this, but it's just as obvious that he likes the direction. "So…"

"So, we'll ambush their ambush."

"Damn," he says, whistling. "You really have learned a thing or two."

"Living in the real world helps."

Again, Soren's happy to let me organize our counter-action, and as he moves toward the position I've assigned him, up in a tree that overlooks the hollow where we let the sentry go, I hear him muttering to his audience.

"Subvocalize if you have to give commentary," I bark. "But it would be better if you focused."

"Yeah," he says absently. "Okay."

I suppress a sigh. If all goes well, I won't need Soren to fire a single shot. Still, it would be a little more reassuring if I knew his head was fully in this.

"Come with me," I tell X3B, and he follows readily enough. Just beyond the hollow, we find a rock outcropping for him to crouch on top of while training both laser pistols on where we expect Otto and his people to show. "I'm going to use your loud-speakers again, so you'll be drawing any fire. If this works out, though, there shouldn't be any."

"Very comforting," he says, and the sarcasm evokes a twinge of nostalgia for my own cybernetic partner.

"Make sure your pistol's charge pack is fresh," I subvocalize to Soren over a wide channel while making my way to the position I've chosen, in a tree opposite his. This way, we'll have the hollow covered from three angles, with the ability to turn it into a slaugh-terhouse if need be. If it's true that the Fallen lack dataspheres, which their use of NVIS radio seems to confirm, then there'll be little hope of them drawing a bead on either Soren or me before we kill enough of them to send them into disarray.

Once I've hoisted myself into my tree and turned on thermal

vision, I subvocalize again over the wide channel: "I'm in position." With that, we wait, soaking in the bathwater heat of the jungle.

The day wears on, the uneventful hours piling up, one on top of the other. Ask a veteran what it's really like to be in the military, and if he's being completely honest, he'll be more likely to describe something like this: long stretches of tense boredom, waiting for something to happen. Victory only comes to the patient. The ones willing to follow a line of action for as long as necessary.

As we wait, strange creatures trundle across the jungle floor, disarmed by the stillness. I try my best not to let them distract me, but a planet's native organisms always hold a fascination for me, and I catch myself glancing down to catalog their anatomy as best I can, with only their heat signatures to go by. Fount, I'm worse than Soren.

A muscular, five-armed thing probes through the hollow, its fifth arm a stumpy protrusion from the front of its head that grasps at the ground with every step. Is it looking for prey, or simply feeling its way through the world? Vision is cognitively demanding —could this creature have gained some evolutionary advantage through navigating by touch alone? It seems unlikely, but then, so do a thousand other beasts I've encountered.

An alert pings my attention from the right hemisphere of my field of vision—thank Fount I set up some datasphere triggers, just in case. I look to see a cluster of heat signatures approaching through the jungle, thirty-one according to my datasphere, their arms in positions that suggest firearms. The weapons themselves aren't visible to me, which just means they haven't been fired recently.

It's a little surprising to me that they're all approaching from the same direction. Yes, they're spreading out as they draw closer, in order to come at the hollow in a wide arc, but clustering together as they are really isn't a good tactic when faced with plasma grenade-carrying Troubleshooters. The approach says one of two things: either I was wrong and Otto does want to work with us, or they've never faced Guardsmen in combat and don't know the danger they're in.

The way they're holding their weapons tells me it's probably the second one. And it makes sense, I guess: Soren only mentioned the Guard bargaining with the Fallen that control Nectar's server room, never fighting them. If the Guard had had the resources to devote to an assault, the Fallen wouldn't be here anymore.

"Stay frosty," I subvocalize to Soren and X3B as Otto's people take up positions, weapons trained on the hollow. "Don't engage unless I say to."

The Fallen hesitate for a few moments, maybe surprised that none of them have spotted any targets yet. After a while, a few of them arc around the clearing, trickling around the perimeter, and I'm about to tell X3B to fall back when they draw up short.

Their entire formation breaks, flowing forward toward the hollow. When they reach it, they mill around it, postures suggesting confusion. I can see a lot of them now even without thermal vision.

"Freeze," I command from Zeb's shoulder speakers, my voice booming through the foliage. "Drop your weapons."

They don't freeze. Instead, they move around the hollow even more spastically. Some of them start inching toward X3B's position.

"Stop moving and drop your weapons," I say again. "Comply immediately or I will fire."

Most of them stop, but a couple are still moving toward the bot.

Sighing, I shoot, hitting a tree just ahead of them. "One more step and I'll end you. Drop. Your. Weapons."

"All right," a man calls, his voice deep and resonant. "Lower your weapons, everyone." I'm impressed by how calm he sounds.

"Pile them in the middle of the hollow and tell me when you're finished," I say.

"Okay," the man shouts again. "They're all in a pile."

"X3B, verify."

The bot leaves his position on the rock outcropping and creeps to the edge of the hollow. None of Otto's people react, so I'm guessing they don't see him.

"A few are still armed," he subvocalizes.

"Paint them," I say, and a second later my datasphere turns five of the figures scarlet.

Steadying my breath, I line up my shot.

The blaster goes off, sounding like a guy-wire snapping, and the white bolt slams into the back of my target's thigh, sending him staggering forward.

"The next shot will be lethal," I snarl, and a few of the Fallen near X3B clap their hands over their ears. "*Drop your weapons. All of you.*"

The red-painted forms all approach the weapon pile and seem to toss their firearms onto it. Then they back away.

"They are now all unarmed," X3B reports.

"Good. Soren, sit tight in case things go south."

"Got it."

I holster my blaster. As silently as possible, I crawl back through my tree's branches and lower myself, taking care to keep its thick trunk between me and the Fallen. Once I'm on the ground, I draw my weapon and lead with it, my left hand cupped under my right to steady my aim.

"We could have talked without you shooting one of my people," says the same resonant voice from before as I draw into view. The speaker is a man with a long beard bound in twine. He grimaces toward the groaning woman lying a few feet away, whose wound is being tended to by another.

"You didn't take me seriously until I fired," I say. "But honestly, that makes sense to me. I talk best with my blaster."

6

"Y ou were moving on us," I say, before whipping my blaster toward a man with bad acne who's getting too close to the weapon pile. "Get away from there." He steps back, and I continue. "I sent your sentry with an offer to work together, but instead you were about to attack us."

Otto shrugs. "Ambushing you wasn't a totally irrational course of action. If it was, I doubt you would have anticipated it."

"Oh, I have plenty of experience predicting irrational behavior," I shoot back. "Trying to ambush us *was* irrational. I saw it coming because I could tell from talking to your man that you have an irrational distrust of Guardsmen."

Otto's shaking his head, his trussed beard wagging back and forth. "You're going to have a hard time convincing me *that's* unreasonable. Humanity wouldn't have been able to retreat from the real world if it wasn't for you enablers."

"I agree with you. But a man's gotta eat, and so does his family. People have done a lot worse in human history for a paycheck. Anyway, there's more to this than whether you trust the Guard or not. Tell me, when you left Sheen, did you take *every* kid in the city with you?"

"No," Otto says after a brief pause, and the syllable sounds forced. "We had to flee before we could get to them all."

"And the kids you did take—are they living better now than they did before?"

"Yes, considering they're not in danger of being traded to a psychopath."

"But their living conditions are worse. I don't know what sort of shelter you've found or built, but I'm sure it doesn't compare to the buildings you occupied back in Sheen. I'm sure the children are much more frightened of predators snatching them in the night than they ever were in the city. And they're right to be."

"What about it? There's nothing to be done about that."

I shake my head. "What I'm trying to tell you, Otto, is that we can help you save those other kids. Not only that, we can help you take the city back from your brother."

The Fallen rebel chuckles. "You and your bot?"

"A single Troubleshooter has an outsized effect on an engagement. I have the tactical and strategic knowhow to increase your people's effectiveness, and I have the superior weaponry to make Rile hurt. Plus, I'm not the only Troubleshooter here. There's another with his laser pistol trained on you right now. Do you think I would have risked approaching so many of you if there wasn't?"

"You're bluffing."

"No, I'm negotiating. And those who lie during negotiations tend to run into trouble when it comes time to make good on their offer."

Otto studies me, his dark eyes seeming to weigh me for a long time.

"How would you propose taking the city from Rile?" he asks at last.

To be honest, I hadn't gotten that far yet, but failing to say anything probably wouldn't do much for my position, here. So I improvise.

"Your tribe must have been pretty big, before the rift between you and Rile." I say. "Judging by how many fighters I've seen."

The Fallen leader nods. "Our numbers were approaching a thousand, altogether."

"What's the main food source?"

"Not cannibalism, if that's what you're asking. I know that's what you off-worlders usually assume."

"It's not what I was asking. I'm trying to learn Rile's vulnerabilities."

"He maintains a farm in an empty lot, guarded against scavengers and pests at all hours. But our main food source has always been hunting. There's no shortage of meat to be had in the jungle, mostly pretty easy game, even without the weapons Rile traded for."

"And how did you folks come by your weapons?"

"Rile armed us. He concealed what he was doing for a long time, and for a while he managed to explain away the children's disappearances by blaming predators and the like. I figured out what was going on, though, and I organized the evacuation."

"Okay. Well, we don't have the numbers for a siege, and threatening Rile's food source doesn't seem like an option."

"Obviously," Otto says dryly.

"How does he maintain control of so many people?" I ask. "How does he keep them so afraid they won't venture outside when Guardsmen are about?"

"They won't go outside under *any* circumstances." As he speaks, Otto's upper lip curls. "Not without Rile's permission, and only under strict supervision. Rile's men have free reign to make an example of anyone who tries to leave the buildings of their own free will. Children are beaten and thrown back inside, and the women..." Otto shudders. "Rile's also had plastic explosives planted underneath their homes, which he promises to detonate if they disobey."

"Do you think it's a bluff?"

"The bombs are for real. As for whether I think he'd set them off...yes. I do."

Based on his evident disgust, it seems pretty clear Otto's telling the truth. What he's saying fits my impression of Rile, too. I've met too many men like him to have any doubt about what they're capable of.

The people standing around us, many of who can't seem to keep their eyes off the weapon pile, show a range of reactions to our conversation. Some are shaking their heads in shame or disgust at the talk of Rile, but others stand stiffly, with a few glaring at me.

I need more time to process what Otto's told me—time I don't have. Still, I feel like we're close to working together. If I can just push a little more...

Might as well go all-in. "The way he treats the tribe's women and children can't be a new thing," I say.

Otto's jaw stiffens, and his expression goes blank. "No," he admits at last.

"Yet he's your brother," I say slowly, "and your group splitting off—that *is* new."

The man's silence holds, but his gaze falls to the ground.

"So you've been tolerating Rile's behavior for a long time. What changed?"

"What's your point?" a youth to Otto's left spits, but the leader holds up a hand.

"Peace," Otto says. "He has a point. An important one." His gaze lifts to meet mine once more. "Rile rules with fear, and any who dare to disagree with him are shot without further discussion. So yes, while many of us considered his actions disgusting, we stayed silent. Because of that, we didn't know who was truly with Rile and who found his actions repugnant. We couldn't find each other. Alone, we weren't strong enough to act."

"And yet," I say, gesturing at the group standing around us.

"And yet...when I discovered that Rile was trading away the children, I approached a few who I thought would stand against him with me. I got lucky, because I turned out to be right. Then they told a few more who they judged would be with us. Not Rile's twisted goons, but people whose goodness glimmered through every now and then, despite the hell my brother created after our father died. And over the course of a few days, we formed a party. Then, we acted."

"Right. But why couldn't you do that before?"

Otto's jaw firms up, but his eyes are narrowed in pain. When he speaks, his voice is soft, and those around us lean toward him to hear: "Maybe it is about time we drag this out into the open. We didn't act before because we were cowards," he says, and now he's talking to everyone, not just me. "We let Rile cow us. We always had the strength to oppose him, to stand up for what we knew to be right. But we didn't use it. Not until our future was threatened."

I think I like the direction this is headed, but I'm a bit confused by that last remark. "Wait—you said the *children* were threatened."

"Yes," Otto said, a slight tremor entering his tone. "Rile trades away the children, two by three by four. But there's something you may not understand, Guardsman. Your employer pays you well, and will look after you in later life. Maybe you'll upload to the Subverse and be taken care of forever. But for us, our children truly are our future. We rely on them not only to carry the tribe forward after we're gone, but also to care for and protect us when we're old and weak, just as we protected them in their youth. For Rile to trade away our children, he's literally trading away our future."

"Does Rile have children?"

Otto nods. "Most of them are forced to stay inside, except for a couple of the older boys, who he takes hunting. But none of his kids have been traded."

"I see. Are you ready to join forces yet and take this bastard down?"

"The decision's not mine alone, and you haven't proposed a

plan to do that yet. I'm ready. But I'm not the only one you need to convince."

The others haven't moved, and their interest in their weapons seems to have waned, at least for the moment. Some of them wear expressions of skepticism, but more look interested. A few look downright eager.

"Okay," I tell them. "Then here's the plan. Most of you will go with my colleague, who'll lead you around Sheen City to where our Broadswords are hidden. With the ships and the combat bot, you'll have more than enough to raise holy hell and draw all of Rile's men to you."

"A distraction, I assume," Otto says, his tone neutral. "Since you mentioned *most* will go with the other Guardsman."

"That's right," I say. "You and I will lead a squad into the other side of Rile's territory. You'll start evacuating women, children, and any men who live in those buildings with them. For my part, I'll plant plasma grenades in the buildings' basements, set to detonate on my command. If Rile's men come at us, we'll lure them past the buildings, then bring them down on their heads and mop up whatever's left."

"It sounds like it could work. I'm with you," Otto says. "Thomas?" he says, turning to the youth near him.

Thomas's eyes still burn with suspicion and anger, but at last he nods. "I'm with you."

"Gordon?"

Gordon, a graying man with a neatly trimmed beard, also nods.

One by one, Otto gets unanimous consent from those gathered around us. It takes longer, but I can appreciate doing it this way. A simple vote might have been unanimous, but it's easy to raise your hand or say "Aye" without meaning it. If you give your support openly, though, with everyone else listening…it binds you. And it strengthens the group as a whole.

"We're with you," Otto says at last. "All of us. Though, you mentioned saving men from those buildings—you should know, Rile doesn't permit men too weak or old for hunting to live."

I nod gravely, and Otto dispatches Thomas to run back to their camp and inform the adults there of what we're planning.

"I wish we could do this right now," Otto says. "But the day becomes evening. Unless you think we should strike during the night?"

"No," I say after a moment's consideration. "We should rest first. Too much risk of injury if we try to navigate the jungle and then the rubble of the city by night."

Otto nods. "Then we make camp. I'd invite you back to ours, but I'd rather not frighten the children with our talk."

"Understood," I say, then switch to subvocalizing. "You get all that, Soren?"

"Loud and clear."

"Are you ready to trust them?"

"About as much as it's possible for me to trust a bunch of Fallen. At least, I don't see why they wouldn't want our help getting the city back from Rile."

"Yeah," I say. "All right, well come down and introduce yourself."

Soren helps Otto set up a perimeter around our camp while I run Otto's people through some basic exercises I expect will come in handy during the fighting tomorrow. Though I wonder how much of my rushed lessons they'll actually retain.

Later, Soren and I are sitting next to a dying fire in silence. Otto sat with us for a couple hours, drinking from a metal flask and offering us nips from it. Soren accepted a couple times, but I refused. I want to be fresh for tomorrow.

I should probably turn in, but first there's something I want to discuss with Soren.

"You said if I help you get access to the servers, you'll help me clear my name with the Guard," I say. "Is that still your intention?"

"Of course," Soren says, turning an easy smile toward me. "It's the least I could do."

"Well, there's something else I want to ask."

He raises his eyebrows.

"Help me take down Rodney Fairfax."

That brings a grimace from my old friend. "Joe, officially, he's an ally of the Guard. If I went against him, I doubt I'd be in a position to help you clear your name."

"You said you've been following my versecasts. That means you saw the slaughter he brought to Tunis. How he consorted with pirates to abduct children."

"Sure, but versecasts can be modified to show whatever you want. I'm not saying *I* believe you modified them, but no one takes versecasts as a neutral account of events. People just choose the stories they like best, and follow the versecasters at their center. Because it's fun to go along for the ride, whether it's true or not."

"So the Guard thinks I have the time to modify versecasts to frame Rodney Fairfax?"

"They probably think it's possible. That, or someone's feeding you fabricated versecasts to distribute. Or maybe they haven't watched the versecasts at all." Soren shakes his head. "You should focus on getting your daughter back, Joe. Fairfax has a lot of clout, and I wouldn't let vengeance blind you enough that you walk into whatever he has waiting for you."

"Vengeance?"

"I know he killed you, back on Arbor. You want him dead for that, right?"

"And for ripping children away from their families."

"Yeah. Maybe that's what you tell yourself it's about. But I know you, Joe. You don't like being bested. You want a chance to prove you're better than him, stronger, if only to yourself."

I stare at him wordlessly. Maybe he's right. Maybe all I care about is vengeance.

Yes, Harmony will be safer Fairfax he dies, and so will the

galaxy. But is that just a convenient justification for seeking revenge above all else?

It doesn't matter. Nothing's changed, no matter what Soren says.

I want Fairfax dead, and I'll make it happen. Whether Soren helps me do it or not.

7

"We're in position," Soren says into my thoughts, projected there by my datasphere. "You?"

"Have been for a while." We maneuvered into position under the cover of darkness, and Soren's timing couldn't be better: dawn has just begun to spread across the city. "Any problems?"

"Negative."

"Told you there was nothing to worry about." Soren is going along with my impromptu plan, probably for entertainment value, but I don't think he's crazy about splitting up, or about leading a bunch of Fallen to our ships.

"Maybe not from Otto and his people. But I have a feeling Rile's capable of giving us plenty to worry about."

Even though we're communicating using the medium of thought, and the squad around me can't hear, I still don't answer him. No need to jinx the action before it's even begun.

We're crouched in the middle of a rubble-strewn intersection—one that offers plenty of cover, but also enough mobility to retreat if needed. I don't think it will be.

Scanning the buildings around us, as well as what I can see of the four connecting streets, turns up no signs of life. Rile's two men may have escorted us out to the very edge of Sheen City yesterday, but under normal circumstances he doesn't seem to maintain a presence beyond the few blocks they've cleared for their tribe. Other than hunting, that is—but we're coming in from the north-west, and Otto says the easiest game is in the east.

"Will we start, then?" Soren says.

"I thought you'd never ask."

Through the pause, I can almost hear the heavy sigh he's probably heaving, though that wouldn't transmit unless he willed it to. "All right, Joe. Good luck."

"You too."

With that, we wait. I can't see them through the truncated stumps of buildings around me, but right now I know my ship's crew will be skimming over the city, keeping formation with the *Hermes* under anti-grav while hugging the building tops as closely as they can. Shouldn't be hard, considering how slowly they'll need to move to keep pace with the group on foot below.

But if he followed the plan, Soren should already be deep inside the city, just a handful of blocks away from Rile's perimeter. Less than ten minutes later, I hear the sound that confirms that: the screech of Javelin missiles leaving their tubes and flying above the cityscape.

Four explosions follow, though to the untrained ear they probably sound like one. The nine Fallen surrounding me tense up, staring at each other with wide eyes as the ground rumbles underfoot. "Are you waiting for a better signal than that?" I yell at them, and it seems to rouse them. They fall into loose formation behind me as we advance together across the intersection, toward the path I scouted an hour ago using my night vision.

The route I've chosen is as clear of rubble as you can reasonably expect from a post-apocalyptic city, and I'm not complaining about the debris it does have. I like having readily available cover. Though Soren's distraction is about as convincing as you can get, there's no guarantee this will be a cakewalk. Hell, if it was too convincing, it could send Rile's men into a panicked retreat, straight into us.

We discussed that possibility with Otto last night, and we decided that other than the opening volley, we wouldn't fire any more Javelins. Especially considering the risk of hurting innocents. Both our Broadswords have a Fallen aboard who's familiar with the area, to serve as spotter—and who's shut out from the ship's systems—but Otto was adamant about this, and I agree with him.

Of course, laser weapons pose a much lesser risk of collateral damage, and as our squad jogs through the city, dodging rubble, the distant crackle of the Broadswords' laser turrets is distinctly audible.

As we near the first block occupied by the tribe, I scramble up the side of an iron fire escape, which groans threateningly as I ascend. Not my best idea, but we need the intel, and I'm ready to throw myself clear if the thing detaches from this hollowed-out husk of an office building. If I injure myself, I'll just have to tough it out and wait for the Fount inside me to work its magic.

Not daring to climb beyond the third story, I peer over the city, letting my datasphere do most of the work. Predictably, it picks out two hostiles before I do, tagging them both blood-red. When I zoom in on them, I see they're both exhibiting signs of anxiety: one of them keeps fingering the butt of his laser rifle, and the other shifts his weight from foot to foot.

I look down at Otto and hold up two fingers, then point to the goons' locations. He nods, breaking off with half our squad to sprint toward a covered position farther down the road—a pile of rubble stacked high near a broken-off building. As they run, I cover them, blaster at the ready to answer any attack. From their positions at the bottom of the fire escape, my fireteam does the same, keeping their weapons up to suppress enemy fire if needed.

Watching Otto's fireteam advance, I try not to wince. Around the campfire last night, they seemed to get the concept of bounding overwatch easily enough, but grasping the principle doesn't equal flawless execution. Not without years of drills and live experience.

Their path forward is far from optimal, leaving them needlessly exposed, even though there's cover nearby they could easily crouch-and-run along. One of them turns to make some grinning remark to the man behind him, as though the protection my half of the squad is providing makes them invincible.

These guys are much worse than I am, and I haven't used squad tactics since I led a bunch of combat bots against a Fallen insurrection back on Vesuvius. Shaking my head, I remind myself that our adversary is just as untrained.

Once Otto's team is in position, he makes a chopping motion forward, and I carefully make my way down the stairs. The three waiting for me on the ground peel away from their positions to advance together with me. As we do, Otto's fireteam covers us. Which doesn't provide me with a whole lot of reassurance, but I guess it's better than nothing.

Unsurprisingly, one of Rile's goons spots us well before we get the drop on him. My fireteam's the one bounding when it happens, but Otto's team actually does a decent job in distracting him with their fire, scattershot though it may be. We reach the parking garage entrance we were making for, and from there we're able to hit the hostile before he can withdraw behind the building he's clearly supposed to be guarding. He goes down and doesn't get up.

The other grunt gets away, and we don't make much effort to stop him. Actually, it's part of the plan: all about making sure Rile realizes what we're trying to do and devotes men to stopping us. Divide and conquer.

"This is one of the places Rile keeps non-fighters," Otto says, gesturing at the long, squat structure.

I nod, and just as we're about to head in, Soren's voice leaks into my thoughts: "We're ready to melt back into the jungle, Joe. How are things looking on your end?"

"Couldn't have timed it better," I send back. "Proceed as planned."

"Roger that."

I take it upon myself to clear our entrance into the building. There's a battered metal door a few meters away, and my squad mates arrange themselves around it as I prepare to attempt entry. When I try the knob, it won't budge, but before I use one of my only breaching charges I decide to try more traditional means, bringing my foot up and slamming the heel into the door. The first kick makes it give a little, and the second sends it flying open to crash against a wall.

It takes less than three seconds to clear the first room, a smallish cube. Then I wave the rest of my squad in, and Otto heads for the doorway into the next room, which lacks an actual door.

I follow right behind him, a little nervous about how cavalier he's being. But the lack of resistance vindicates his comfort level —for this situation, anyway. Not as a matter of principle.

But what the next room holds makes all thought of combat theory fly from my head. Long and low-ceilinged, it appears full of living corpses. Sallow-skinned things laboring for air, their eyes sunken like embers through snow. My datasphere quickly calibrates my night vision to the room's dimness, and I see that bald patches dot most of their heads.

"These people are suffering from extreme malnutrition," I say to Otto, my voice coming out flat.

He nods, his mouth a grim line. "These people are in the worst condition. The ones who live closest to Rile—the ones he considers most attractive—are better fed and cared for. These are the ones he thinks are ugly, or who've fallen from his favor. He keeps them out here on the perimeter, where they're most vulnerable to predators."

Something flickers outside, and seconds later a low rumbling emanates from the direction we came. Otto's head snaps toward it, his brow furrowed. " Is that a storm? The sky was completely clear just a minute ago."

"Sounds like there's one anyway," I snap, unwilling to let something like weather distract me right now. Instead, I'm focusing on my hatred of Rile, as well as keeping the bile from rising any farther than it has. "Tell the rest of the squad to start evacuating these people. Then come back here. I want you to take me downstairs, to where Rile keeps the explosives."

A couple of the sickly creatures gasp on hearing my words, and a few others stare at me, but most of them seem unconcerned with pretty much everything in their lives, even the sudden appearance of a strange Troubleshooter. Otto gives a curt nod and trots back to the front room. A few seconds later he's back, leading me through the long room, toward a stairwell.

"Rile keeps them from tampering with the bomb by checking it every night," Otto says as we trot down two flights of stairs.

"Figured," I spit. The fear of blowing themselves up probably does that too—themselves, and those who sleep beside them on the dusty concrete at night.

The sound of laserfire from above brings us up short, and we stare up the stairs the way we came.

"Rile's men were quicker than expected," Otto says.

"Yeah," I say, trying not to grit my teeth. "Just point me to the bomb. I'll go it alone from here. You go back up top and help your people hold off Rile's men."

"The plastic explosives are in a room at the end of this hall," Otto says, pointing. Without another word, he turns and sprints back up the stairs, laser rifle at the ready.

I'm already running down the hallway, slowing only to dodge some nail-ridden boards halfway along its length. Even at this remove, I can hear the amount of laserfire being exchanged above, and I can estimate the number of Rile's men. Sounds like we're pretty outnumbered.

Then I'm barreling through the door at the end of the hall, head whipping around to search the floor and walls.

Then, I see it. Not the explosive, but where it was. Strips of adhesive on a metal girder, hastily cut away, leaving only ragged strips where the bomb once was.

"Soren," I breathe, not bothering to subvocalize.

"Yeah? What's going on?" He isn't subvocalizing either, and I can hear the sound of laserfire behind his words.

"It's not here. Rile moved the bomb, and I'm pretty sure his men are up there surrounding Otto as we speak."

"Ah, shit," Soren says. "Fount damn it."

"I need you to pack both ships with Fallen and come back us up."

"Uh…you're in the building's basement, right?"

"Yeah, but I'm going back up."

"Just stay down there, Joe. Find somewhere to hide. I doubt Rile's idiots expect anyone to linger down there. They'll overlook you."

Above, thunder sounds loudly enough to drown out the laserfire momentarily. "Otto would die if I do that."

"Let him. He's just a Fallen, Joe. He was willing to kill us, yesterday. Let him die."

I stare at the girder, where the plastic explosive used to be. No bomb, no plan. And Otto has no idea.

The storm rages louder. It really is strange how fast it picked up.

"Soren," I growl. "Get your ass over here, *now.*" With that, I end the transmission and turn to race back down the hall.

8

When I reach the ground level, the laserfire's only coming from one side of the building—the side we approached from.

Fount damn it. Rile's goons have already pushed Otto and his people that far?

Somehow, I doubt they kept the presence of mind to implement the center-peel retreat I tried to teach them yesterday, and anyway, it probably wouldn't do much good with a herd of civilians to protect.

I find the porch where we entered empty, but through the open door I see what I feared:

The street's littered with the still forms of the people Rile allowed to get so close to starvation. Three of the squad are dead, too lying where the laserfire threw them, and the other four are firing desperately from random spots amidst the rubble, with no sense of cohesion. The skeletons we 'liberated' cower nearby, against buildings. They seem too afraid to run, but I doubt their decision to remain here will win them any mercy from Rile.

At least Otto's alive. For now.

The enemy's backs are to me, and they aren't bothering much

with cover. There are nearly fifty of them, and only four of Otto's people are still alive, crouched behind anything that offers some protection. Rile's men can afford to stand around in the open and wait for the rebels to screw up, which I'm sure will happen sooner than later.

One thing's for sure: if Otto dies, conditions aren't going to get any better around here. Chances are they'll get a lot worse.

A voice in my head is yelling at me, trying to tell me that my anger's going to get me killed. I need to suppress it.

But that's not the Shiva way. The old Shiva Knight would say to embrace my emotions—to channel them. According to him, if channeled correctly through the Fount, emotions can shine light on the optimal path forward. Observe them, accept them, do not try to change them.

Focus on them.

As I do, a rushing sensation fills me, starting with my chest and quickly extending to fill my limbs. My field of vision seems to narrow to a point—the back of the nearest henchman. Everything else is still there, but I prioritize that one thing, and my hand moves to my holster, unsnapping it and drawing my blaster in one smooth motion.

As its muzzle rises toward my target's head, I suddenly remember standing in one of Arbor's ways, facing Fairfax.

A single bolt lances forth, and I don't bother waiting to watch its effect. I already know it will strike true, as surely as I know the rain that's just begun to fall will hit the ground. Every drop.

My arm's already swinging to the next goon, my finger squeezing the trigger before I switch to a third target.

The first bolt I fired hits home as I'm selecting a fourth hostile. Blood and bone exit the goon's head, spraying into the air, and then Rile's men start collapsing as uniformly as dominoes as more bolts hammer home.

Eight men lie dead before the first seems to register what's happening. My blaster, already twitching toward another target, switches trajectories. The first man to notice my presence dies before he can speak.

Two others see him fall, and they die, too, as they're turning around.

Some distant part of my mind remarks on the fact that at any given moment, there are four white blaster bolts in the air, enough fire that it looks like a full fireteam should be firing from the doorway.

But the brunt of my cognition is divided between shooting and monitoring the awareness levels of each hostile. When instinct shouts that a goon is about to turn, he dies, his head or neck or back burst apart by a blaster bolt.

Everything has slowed, like I'm seeing reality at a faster frame rate. Every sound is crisp and audible—not only the laserfire and the crescendoing thunder, but my own heart beat, and the scuffling of dozens of pairs of feet.

A deep calm accompanies the slowing, and I'm able to think full thoughts between firing each bolt. Fighting like this reminds me of playing chess.

The fact that Rile took the bomb has become irrelevant. I've become a human explosion.

As the eighteenth man falls, too many others become alerted to my presence, all turning as one. I withdraw into the room to cut off their lines of fire. I'm able to fell three more before too many hostiles turn their attention on me, rushing the porch and forcing me back into the main room.

I'm able to waste two more as they push into the porch, but then their fire becomes too great, and I withdraw farther, turning sharply to inch backward along the wall, toward the staircase.

The henchmen burst into the darkened room, six of them charging one after another, spraying their fire all over in a desperate attempt to hit me before I can hit them. Their neon-blue laser bolts come nowhere near me, and I smoothly unleash a barrage of blaster bolts, anticipating their positions as telegraphed by their speeds and trajectories.

As the fifth bolt leaves my weapon, my first target falls.

The initial charge fails, but it buys time for the rest of Rile's men to enter the long, low room, while still others are entering from the other side—their reinforcements have arrived. My blaster fire has given up my location, and their weapons are turning toward me, the first laser bolts crackling through the air to slam into the wall around me.

I abandon the stairwell as my destination, instead pushing off the wall and heading toward the cracked and battered furniture that litters the center of the room—threadbare couches, moth-eaten armchairs, uneven tables and chairs held together mostly by hope.

My datasphere lights up with dark circles to indicate beads drawn on me by Rile's men. I use its data to evade their fire, since even my overclocked instincts can't seem to process all of it at once.

I dive, rolling and coming up behind what looks like a church pew. It starts to smoke and crack with laserfire right away, but I'm already scrabbling to the left, behind a couch, and then underneath a dining table. From under it, I take down three more hostiles before they realize where I've gone, and I scrabble back on the diagonal, using the furniture to conceal my path. The fact that they don't have night vision is definitely giving me an advantage.

I lead them through the maze of bedrolls lying on concrete, couches and benches laid with bedding, and other objects these people have made into beds. Pop up here, where they'll least expect it—unleash a barrage of pure white blaster bolts. Duck back behind the paltry cover and retreat through the furniture to the place where I'll unleash my next attack.

It isn't long before I have to swap out my depleted charge pack for a fresh one. It takes precious seconds to fish the charged pack from one of the pockets on my belt and drop the spent one into it, with laserfire lighting up the room all around me.

Then, I reach the end of the furniture. The place where I'll have to make my last stand.

As I lift my blaster above the mess of furniture, a distant whine reaches my ears, growing louder with every second. I'd recognize that sound anywhere: the high-pitched hum of a Becker drive.

My night vision makes targets jump out in the gloom, and I swing my blaster between them, loosing bolts of light aimed to anticipate their near-future positions. Several go down, but many more are closing in across the room, some circling around the sleeping area.

"We're here," Soren says inside my head. "I don't know if we're going to get to you in time, though. At least a couple hundred hostiles are swarming toward your location, and I don't think the Fallen I brought with me will be able to fight through them."

Sighting three more targets, I let my hands do the work as I glance backward to my left. There's an exit about twenty meters away, but whether it leads outside or to a dead end, I can't say.

I tag it with my datasphere, and when I face forward, all three of my targets have fallen. I switch to the next batch of hostiles.

"See the point I just tagged?" Two more hostiles go down, one with a bolt to his neck, the other with his skull and brains laid bare. "Can you tell me if that leads outside?"

"Negative. It's close to the building's exterior, but I don't see an exit. Must just be another room, though I can't see any windows."

"Make me an exit."

Soren pauses—precious time I don't have. I let fly five more blaster bolts in quick succession, then I'm forced to stop firing as I roll backward to avoid enemy fire.

"You want me to use another Javelin?" he says at last.

"Yes. Now."

"We agreed with Otto only to use four."

"Soren, *fire the Fount-damned missile!*"

"On it."

I'm in the open now, performing a bizarre dance with no rhythm in order to dodge the multiple laser bolts my datasphere's telegraphing in any given second. There's barely time to get off any blaster fire at all, though I do manage to put down three more targets

The sound of a Javelin screaming through the rain reaches my ears, and the enemy flinches collectively, allowing me to straighten and neutralize more of them, the walls flickering with the light of my blaster fire. But there are dozens of hostiles in here now, and my kills barely diminish the barrage of lasers.

The missile hits, sending tremors through the building, and I jog sideways toward the door, which has buckled in its frame but hasn't come free.

At last I'm there, yanking on the handle, but it won't budge. That's the closest my calmness comes to shattering, and somehow I'm sure that if I let the stress get to me, I'll fall out of my over-clocked state. But the calm holds, and I jerk the handle again as neon-blue laserfire scores the walls and floor around me. It opens, then I'm through, emerging into a smoke-filled, smoldering room that sports a new hole in its exterior wall.

No time to stop. As I emerge into the downpour, I notice a mass of Rile's men clustered to my right, pushing past each other to be the first to get inside the building I just left. To get at me.

None of them spot me, at least not yet, and I take the opportunity to eject my blaster's charge pack and swap it with a fresh one. That done, I level my blaster at the mass of enemies, left hand cupped under my right, and I start raining hell on them as I side-step toward a building across the street.

Ten bolts are in play by the time the first hits, and when the shots start connecting, they prove accurate. Each one picks an indi-vidual out of the crowd, blasting him backward into his fellows and causing immediate confusion. I'm progressing slowly up the side of a rubble pile, and when my pursuers start emerging from the building after me, I'm forced to throw myself over the top, neutralizing the first few to exit and then scrabbling backward toward the cover of the building behind me.

That's when both Broadswords start opening up on the mass of hostiles trying to push into the building, laser turrets hammering them from above. The carnage is absolute, and I can pick out each individual scream of fear and rage, each shriek of pain. In the meantime, a headache is starting to build inside my skull, the pressure mounting. Lightning flickers, and the rumble of thunder follows a couple seconds later.

I don't make it to the building, crouching against the pile of rubble instead, firing at my pursuers over the edge. They're forced to come out one and two at a time through the gap, and it's hopeless. My aim is too good, and they're mostly mowed down before they can return fire.

Even so, my accuracy's deteriorating. That's not all—my body is starting to shake. At first, it's a barely noticeable vibration, but then tremors start to rack my body.

The old knight's words come back to me, then: *Overclock for long enough, and you will fall into a deep unconscious state, helpless before your enemies.* Have I already been overclocked for too long?

My vision's as crisp as it has been for the last ten minutes or so, but the periphery's beginning to blur. Then, the darkness starts edging in, and it takes all my will to keep it at bay.

The blaster tracks its next target. My trigger finger squeezes, and a bolt leaps out to seek flesh. Soon, my consciousness is reduced to only this. I forget where I am. I forget my name. I exist only to shoot and kill.

A ship lands nearby, sending up dust despite the downpour. With that, the darkness wins out, and the last thing I feel is my body slumping against the rubble.

9

I'm stumbling through a city that tries to dazzle at every opportunity. I'm leering at passersby, who mostly keep their distance. My head feels full of fog, but through it I can grasp at memories, though they slip away as soon as I try to pin them down.

"This isn't real," I mutter at a girl on the cusp of adulthood, and she shies away from me.

That's the one thing that seems certain, at the moment: this isn't real. It can't be, because I remember dying thousands of times, maybe millions. I remember sprees of senseless violence that end with my death, which I mostly embraced.

That was a prison of some kind. I think. Everyone seemed afraid of me, there.

Not everyone's afraid, here. Some people don't shy away— instead, they hold my eyes till we pass each other, as if daring me to make a wrong move. That isn't how people reacted to me, during the endless cycles, the day-long periods of life and killing and death. Everyone was afraid of me, then.

Marissa. She's the only reason I was brought to this place. A voice speaks up in my head, telling me she's the only reason I exist at all, but I push it aside. That's stupid.

I don't know why I'm being allowed to walk through this shining city, with all these normal-seeming people. A memory tugs at me from the corner of my mind—I think I was freed from my prison, somehow. But the details still lurk behind the haze.

One thing does take shape as I lurch from sidewalk to sidewalk: the desire to inflict as much damage on this place as I can. To try to cultivate some actual *consequences*, to remind everyone what it's like to actually live. These people don't know what life is. They might as well be dead.

They *are* dead, as far as I'm concerned.

So what difference will it make if I kill them?

There are safeguards against violence, I remember. Something in the code.

Code?

Yes. This place is artificial. A program. A simulation. They call it…the Subverse.

It's coming back to me now. How Marissa brought me here. Copied me against my will, a bastard child of a father—myself— the real me, who didn't even know I existed.

But I'm him, too, now. Somehow. How can that be?

One thing at a time. I found ways around the safeguards, before. The simulation's pathetic attempts at realism offered byroads around the protections. Pain can be inflicted. Why would they simulate pain? Because they know life is nothing without it.

Except here, you can feel pain for an eternity without ever dying. The pain leads nowhere—it has no logical consequence. There's only the pain, unnatural pain, culminating in nothing.

I'll find a way to inflict it again. And they'll send me back to the looping hell. Fine. It's worth it, to make my point.

Words appear before me: an invitation. "YOU ARE INVITED TO THE RESIDENCE OF ARTHUR AND ZELAH ELIOT.

INCLUDED IS ONE COMPLIMENTARY TELEPORT, COUR-
TESY OF THE ELIOTS."

The invitation is totally unexpected, which makes it novel.
Novelty is the only thing that comes close to tempting me like pain
does. So without considering the decision at all, I accept the
invitation.

Instantly, I appear in a structure where the laws of physics
don't seem to apply. But why should they? Why bother with such
paltry things as limits in this sham utopia? Humanity has tran-
scended those, right?

Transcendence. I'd spit on the idea, but I seem to have lost sali-
vary privileges the moment I entered this house. I'm standing on
the wall, at the moment, on top of a painting I likely have no
ability to damage.

Not under the usual rules, anyway. But I can find a way to
damage anything. It's a talent of mine, just as it was in the real.

The ceiling—well, it doesn't exist. There is no ceiling, and
instead it looks out on a white void. Standing on a wall, I peer out
at it, then I walk toward it.

"You can't pass through," a quiet voice says, and I turn to find
a woman with blond hair that tumbles in waves past her shoulders.
She has eyes like sapphires, and she wears a pink sundress. "It's
just for show."

"Isn't everything?"

"I suppose. Please, Mr. Pikeman. Won't you come in?" She
gestures toward a doorway set in the same wall I'm standing on,
and it opens, seemingly by itself.

Wordlessly, I let myself fall through the portal. I arc through
the air, flipping end over end, and find myself standing on the
other side of the wall, in the next room. "So you live inside a video
game," I say, gazing around at the cheap wonders this room holds.

The woman lands on the other side of the door. "Don't we all?"
she says with a small smile. There's a hint of sadness, there. Well,
she'll feel much more than sad when I'm through with her.

The room is all floors—there's no wall, no ceiling. Every surface is a floor, covered with luxurious rugs, gleaming furniture, satin sofas, priceless ornaments and artifacts.

Looking up, I can't see the floor above me, the one opposite the surface I'm standing on. Instead, in the cavernous room's center hangs the void of space, littered with countless stars. It blocks my view, and when I walk to the edge of the surface I'm on and up the next, I find the void is continuous.

"Quite the impossibility, isn't it?" Zelah says, though she sounds bored.

"Yes," I say flatly, taking a moment to wonder at the idea that someone could become bored of this. When you keep the impossible hanging in your drawing room, and you see it every day, then what remains in life to widen your eyes?

What an excellent metaphor for the Subverse. They say humanity has fallen in the real, but the actual Fall happened when humanity uploaded itself to this sham heaven.

"I looked you up, after the day you chased me through Sheen City," she says. "I researched you."

Turning to her, I squint. "Chased you?" I don't even know her. Or do I? Something stems from the back of my mind, like the sound of someone screaming to be heard, though it manifests as lower than a whisper.

"Yes," she says, pausing as confusion flickers across her face. She takes a seat in an armchair sitting on the wall perpendicular to mine. "Won't you sit?"

I drop to the floor where I stand, cross-legged, and grin at her. She blinks. I'm sitting on a sumptuous rug, its strands trailing up my legs like tiny plants on an ocean's floor.

"I have to admit, you're not what I expected, based on my research. I know we're well-acquainted in the real, but this isn't the tone I thought our conversation would take."

"We're…acquainted?" I repeat. "Can you remind me of the nature of our relationship?" My grin's intact, mostly because I can tell how unsettling she finds it. I let my gaze wander around the room, wondering how I can exploit this house's rules so I can get around the pain protections.

Zelah is frowning. "You saved my daughter, Faelyn. According to your versecasts, anyway, as well as those put out by my biological self."

"Ah…yes," I say absently. "Faelyn. Beautiful girl."

"Her consciousness resides in a bot's body, now."

That jogs something in my memory, and my gaze snaps back to Zelah's face. In my mind's eye, I see a featureless face of dark metal. It belongs to a bot, cowering on the bridge of a Guard ship. The bot holds its head, weeping silently, its whole frame shuddering. Amazing that the capacity to cry would be programmed in. Or was it programmed? Could the ability to cry have been something the girl brought with her when she was transferred over?

"There's something off about you," Zelah says slowly. "Are you the same Joe Pikeman that saved my daughter? Or are you a copy? I was under the impression he has no copies."

"He doesn't," I say haltingly. "Or, actually…." I'm staring into space as memory trickles back into the leaky vessel of my mind. "He does. I am one. And so is his TOPO."

"TOPO?"

"Trajectory Operations Officer." The title rolls off my tongue, easier than it should. Except… "I'm not really a copy, though. I mean, I was, but we melded, somehow. I'm just remembering that. I—" I clear my throat, shaking my head. "I'm not sure what's happening to me."

"You…melded," Zelah said, inclining her head toward me. "And so, anything I say should make it back to Joe?"

"I'm not sure. I don't know what's happening. I'm getting memories from him, memories of *being* him. But I also remember feeling suppressed. Like he was holding me in the back of his mind, trapping me, so I didn't destabilize him. But I think I'm destabilizing him anyway. I think that's why he's here. He over-clocked, and—"

"Overclocked?" Her head tilts sideways.

"Something the Shiva do."

"But if I tell you something, there's a good chance he'll remember it."

I shrug. "Hopefully. I think…I think he remembers everything from my existence. But for some reason, I'm blocked from his memories."

The way she's looking at me right now, I can tell she doesn't think I'm well. And I think she's probably right. This place, the Subverse, it did a number on me. The fact that I seem to have escaped into the real Joe Pikeman's head…that's probably a blessing, even if I am a prisoner inside his head. It's good for me. I'm sure it is.

But the desire to hurt Zelah Eliot remains. To hurt anyone available. But she's so beautiful, too, I…I had a thing for her, didn't I? The real Joe, I mean. He didn't even admit it to himself, but *I'll* admit it. Lust rises up inside me, and it clashes with my desire for violence, generating twisted visions in my head.

"I'm going to tell you what I discovered," she says, nodding, as if to herself. She rises from her chair, then crosses the room, the gravity seeming to shift to accommodate her as she steps from one wall to the next.

When she reaches me, she sits across from me on the rug, also cross-legged. I'm sure it's not a good idea to be so near me, but I also won't complain. My old tricks for circumventing the safe-guards against pain are starting to bubble up through my thoughts.

"I don't think the brainprints are reliable," she says, snapping me out of my reverie.

"Hmm? What?"

"The brainprints. Sent between Subverse residents and people in the real. I believe they're being tampered with. Either Bacchus Corp, or the Subverse's algorithms—whoever's doing it, I'm not able to communicate properly with my double in the real. With the biological Zelah. My husband doesn't believe me. He completely discounts my suspicions, along with pretty much everything else I say. But I'm sure it's true."

"What have you tried to tell the real Zelah?"

"That I don't think this is how humans should live. That I think this place makes us unhappy, and then crazy. But it doesn't get through. Anything negative about the Subverse gets edited out."

"Where is your husband now?"

She narrows her eyes slightly. "Gone. For months, now. He plays the Great Game. He's on deployment with his faction in the Nightmute System, battling the Ocher Faction for control of asteroid mining in the region. Why do you ask?"

In answer, I lean forward and press my lips to hers, so tenderly that it surprises even me.

Zelah jerks back, eyes wide, blinking at me in surprise. I wait, something very close to panic coursing through me. What am I doing? Whatever it is, this is the realest thing I remember feeling in the Subverse. Ever.

Then she leans forward, kissing me back.

We intertwine, sinking to the rug, and soon her straps are slipping down her bare shoulders.

Hours later, as she's lying in my arms, I fade away. Without warning.

My last memory is of intense longing, with a bitter note of sadness that I'm leaving her.

10

I wake, blinking into the light filtering through a grimy window. This looks like the shed where me and Soren slept during our first night in Sheen City.

Then I give a start, as the memory of lying with Zelah Eliot comes crashing back. Right after she told me her suspicions about the brainprints. That wasn't a dream, was it?

"Was that your first time overclocking?"

My hand darts instinctively to my blaster, but it isn't there. Though my body aches everywhere, I manage to push myself to a sitting position. It doesn't seem like I'm in any condition to meet an attack, if the speaker wanted to attack me, but it's just the old Shiva, standing in a shadowed corner.

"The second time," I grunt, pushing myself backward to learn against the rough wooden wall. A splinter pokes out into the small of my back, but I don't have the energy to shift myself just yet.

"You aren't ready. Your training hasn't progressed enough. You're lucky you aren't dead."

"I would be dead, if I hadn't overclocked."

"Not if you'd stayed in that basement, as Soren suggested."

The old knight meets my glare with a neutral expression.

"Is that what a Shiva Knight would have done?" I ask.

"No," he says without hesitation.

"Good. Because if it is, I don't want to be one."

"Even still," he says. "You must avoid situations that require you to overclock in order to survive. You didn't have to come to Sheen City at all."

"If I hadn't, Rile would have kept his power over these people. We beat him, right?"

He nods.

"And because I'm helping Soren, he'll help me clear my name with the Guard. That'll make traveling through this sector a lot less complicated."

"I'm surprised you think that's going to work out so cleanly."

"Soren says he can do it. If he says it, then he can."

"If you say so." The door opens, and the old man vanishes before Soren gets far enough into the shed to see him. He stands with his hands on his hips, wearing a wry grin as he studies me.

"Well, I'd say it's a miracle you're still alive, but...I've never seen anyone fight like that, Joe." The silence stretches on, and his grin fades. "Sorry you woke up in this place. Even though we saved them—you saved them, really—I figured we should try to stay out of the aftermath as much as possible. Let them decide where they'll go from here. I figured that's what you would have argued for, anyway. So I moved you here."

"You were right."

"Okay. Good, then." He clears his throat. "I did a little negotiating, too, of course."

I shift away from the splinter, wincing. "To access the Subverse server room?"

"Yeah. They're going to continue controlling it—they don't trust the Guard enough to hand it over completely. I guess they're afraid we'll swoop in and exterminate them the moment they do. They don't know we lack the manpower to do that."

"So what's the deal?"

"Trade. We keep them provisioned in food and supplies, and they grant us access to the server room when we want it. No more coercion, no more demands like the ones Rile made, to hunt down his brother. Just trade."

"So they won't need to trade with Fairfax anymore. They won't need his weapons."

"That's the idea. I doubt Otto would allow that to continue, anyway."

I breathe a sigh of relief, at that. Otto's still alive, then. That's good.

"I know what you're thinking," Soren says. "I'm surprised Otto didn't get whacked, too. When he saw you draw the attention of the force attacking him, he laid into them like a devil, and what was left of your squad did the same. But Rile's men seemed fixated on you. You were like a god, Joe, and every man of them wanted to be the one to slay you."

I wave my hand. "Cut the melodrama. I'm not in the mood for you to massage the truth for your versecast right now."

"No massaging. I'm being serious."

"Are the women and children safe?"

Soren frowns. "A lot of the ones in the building you entered died. But a lot of them survived, and the people in the other buildings were untouched. They're grateful to us, Joe. They want to throw a feast for us."

"We don't have time to feast."

His frown deepens. "Thought you'd say that."

"We'll let them restock our Broadswords, then we're leaving."

"Yeah. Okay. We should get going, anyway. I think Fairfax is planning to ramp up his plans for this sector."

That makes my eyebrows climb. "You're taking the threat of Fairfax seriously, now?"

"Well, Otto told me something while you were unconscious. Apparently children weren't the only thing Rile was supplying to Fairfax. He also gave them…specimens."

I squint at him. "Specimens?"

"Yeah. From a cat-like species here, which Otto called the Kitane. They're most like Earth jaguars, except with antennae that give them a couple extra senses, including what sounds a lot like echolocation, for the nights under the thick jungle canopy."

I nod. "What do you make of it?"

"Well, I saw the versecast of your battle with that giant snake. A lot of people say you had your ship's computer generate the entire sequence, but I know better. Do you think Fairfax's next mutant might be based on the Kitane?"

"Possible," I say as my fatigue spikes. "Either way, we need to get off Anaconda and get to Gauntlet."

"Agreed. If I back you up, hopefully we can convince the brass to lend us some troops to deal with this."

"I thought you said they consider Fairfax an ally."

"Not after this. I'm sure they won't. Not after what he was doing here."

"I hope you're right."

"I'm going to back you up, Joe. I'm going to keep up my end of the bargain. And after we clear your name, we'll tackle this thing together."

That sounds like the old Soren to me. I manage to get to my feet, using the wall for balance, and I grip his hand firmly. We exchange grim smiles.

Before we leave, and as Otto's people restock our ships under Soren's and X3B's supervision, I learn from one of my recent squadmates that Rile is still alive, and being held in custody. I ask Otto to let me see him, and he agrees. I guess he wants to set a good precedent for his relationship with the Guard, going forward.

They're keeping Rile in a room where he'd positioned one of the bombs meant to blow up his subjects if they defied him. He's under heavy guard, but the men and women at the door forget to take my blaster as I go in. That, or they were never ordered to.

Either way, when the door closes behind me, I draw the blaster and level it at the scrawny man sitting in the room's corner, leering up at me through hooded eyes.

"Otto send you to do what he couldn't?" Rile asks.

"No," I spit. "I thought I'd do him a favor."

"Well, go on, then."

I stand there for a long time, weapon trained on the monster crouched before me. Rile is way worse than Arthur Eliot—and probably worse than most of the people I've ever killed. If anyone deserves to die, it's this bastard.

"What are you waiting for?" Rile asks, and a sneer begins to shape his mouth. "You can't do it either. Can you, Troubleshooter?"

What's wrong with me? I just slaughtered dozens of Rile's men, neutralizing them one after another. What's one more kill?

But I fought Rile's men to defend myself, didn't I? And anyway, part of me know that even those kills will come back to haunt me, eventually.

I should be able to put down Rile without a moment's thought. The sims they put me through on Gauntlet were supposed to make me into a cold killing machine. And they did, for a time.

But Rile is crouched there, defenseless. This would be an execution, not a fair fight.

I lower the blaster. "Fount damn it," I mutter.

With that, I leave the room. Rile's cackling laughter follows me out.

ARES

1

The interlude in slipspace gives the Fount coursing through my body time to repair it, and I give myself lots of rest to help things along.

That said, I still limp through my usual workout regimen as best I can, confident that if I screw up and injure myself further, the Fount will compensate.

That's the thing—I've always taken the Fount's restorative properties for granted, and it's led me to take on more risk than I probably should have, even as a Guardsman. But these new capabilities…the ability to disguise myself, and overclocking…they're something else entirely. Overclocking gave me an incredible advantage over Rile's men, almost an unfair one.

Except, maybe it *was* fair, in one sense. According to the old knight, my body paid for it. Overclocking always takes time off your life, according to him. Sometimes days, sometimes years. Between that and my refusal to enter nanodeath during slipspace voyages, it seems I'm not going to live very long.

"The journey to Gauntlet involves two legs in slipspace," Belflower says. She requested a private meeting, and I granted her one. I'm not willing to succumb to any attempts to blackmail me, but there's a difference between that and willfully pissing her off. She does have sensitive information, and I doubt Marissa would be pleased if I failed to respect that. "Our course intersects the Barrow System—" She indicates a point on the shared star map that's spread throughout the bridge, projected by our dataspheres. "We'll arrive there in just a few week's time."

"And?"

"Barrow has multiple slip points. We could use one of them to ditch your friend and continue searching for the bots."

The corner of my mouth twitches. "How would that work? We'll be entering Barrow at the same time as Soren."

"We let him leave first, then simply head to another exit point."

" And what makes you think I'm going to abandon clearing my name with the Guard just so you can check on the uprising sooner?"

"What makes you think Soren will make good on his promises?"

"Because he's my friend, and I trust him."

"People change in ten years, Captain. Some people change a lot. And I'm thinking maybe you distrusted him to some degree, even when you were in training together."

I frown at her, partly because of the impertinence of the remark, and partly because she's right.

"Besides," she continues, "as I've already pointed out, we have every reason to believe we'll find your daughter involved with the uprising somehow. Whether she supports it or opposes it."

I shake my head. "Just because you're obsessed with this thing doesn't mean Harmony is. There are other things happening in this sector, and we're going to take them one at a time. We're trusting Soren. Ship, deactivate Engineer."

She vanishes from the bridge, and I recline in my chair, enjoying the silence. Humoring her is one thing, but she was starting to get on my nerves.

That's when the old man crosses into view from my left, and I groan. "You'd think I'd be able to get a moment's peace, traveling alone in a Broadsword going faster than light."

He grunts. "Did you also think you'd get a holiday from your training? Since you seem so intent on barreling headlong into things you don't understand, I would think you'd feel even more strongly about continuing."

"Oh, I intend to continue the training. I was just waiting for you to show up. It's not like I'm able to message you."

"If you speak, I will hear it. I'm currently encoded in the Fount circulating through the *Ares'* oxygen filtration system."

"So, I'm breathing you in as we speak?"

He grimaces. "It's probably best not to think of it like that." He clears his throat. "Do you realize what happened, in Sheen?"

"I killed a lot of people, and we stopped a tyrant."

"Not that. I'm talking about the storm."

"What about it?"

"Didn't you notice how it came out of nowhere, on a perfectly clear day?"

"I was a little too busy with other thing to play amateur meteorologist."

"But you recall how shocked Otto was at its gestation."

"Uh, yeah. That storm's 'gestation' really threw him for a loop." I make a face.

"This is no laughing matter. Joe, I'm beginning to think you've been Chosen."

Tilting my head, I say, "Sure, but haven't we been over this already? You already said the Fount chose me to be a Shiva—to head for the center of the galaxy, restore it and all that."

"It's more than that. The land has begun to reflect your state. The storm only began to form once you became angered by the condition of the people in Sheen City."

That makes me blink. "You're kidding, right?"

"Have you known me to kid?"

"Well, no. Definitely not. But to suggest that was anything but coincidence—"

"Obviously, you haven't grasped how integrated the Fount has become with the galaxy. Where there is life, there is the Fount. Just as viruses and bacteria circulate through the atmosphere, so does it. Do you not think it could affect the very weather itself, and bend it to the one it considers a vital agent of balance?"

"I think this is getting way too mystical for me."

"Joe, we live in a time of great need. Galactic balance was meant to be restored decades ago—by me. I failed, as you so enjoy pointing out. But you must not fail. The future depends on your actions."

Now that's a scary thought. I messed up being a dad to Harmony—and now I'm expected to take care of the galaxy? "Tell me something," I say. "Did you die from overclocking?"

His lips firm up for a moment. "That's how I was meant to die," he says, his voice low.

"How do you mean?" I ask, hesitantly.

"Every Shiva's quest is to restore the galaxy. To do that requires overclocking for so long that recovery becomes impossible. That's why a living Shiva is such a rare thing—every last one dies accomplishing his quest."

"And that includes me," I say flatly. "I'm expected to die, too."

The old man doesn't answer, and I get the feeling that he hadn't intended to divulge this tidbit just yet.

"I need a drink," I say, standing up from the command seat.

Typically, I never drink. But included among the provisions Otto gave me are ten bottles of the best homebrewed wine Sheen City has to offer.

After what the old man just told me about what I'm actually expected to do in the galaxy's Core...I intend to hit those bottles hard.

2

I keep up my training. I'm not saying I'm on board with the whole dying thing, but what the old knight's teaching is bound to come in handy either way. If I'm gonna go head-to-head with Fairfax, or beat the giant cat-thing he's apparently engineering, I'll need his training.

The training itself still involves a lot of sitting around and meditating, though we are working in some physical exercises. The old man has me trying to come as close to overclocking as I can without actually doing it. Remembering how it feels, focusing so much that my reflexes are razor-sharp, even in my normal state. Obviously, I'll never reach the level of performance I did against Rile's men without overclocking, but the old knight says this will prepare me for when I do overclock.

Training doesn't take up all my time, and I spend some of the leftover hours researching the Kitane. The animals are the color of wheat by default—except for the insides of their ears, which are pure white—though apparently they can camouflage with their surroundings by altering the color of their fur. Except, a Kitane doesn't actually have fur. It resembles fur, but each tiny wisp is actually a protrusion of scaly flesh, which it can alter just like an iguana. Kitane are kind of like a cross between a snake and a cat. Truth be told, they freak me right the Fount out.

On top of all that, Kitane can use echolocation, while their antennae make them super-sensitive to disturbances in the air. Their retractable claws are long enough to remind me of a comic book character that still gets trotted out in the Subverse sometimes, and their teeth look about as fun as a bear trap. They put a lot of Earth predators to shame, meaning there's nothing in humanity's evolutionary history that could possibly prepare me to face one— let alone one that's larger than the *Ares*.

But I try not to dwell on that.

Other things I'm trying not to dwell on include the way Marissa's been avoiding me. I'd expect her to be lecturing me regularly about not going to look for Harmony, but if I had to guess, I'd say she's given up.

Moe's been acting weird, too. They were both pretty subdued during the trip from Sheen City to the slip exit coords, out past the Nectar System's sixth planet. And when it came time to cooperate with Belflower to perform a full systems check, they delivered their reports in clipped words, exchanging glances every so often.

Whatever. Between training and learning about the Kitane, I have plenty to keep myself occupied. The cat is becoming something of an obsession, which I start to realize after the fourth straight evening researching it. I decide to take a break by watching some of Soren's versecasts from the time before I met up with him on the Amydon Shipyards. I start with his first encounter with Rile.

It went exactly how he said it did: Rile asked him to headhunt his brother, and Soren said he would need back up and knew where to find it. Even though the tyrant apparently hates the Subverse as much as I do, in the versecast he seems amused by the spontaneous asides Soren launches into mid-conversation, meant to keep his versecast audience engaged.

As I continue back through his history, I learn that Soren leans on his audience's anti-biological bias a lot—even more than he did around me. He calls biologicals "backward," "uneducated," "naive," and "a necessary evil."

A necessary *evil?* Soren is a biological, for Fount's sake!

The guy must know what he's doing when it comes to cultivating a Subverse audience, since he's been doing it nonstop for most of his life. But to sell out your principles so completely, just to get more followers…

I wonder if it happened gradually, or he just decided overnight to go against the real and everything it stands for. Probably the first one. That's normally how selling your soul goes—you dole it out piece by piece, rarely all at once.

I wonder if Soren's family ever watches his versecasts. They must. He was always their golden boy, and they credited him with lifting them out of poverty. The money he made versecasting paid for his younger brother's education in the arts, not to mention replacing his father's leg when he lost it trying to repair a threshing bot.

But how do they see his prejudice against his own people? Do they turn a blind eye, or does Soren assure them it's all necessary to maintain his audience?

Either way, the versecasts give me a lot to think about. Little of it pleasant.

The training and the research continue, and the days roll by. At last, the time comes to exit slipspace into Barrow, the star system Belflower suggested as a good place to ditch Soren, if I was so inclined.

"Activate crew," I say, and they all appear at their respective stations. Belflower and Asterisk look eager to be underway, but Marissa and Moe both wear grim expressions.

"Prepare to exit slipspace," I say. "Everyone perform one last superficial check of your station. Our next exit point is on the other side of Barrow System, so we'll be in realspace for about nine hours, provided we don't run into any surprises."

"Exiting slipspace now," Moe says.

I turn to Marissa. "OPO, do you see the *Hermes*?"

"Affirmative," Marissa says tersely. "She's already here."

"Very good." I will my datasphere to contact Soren's. "How was your trip?"

"Fine," he answers, sounding distracted. "Looks like that's about to change, though. I'm getting a distress signal from the Midtown in this system."

I glance at Marissa, who's studying her station intently. She must have gotten the same signal. "What's going on?" Midtowns are the Mid-System equivalent of Brinktowns.

"Well, I'm not sure I trust the contents. Apparently, they were attacked by a pack of bots. If that's true, it's the first time it's ever happened."

I feel my pulse accelerate, and a tendon in my neck starts twitching. "We'd better investigate."

3

By the time we reach the Midtown, the houses have stopped smoldering, but it's not hard to tell the damage is fresh. I peer through a belly sensor as our Broadswords fly in tandem above the walled village, and I can see several streets coated in ash. Many of the structures are nothing but burned-out husks.

The spaceport was wrecked too, so Soren and I put down in the middle of town, in the center of the cobbled main square.

"Where's the server room location?" Soren asks the gathered throng as he emerges from his airlock. "Do any of you know?"

Although they've clearly come to greet us, many of the residents seem in varying states of shock, their eyes wandering across the hulls of our ships even as Soren speaks to them.

"We don't," a young man says, who's more clear-eyed than the rest. "The bots made us show them the terminal, but they went off again. My guess, they hacked it for the server location and went off."

"So you were really attacked by bots?" Soren says, eyes narrowed.

"Aye. Their ship left the Barrow System just before yours

entered, it from what our satellites are telling us. Though I'll tell you, these things didn't act like any bot I've ever seen."

"How did they act?"

"Like people. People trapped inside bots."

"Is the terminal still operational?" I say, before Soren can ask any more questions. I'm wary of his versecast audience learning too much and then spreading misinformation across the galaxy. Clearly, I need to have an offline conversation with him, very soon.

"Aye," the boy says. "They didn't harm it."

Soren's looking at me. "I'll get the server location from the terminal," he says. "Then I'll go check on the servers. You stay here and help these people."

I know that "help these people" is code for "find out what happened," but I also plan to do whatever I can for them. That said, I doubt there's much I can do.

"You sure you don't want backup?" I say. "In case the bots left a nasty surprise for you?"

Soren grins. "I'll send X3B in first. Patch his feed through to my versecast, and—"

"Got it," I cut in, doubtful these people are interested in hearing about his versecasting techniques right now.

The boy shows Soren to the terminal, and he returns after ten minutes with the server's location.

"I'll be back inside two hours, if all goes well," he says. "If it doesn't, I'll get in touch."

"Good luck," I say. "And stay frosty."

"Hard not to," he says, putting his hands to his biceps and chattering his teeth comically. It's winter here, apparently. Unless it's always this cold. I've heard it said that Mid-Systems planets tend to be colder and rougher, though I've always figured that as bluster from Midtown natives trying to show Brinktowners up.

The *Hermes* takes off, and I secure my ship against the locals' curiosity, leaving orders with the crew to warn off anyone who gets too close, and to contact me if they do. I'm here to help, but I'm not here to give tours of my Broadsword, or let anyone paw at her as if she were an interactive exhibit.

The boy and I take one of the streets branching off from the main square, which ash covers in random lines and swirls. Despite the recent trauma, he's chatty enough, so I mostly let him talk. He has an earnestness that makes him believable, in a way most overly talkative people aren't. I guess that sort of person usually seems nervous, like they have something to hide behind their torrent of words, but not this guy.

"A few dozen died in the attack," he says. "My pa was one of them."

"I'm sorry."

"Yeah." He raises a finger to his eyes and wipes something away, but other than that he stays composed. Tough kid. "I was unlucky. But as a town, we were fortunate. Not too many deaths. The bots didn't seem all that concerned with killing, not once they got what they wanted. The reason you don't see many of us around is because most of us are out repairing the walls so the horse raptors don't get in."

Right now, I'm trying to picture what a horse raptor must look like. Some species just aren't worth meeting, no matter how interested in xenobiology one might be.

"I tried to pitch in," the boy continues, "but they wouldn't hear of it. Said I needed time to process what had happened." The kid looks up at me, and I can see more tears welling up in his eyes. "Pa was due to upload next year. I would have been able to spend eternity with him and ma. Now it'll just be me and her alone, forever."

I clear my throat, not feeling confident about dealing with a situation like this. Kid needs a long bout with a therapy sim, but then, I'm not one to talk about that. "What did they want?"

"Huh?"

"You said the bots left everyone alone, once they got what they wanted. What was it?"

"Ludmilla Cadogan, seems like. Though they took all our bots, too."

I shake my head, eyes narrowed slightly. "A Cadogan?"

"Yes sir. And they took her, sure enough. That's why this many people died—we wouldn't give her up, not until the bodies started really stacking up. She wanted to give herself up from the outset, but we wouldn't hear of it. We all loved her, mister. She was dear to us. Seventy-two, but as spry as a thirty-year-old, near enough."

"Hm." The Cadogans are the best-loved of the Five Families, and the most trusted. Which makes me trust them the least, just as a matter of principle. They're the ones who created the Fount, and as such they've fallen on hard times in recent centuries, since the Fount finished serving Bacchus Corp's purposes a long time ago. Even so, like the rest of the Five Families, they have guaranteed spots in the digital heaven, available to them whenever they wish. But I've heard about a lot of them remaining in the real, pursuing various branches of physical science, in a galaxy where no one cares about the physical anymore.

You'd think that would endear them to me, and it would, if they hadn't also been one of the key architects of humanity's downfall. I don't trust the Five Families, period. Which I guess you might call ironic, considering I bedded one and got her pregnant.

Anyway. If a Cadogan was living here in Midtown, for long enough to become loved by the people, then I'm given to wondering exactly how she was manipulating them, and how they played into her experiments. Come to think of it, I *have* been getting this weird, creepy vibe ever since stepping off the *Ares*.

Then, it hits me, and I can't believe I didn't pick up on it before: "Where are all the children?" I ask.

The boy opens his mouth to answer, but at that moment, some sort of demon charges into the road up ahead of us, emerging from a side street. It has two limbs protruding from its front like great green lobster claws, which it uses to snatch up two pedestrians at once as they shriek in surprise, and then pain. The sound of crunching bones floats past the buildings toward us.

"That a horse raptor?" I ask. But the boy's gone from my side, fled to a nearby house to pound on the door.

The noise draws the thing's attention, which is just as well, since I was about to do that with my blaster anyway. Kneeling in the ash and dirt, I cup my left hand under my right to steady my aim.

It drops its victims, and they tumble limply to the ground, sending up puffs of black dust. Then it charges.

The term "horse raptor" made me envision a perfect cross between those two creatures from Earth's evolutionary history, which was horrifying enough. But, as these things often go, the reality's even more horrible.

The thing barreling toward me past the Midtown's cubic metal buildings looks more like a praying mantis on steroids. Each of its four black eyes holds a searing red pupil in the very center, and its lobster-claw appendages hang at the end of tree-trunk limbs. Its four spindly legs appear to perform an impossible task as they flick its entire frame forward in bounding leaps, covering meters at a time.

It doesn't take long for me to empty my charge pack into its face, spamming the trigger as fast as I can. Three of its four eyes burst apart in gouts of orange ichor, and I manage to take out the fourth just as it reaches me.

I roll to the side from my kneeling position, and its thin, razor-edged foot just misses slicing me open. A nearby alleyway provides some cover, and I back into it, slapping in a fresh charge pack and opening up once more on the beast's thick carapace.

With its vision gone, the horse raptor starts laying about with its lobster claws, smashing and crashing them into whatever it can find—rooves, doorways, a bicycle, and the ground. Across the street, the boy has plastered himself back against the door he was knocking on, which has failed to open. His face is the color of snow, and a dark patch is spreading through his trousers.

My breathing steady, I continue to fire, aiming for the thing's joints. Three times, I'm forced to change position, side-stepping down the street ahead of its claws.

Finally, the horse raptor begins to slow down, and near the end of my third charge pack it collapses under its own weight to lie there twitching in the sooty street.

I walk to the porch where the boy still stands, shaking, and I clap a hand on his shoulder, guiding him around the spasming demon. "Anyway. You were saying?"

He raises a shaking hand to point at his dead neighbors up ahead, their bodies misshapen from the bone-crushing squeeze. The boy's chin lifts toward me, his mouth open and trembling.

"Hey," I say, gently tapping his head with two fingers. "This is not the worst thing that happened to you today. Where'd the tough guy go who I was talking to a few minutes ago?"

We sidestep the bodies, which have already attracted a group of people who've emerged from their hiding places to gather around. The boy can't seem to avert his gaze—probably he knows them well—but I guide him by the shoulders till we're past them.

"What's your name?" I ask him.

"Uh, Percy. Percy Oliver."

"Okay, great, Perce. Can I call you Perce?"

Percy frowns. "I'd rather you didn't. Sounds like 'purse.' Like a lady's bag."

"How about 'Murse?'"

His frown deepens, and I chuckle. "Percy it is. You were just about to explain to me why this place has no kids."

"Oh. Right." He blinks, and I can almost see it as he pulls himself back together. "That's 'cause no one's had kids here for over fourteen years."

That makes me fall silent, as I consider the implications of that. Tumbling birth rates aren't news—ever since the Fall, people have been trying to make enough tokens to upload to the Subverse as early as they can. The expense of raising children doesn't exactly hasten that process. But I've never heard of an entire town giving up reproduction for any length of time, let alone over a decade.

One thing seems certain: Ludmilla Cadogan is behind all this.

I'm about to ask Percy how, exactly, when Soren's voice enters my thoughts: "Joe, I'm at the server room. Got soaked doing it—it's accessed through a covered hatch in the middle of a swamp. I think moss conceals it under normal circumstances, but it looks like the bots scorched that off."

"What did you find?"

"Nothing. I mean, no damage. They didn't touch the equipment itself."

"Any tampering?"

"Nothing physical. The log shows they made off with petabytes of data, though, and it looks like they deleted that data off the servers. I'm getting messages from my audience with clips from local news—apparently, thousands of people vanished from the Subverse in an instant, without warning. That must be the data they took. The consciousnesses of those people."

"Fount. We need to report this to Gauntlet, yesterday."

"I know. It'd be better if we could take a resident from here with us—a first-hand account of the attack would make them take this more seriously."

I pause. Percy's staring at me looking slightly confused, and it's not hard to tell why: since this conversation's all subvocalized, it looks to him like I'm just standing here, staring into space. "You really think that's necessary?" I ask Soren.

"The Guard needs a lot of motivating to allocate troops to anything these days, Joe."

I nod, though Soren can't see that. "These people could use some sort of relief effort," I say. "Plus, the Guard might want to look into what's going on with them. There's something weird about this place."

"Yeah? Well, we're out of time for getting involved. Have you met anyone you think we could drag through slipspace with us?"

My gaze falls on Percy again, who's looking up at me with questioning eyes.

"Uh, yeah. I think I might have someone."

4

"This is so cool," Percy says, wandering the bridge, gazing around at it wide-eyed. He pauses near the command seat. "You mind if I—?"

Before I can answer, he deposits himself into it, straightening up to peer forward with an air of determination.

I bite off some cutting words before they can make their way out, reminding myself that this kid just lost his dad.

His mom was accommodating enough. She seemed eager to send Percy to Gauntlet if it meant getting to the bottom of what happened, and finding Ludmilla. She seemed a lot more concerned with that than she did with avenging Percy's father. Based on their reactions to his death, I'm getting the impression he was a bit of a shit, or at least shiftless enough that his absence doesn't seem to make much of a difference to them.

The crew are all already at their posts, but since he's not a Guardsman, Percy's datasphere doesn't have access to them. "Get us off this planet and to the exit coords," I say to them, subvocalizing so Percy can't hear. "Full system checks en route."

They subvocalize their acknowledgments, following my lead,

which pleases me. As aggravating as this crew can be sometimes, I have to say, they're the most obedient I've had to date.

I tell Percy to strap in for the ascent through the planet's gravity well, then I head for the cabin to lie in my bunk and ride it out there as best I can.

The *Ares* bounds into orbit. Once she switches to positron reactor propulsion, about five minutes after leaving Midtown, I get up and head back onto the bridge.

I walk toward Marissa's station, and she looks at me askance as I turn to lean back against her circular railing. "Listen," I say to Percy. "Can you tell me why Ludmilla Cadogan was so popular among you and your neighbors?"

"'Course I can," Percy says, nodding vigorously. "It's 'cause she could do so much with the Fount."

"What do you mean—like, Fount engineering?"

"Sure. Well, she didn't figure out how to change it, exactly. It's designed to be basically tamper-proof without the access codes. She must have explained all that to us a thousand times. Redundant, iterative layers of security, dispersed across thousands of nanobots residing inside dozens of people, right?"

"Yeah."

"But she figured out how to control what the Fount *does* to people. Using drugs."

"Uh huh. What did these drugs do?"

"Only what everyone's secretly wished for ever since the Fall. Everything our biology would normally make us want—all that's gone."

"Everything?"

"Yeah, you know." Percy shifts uncomfortably. "Not like food, I mean. Nothing important for our survival. But, uh…sex drive?"

"Right," I say, wondering what Percy's age is. He seems kind of old to be so uncomfortable around this topic.

"She made the Fount flatten out our hormones, too. So, for

example, the men lost our natural aggressiveness. That's gone, plus competitiveness, and so on—we all work together, now."

"To do what?"

"Well, the changes also made us more creative, so we could make more art for the Subverse."

I find myself shifting against the railing. "How did she manage that?"

"She made it so the Fount stimulated the right side of our brain, and suppressed nor—uh, noreh—"

Unbidden, my datasphere supplies the word he's likely trying to say, along with the context it considers most relevant: "NOR-EPINEPHRINE. A NEUROTRANSMITTER ASSOCIATED WITH LONGTERM MEMORY RETRIEVAL. ITS SUPPRES-SION MAKES IT EASIER TO FORM NEW CONNECTIONS AND IDEAS."

"Norepinephrine?" I say.

"Yeah. That's the one. Plus, it suppressed some things the fronts of our brains do. If it didn't, we'd be too hard on ourselves while we were creating."

The boy's face gleams as he tells me about all this, as though he's describing some lasting utopia—like he gets to live in Earth's most famous theme park, Disneyland, all the time.

What I'm picturing right now is a barn full of creative cattle, tricked into thinking they're living fulfilling lives. Painting with brushes affixed to their skulls with heavy metal braces.

"So, no one has sex anymore? No babies?"

"That's right," Percy says, nodding in that over-enthusiastic way he has. "It might sound strange to you, mister, but it works. We're all richer than we could have imagined—we're well on our way to uploading to the Subverse. But no one's richer than anyone else, see? We made an agreement to share any wealth we made, equally, among everyone. No competition. Only cooperation, till we all get into the Subverse and live together, happy, forever."

"Uh huh. And Cadogan? Did she receive an equal share of the wealth, too?"

The boy frowns, as if sensing for the first time that I might not be in total admiration of the world he's describing. "Well, don't you think she should be paid for what she created?" he says.

"I think people should get paid proportionate to what they contribute, yeah."

"Exactly. So of course Ms. Cadogan got more than the rest of us, since she created the whole thing!"

"How much more?"

"Five shares. She's always been very open about it. She wanted to take less, but we wouldn't hear of it."

"I'm sure she did," I mutter.

"The system works, mister. Maybe it's not somewhere you think you'd want to live—there were some hold-backs, at first—but eventually everyone got on board, once they realized it was the way things were going. That's not all, either. Our way of doings things is spreading to other Midtowns already. I've heard of three who've already started changing over to our way of life."

"Your town will die."

"No it won't," Percy says, sounding genuinely baffled. "The opposite of that. It's going to live forever."

"In the real, I mean. Your Midtown will become a ghost town."

"Who wants to stay in the real, anymore? I haven't met a single person who does."

I do, but I don't say that. Why bother? Instead, I say, "If the entire galaxy followed your model, there wouldn't be anyone left to tend the infrastructure that makes the Subverse possible. The entire system would collapse."

"Maybe it needs to. Maybe we can find a way to trust the bots to take care of it for us. Ms. Cadogan says the real is a dead place. Think about how we've never met any other species as smart as us, for instance. The space between the stars is as empty as it's possible to be. Ms. Cadogan says the future's in the Subverse."

She's right, in a sense, but not in the way she hopes. The future's waiting in the Subverse, all right. But it's fighting tooth and nail to get out, and once it does, humanity will learn what pain really means.

GAUNTLET

1

We get the first distress signals three hours out from Gauntlet—just an hour after we entered the Needle System.

"Fount," Soren says. "Is the entire galaxy burning down?"

"Not yet," I say, since I'm pretty sure we've only been witnessing the initial sparks.

"Looks like Midtown was just a warm-up for these assholes." Soren sounds genuinely angry, in contrast to his usual cavalier attitude. I wonder how his versecast audience will respond to this genuine emotion. Probably, they'll lap it up.

I'm studying the transmitted images that accompanied the distress call: bots marching in orderly ranks, firing on turrets and Guardsmen confronting them across Gauntlet's sunny plains. Percy said they acted like humans, but these look pretty regimented. There is disorder, though. They don't march in perfect tandem, and the footage shows some of them exchanging gestures of encouragement and support. Just like humans would.

One bot runs ahead of the rest, waving his comrades on. The Guardsmen gun him down, but his sacrifice seems to buoy the others, and they charge forward with renewed vigor.

They look like revolutionaries.

"I'm guessing they've hit a few Midtowns recently," I say, silently cursing how slowly news travels through the galaxy.

"Why do you say that?" Soren asks.

"Look at their numbers. They took all the bots from the Midtown we visited, right? Where else would they be able to swell their numbers by so many, unless they hit a Lambton factory cylinder?"

"Fount," Soren says, barely above a whisper. "Do you think they'll hit that next?"

"If they haven't already."

We spend the rest of the trip across the system formulating a plan of attack. We're close enough for real-time communication, so we meet in a simulation of a war room. The room has no doors, just a holographic display in the center, which we stand around.

The bots are hitting Control, the mechanized city where the admiralty administers the entire Galactic Guard. It's built to resemble its Subverse counterpart as closely as possible: all sleek, gleaming metal and cold, blue lights, though much of it needs a good wash, and a few buildings look like they're on the verge of corroding through and collapsing.

The city's blue lights remind me of Rodney Fairfax's eyes—the way they blazed during our duel on Arbor. I always thought Control looked out of place amidst Gauntlet's calm, natural beauty.

The city's dark central tower rears against an eternally clear sky, surrounded close-in by shorter towers with rounded, bulbous tops that always reminded me of tumors. The rest of the city is mostly flat, comprised of data centers and admin buildings, with the dwellings for the city's round-the-clock staff of almost thirty thousand situated mostly underground. Officers live up-top, of course—that is, the few that are biological.

The thought of so many humans living in one place in the real always blew me away, and it still does. Still more live elsewhere on Gauntlet: Guardsmen-in-training, instructors, reserve troops, and so on. The Guard draws its personnel from all over the galaxy, so it makes sense, but I still have trouble wrapping my head around it.

"That distress signal was twenty minutes in transit," Soren says, "so by the time we get there, the battle will have advanced over three hours from that point. Think they'll keep the bots out of Control for that long?"

"I hope so," I say. "How many Troubleshooters does the Guard keep stationed in Needle System, these days?"

"None."

I glance up from the display. "Come again?"

"They don't keep any here, Joe. As it is, they have enough trouble finding Troubleshooters to deploy to problem areas."

"I see," I mutter. "In that case, the biggest difference we can hope to make to the engagement is to strafe the bots with our Broadswords before they enter the city. If we arrive after that, we're just another couple troopers chasing bots through Control. We can't strafe them after they enter the city—the brass will string us up from Module's highest spire." Module is the Control's central tower. I gesture at the barracks surrounding Control, designed to match the city's aesthetic, but really just a place to stuff a bunch of meatspace soldiers. "Tell me every bunk in the barracks are still kept full."

"Mostly," Soren says, meeting my eyes.

"Fount," I breathe. Just how chaotic have the Mid-Systems gotten, for the Guard to have to draw on the Control garrison? "How long should it take for the reserve forces to deploy?"

"I'm sure they've already joined the battle."

I nod. "In that case, we should find them still fighting outside the city. They have enough men to keep them at bay for that long."

"Hell, maybe they'll even have the bots mopped up by the time we arrive."

"Maybe," I say doubtfully. The bots shown in the images

weren't all combat bots, so that's something. They sure looked determined, though, and they're all packing heat.

As for why they're acting like humans…I don't know what that signifies. Are they human minds inside bots, or just corrupted units? Either way, if they have full access to the combat bots' battle protocols and arsenals, they're going to give even the Guard reserve forces a hell of a time.

We make it to the planet at last and start burning through layers of atmosphere. Gauntlet's reputation for serenity is a bit misleading, when it comes to rides down its sky. The upper atmosphere is overly thick with dense gases, and the winds blow hard there. My crew stay intent on their stations throughout the trip down, which I appreciate, since the turbulence doesn't affect them one bit.

Finally, we're through—both Broadswords swooping in from the west toward the clashing armies. Zooming in using a forward sensor, I see the bots are taking full advantage of Gauntlet's gentle hills—crouching and lying behind them to fire on the reserve forces.

That may protect them from the turrets and Guardsmen shooting them from near the city's edge, but it won't do anything about laserfire from above.

A few of the bots toward the oncoming ships; something real bots would never do, since they could simply peer out of a sensor on that side without turning. Definitely humans consciousnesses, then, still getting used to their new metal bodies.

"Let's say hello from the Troubleshooters," I say.

"Roger that," Soren says.

"Asterisk, you're in charge of starboard and port-side laser turrets—whichever's facing the enemy at a given time. Use macros when needed."

"Aye, Captain," he says.

With that, I drop into the sim for controlling the *Ares'* belly turret, which folds down from the hull from its position amidst her landing gear. I line up my shot using composite video from multiple sensors surrounding the turret, and I let a line of bots have it. Before firing, I paint my targets and send the data to Asterisk and Soren, to avoid redundant shooting. Then the grips are thrumming in my hands as I unleash a series of staccato laser bursts.

I know our first strafing run is a success before the shots land. An instant later, my assessment is confirmed as the bolts slam into the metal fighters, hitting heads, shoulders, and torsos. Some of them are crumpled to the ground by the bolts, others flick end over end across the field of battle. A couple manage to dodge the attack, but most are hemmed in by the blue bolts and the cover they've chosen.

Nearby, Soren conducts another successful strafing run, though his timing's somewhat off, and a few of his shots go wide. That would have been me, just a few months ago. As much as I complain about the old knight, he was right: when I relied on my datasphere during combat, I was well short of my full potential. His training has brought me to a new level. All the more reason to keep him on.

Answering laserfire sails into the sky after us, but from what I'm seeing, the bots have nowhere near the artillery required to shoot a Broadsword out of the sky.

So they choose another tack. As we begin our second pass, the bots suddenly break into a charge. At their front, a towering figure leaps out of a hollow to lead them, midnight cape billowing out behind him.

Fairfax.

The bots' laserfire multiplies, concentrating on a confined group of Guardsmen. Grenades arc out toward the same spot, and in the front ranks, only a few manage to flee before the explosions. Smoke and fire spurt upward, sending dirt, grass, and body parts flying.

"Aim for the figure in the lead," I say over a wide channel shared by Soren and Asterisk, painting the target with a scarlet crosshairs for them. "That's Fairfax."

But we're too far along our second strafing run to efficiently readjust now, and my order just ends up wasting a lot of energy in the form of laser bolts that eat nothing but ground.

"Damn it," I bark, though only to myself, inside the sim. No Troubleshooter worth his salt would willingly share negative emotions with his crew and allies. A wild impulse rises inside me, to send a Javelin after Fairfax, but that would put the Guardsmen below in too much danger. Over the wide channel, I say, "They know they can't win out in the open, now that we're giving our ground troops air support. So they're making a push into the city."

"They'll take heavy losses doing that," Soren says, sounding a lot calmer than I am. "Look at the fire they're taking already."

It's true. Led by Fairfax, it's like the bots are flanking *themselves*. They're willfully barreling into the Guardsmen force, and the air's filled with neon-blue laserfire hammering down on them from both sides. It's a testament to Basic training and regular practice that no Guardsman has yet fallen to friendly fire.

"I don't think they care about numbers," I say.

"What? That's ridiculous. Numbers have mattered to every insurgency in history."

"We've never had an insurgency like this one, Soren. Think about all the bots in Brinktowns and Midtowns, all across the galaxy. We already know the average town's defenses pose no threat to them, so they have the ability to reinforce their ranks pretty much without limit."

"Still—"

"Look at them, Soren. They must know this is a suicide mission. Which means there must be something in Control they consider worth losing their entire force for. We need to put down and chase them. We need to stop them."

"You think the two of us plus X3B can stop Fairfax?"

"I don't think we have a choice."

"All right, buddy. We're in this far, I guess."

Percy's still in nanodeath—I got him to set up his datasphere so that he'd only come back to consciousness at a prompt from me. He should be fine to stay under during the battle, I figure. Hell, the *Ares* might be the safest place for him.

Both Broadswords plummet toward Gauntlet's surface, landing amidst the swath of destruction Fairfax and his bots have carved for themselves.

By the time I'm exiting the *Ares'* airlock, the invaders have already disappeared amidst the low, bulky structures of Control City.

At that moment, every mindfulness technique from the old knight fails me, and a surge of anger rises up at Fairfax's audacity. Kidnapping children, sacrificing them to make his powerful friends happy, and now hitting the very heart of the Galactic Guard. I'm not going to let him get away with this.

I clamp down hard on my rage, smothering its fire and replacing it with determination.

Something hits the *Ares'* hull behind me, then pings off and falls to the ground. I stare at it in disbelief.

It's a piece of ice, similar in size and shape to a ping-pong ball. But Gauntlet hasn't had any hail in decades.

2

The old knight's words echo through my thoughts: *The storm only began to form when they angered you…*

I shake my head. Even if that could possibly be true, now's not the time to dwell on it. As I'm jogging around the *Ares* to meet Soren, whose ship put down on the other side, I'm approached by a Guardsman. His face is covered in sweat, and the uniform of his shoulder is scorched by laserfire, but his spidersilk armor appears to have absorbed most of the bolt.

My datasphere provides his name and rank: Second Lieutenant Anthony Breen.

"Afternoon, Lieutenant," I say, and he blinks, maybe surprised at the casual greeting.

"Good afternoon, sir," he says, saluting. He flinches as an ice chunk beans him. The hail's picking up, now, and I don't see it making things any easier when it comes to running down the bots. At least we're wearing helmets…though if I run into Fairfax, I'll be removing it first thing. The extra protection isn't worth how limiting it would be be in a fight with him.

"I trust we'll be chasing that mob of tin cans through Control together?" I say.

Soren joins us, helmet sealed to his shipsuit.

"About that, sir," Breen says. "Major Yohn was in command of the contingent on this side of the city, but the bots got him. Our other field officers are too far away to get here in time. Are you okay to take command?"

I exchange glances with Soren, who shrugs. "Go ahead," he says, though I'm sure I can hear a note of resentment in his voice. It brings me back to putting down the pirate assault during Assessment and Selection. Funny—he was fine to let me take the lead in the jungle surrounding Sheen, but in front of other Guardsmen he seems to balk at the idea.

"Wait a second," I say. "You do know who I am—don't you, Guardsman? I mean, you recognize the birthmark, right?"

The lieutenant nods, seeming to avoid Soren's gaze, which is who he probably should have offered the command too. "You're Commander Joe Pikeman. And if your reputation's any indication, there's no more effective Troubleshooter out there."

"Do this right, and it'll go a long way with the brass," Soren says, though he still sounds grudging to my ears.

"All right, then," I say. "We have no time. Let's cross our fingers that those bots get lost in the city and start going in circles. That may be our only hope for stopping Fairfax from reaching Module and accessing Control's mainframe."

Breen nods. "What do you want us to do, sir?"

"First, let's establish lines of communication. Here." I send him a code for a command channel. "Give that to every platoon and squad leader on this side of the city. Tell them to get in touch with me the moment they run into something our plan doesn't account for."

"What's our plan?" Soren says.

"Quick and dirty, by necessity. Breen, have the troops spread out and cover every route between here and Module. Miss one, and there's a chance of letting the enemy slip through the cracks. Meantime, send me this contingent's eight top-rated soldiers. I'll meet them right there." I paint a spot beside the city, where the surrounding grass ends and Control's metal streets begin.

"Squad of ten, then?" Soren says as we jog toward Control. "Is that tenth spot for me?"

"Of course," I say. "Think I'd leave you out, ol' buddy?"

"Stop it. You're gonna make me blush."

To the Guardsman Reserve's credit, my orders are executed inside of ten minutes. My squad assembles, and the entire contingent's just about ready to start pouring through the hail-strewn city streets and alleyways. Unfortunately, it takes less than an hour to get to the center of Control from the perimeter, as long as you can move at a decent clip. That means we have some catching up to do, fast.

"Let's go," the moment the last soldier of my squad shows up. The rest of the contingent's still milling about, but I'm sure they'll follow soon.

Spongy grass gives way to hard metal, and as we run our combat boots rap across it with an unseemly clangor. Control wasn't built for fast, stealthy passage; hell, it wasn't even built for battle. If enemy forces reach here, then something's gone seriously sideways.

Of course, the existence of an enemy force strong enough to pose a meaningful threat to the Guard shows just how south things are going for the galaxy. Sure, pirate assaults have been a serious consideration for decades, but this is something else entirely. The shit has bypassed the fan and blown through the roof.

The ice isn't doing much for our footing—with how fast we're going, we're already risking falling flat on our asses, though everyone's manged to stay upright so far. Luckily, the boys don't seem like complainers. I don't think I'd have the patience for that today.

We're all focused straight ahead, and I think we expected our first glimpse of the enemy to be the glint of their metal heels fleeing in the distance. That explains why the bots are able to take us by surprise with an attack from opposing alleyways.

Their laserfire crackles from both directions, and my datasphere throws up a warning just in time for me to lunge out of the way.

All of our dataspheres would have given such warnings, but two of the boys aren't fast enough, and the bots cut them down.

Recovering my balance, I spin, ripping a plasma grenade from my belt. I cook it for a couple seconds, then toss it hard against the wall of the alley I can see. "Grenade!" I yell, and the surviving squad members sprint forward, away from the alleyways.

The blast lights up the street with an ethereal blue, and the sound of metal parts hitting metal brings a spike of satisfaction as I turn my attention to the bots in the opposite alley.

"Soren, take the corner and get ready to toss a grenade if you have an opening," I say, my subvocalized words coming rapid-fire. "The rest of you, we're center peeling across the alley mouth, slowly. As soon as the first soldier engages, the one farthest from the alley gets behind him and adds his fire. And so on. Understood?"

In answer, they get into position. Despite that two of our number are down already, I'm grateful to be commanding professionally trained troops. As dedicated as Otto's men were back in Sheen, they had nothing on Guardsmen.

Soren gets into position, popping out to fire before ducking back. As he does, the first Guardsman "peels back" to the rear of the formation and begins laying down suppressing fire. The next scrambles into position.

I'm next, and as I peel to the rear of the formation and open fire, I can see we're having an outsized effect on the enemy. They're in disarray, rushing for cover that isn't there. Now that their initial ambush is spent, and they're facing a Guardsman tactic that comes to us as easily as breathing, they have nothing.

Two bots go down right away. "Soren, grenade," I subvocalize.

He takes one out, cooks it, and lobs it into the alley. The rest of us melt away down the street, firing all the while, and then the grenade blast comes, with the squad all safely behind the building. The alley mouth belches fire and smoke, and the metal street rumbles beneath us, but the squad stays safe.

That said, we're down to eight now, and we just spent time we don't have. "Let's go," I bark, not bothering with subvocalizing. Sometimes, nothing can replace a spoken order.

The others show they understand the need for urgency by responding immediately. "Double-time," I say. "But keep your eyes peeled for ambush."

I'm hoping the bots only try going on the offensive once, since they're in foreign terrain. But we have no such luck. A few minutes later, another group hits us from the roof of a two-story data center, from where they have the clear advantage.

The entire squad manages to get by uninjured, laying down suppressing fire as we move through, but it's clear that going forward, we'll have to divide up our squad and switch to bounding overwatch, for safety.

I was hoping to avoid that. It's a more secure way to maneuver, but with only one group moving at a time, it'll slow us down considerably. Not only that, with a group of undefeated bots somewhere behind us, we'll need to stay extra frosty.

"Lieutenant Breen, report," I say over the command channel.

"The whole contingent's meeting with resistance, sir. Looks like they scattered bots all through the city to intercept us. It's like they know the best positions to maximize damage, and they just wait there."

"Tell all squads to switch to bounding overwatch," I say. "One thing's for sure: whatever these tin cans came here for, they're not leaving with it alive."

"Roger that. The rest of the Reserve forces present are sweeping the city from other angles, and the turrets around the city are on skywatch. No evac is getting through for them."

Our squad presses through Control while executing bounding

overwatch as tight as we can. We advance past data libraries, offi-cers' quarters, and admin buildings.

It occurs to me that Control was built to match its Subverse counterpart as closely as possible. Might the bots, or whoever's controlling them, have Subverse access? It doesn't seem that unlikely. And if they have that, they almost certainly know its layout, not to mention its defenses.

Getting that kind of intel would involve infiltrating the Guard's command structure—a scary thought. But I've had cause to think scarier things, recently, and it really doesn't seem that far-fetched.

At last, after an hour of pitched combat, we reach Module. The plaza surrounding it has very little cover—just some bridge-spanned trenches, too deep to realistically use.

Given that, there's no choice but for the entire squad to run across as fast as they can. We're down to five members, now, including me and Soren. Not bad, given the number of hostiles we've taken out today, but then, fifty percent casualties doesn't sit very well with me.

Module doesn't have doors—just massive openings, like caves in a cliff side. If caves were perfectly symmetrical, that is, and covered with thin blue lights that stretched, parallel, for dozens of meters.

The ground surrounding the tower features grates interspersed at regular intervals, where the water flows when it's raining. Currently, chunks of ice congregate around each one.

We barrel inside the tower, weapon muzzles roving in search of targets. The foyer is littered with the bodies of Guardsmen and bots, the former bleeding, the latter emitting sparks and fluids. Nothing moves, and so we press on toward the central chamber.

An elevator big enough to carry freight stretches up through the tower's center, and surrounding it we find Fairfax and a squad of bots, locked in a fierce firefight with some Guardsmen on the chamber's other side, using the elevator's massive tube for cover. The bots' backs are to us.

Did the elevator's security deny them, even after they got this far? Not that I'm complaining. Right now, Fairfax and his friends are sitting ducks.

"Paint your primary and secondary targets," I tell my squadmates, subvocalizing. "Be ready to concentrate fire on any hostiles still standing after the first volley." We've stopped near the entrance, so that we can withdraw to cover if needed, but I'd prefer to just take down the hostiles in one go if we can manage it. That said, I have my doubts.

The target I paint wears a flowing black cape—Fairfax.

"Fire," I subvocalize, and bolts fly across the colossal chamber: a single stream of blaster bolts amidst five of laser. Some of us stagger our shots, in case our targets move, but it turns out not to add much, since our targets mostly stay put.

The bolts slam home, throwing the group of bots forward onto their faces.

"Forward," I yell. "Keep shooting." A thrill shoots through me at the thought of taking down Fairfax. But as I approach, that thrill turns into the sense that my stomach is sinking toward my feet.

Our bolts continue to fly, until we're satisfied the hostiles aren't moving. Even so, I approach Fairfax with caution. When I reach him, I kick him twice in the side, hard. My boot meets metal, and he doesn't move.

Then, I flick the body over with my foot, so that he lies on his back.

A combat bot's face stares up at the ceiling, partially melted. No coldly glowing sapphire eyes. No pill-shaped breather.

Though I already know I've been fooled, I pull back the cape to check the forearms. Darkly gleaming metal—not flesh.

This isn't Fairfax. But why go through the trouble of pretending it was?

The group of Guardsmen who'd been engaging the bots from the opposite side march forward, with a man at their lead who my datasphere identifies as Major Gregory Defoe.

"Commander Joe Pikeman?" he says as he approaches.

"That's right," I say, awaiting his salute so I can return it. Since I outrank him, custom says he should go first.

Instead, he produces a pair of restraints. "Your court-martial awaits. Will you go peacefully, or will it be necessary to use force?" He gestures with the restraints.

I exchange unbelieving looks with Soren. Didn't we just save their asses?

But I guess he's only following orders.

"I'll come peacefully," I say.

3

"Are you sure Chief Shimura can be objective, here?" I mutter to Leeroy Johnson, my civilian counsel, as I cast an eye across the jury benches.

"Oh, definitely," Johnson says. The pudgy lawyer wears a wrinkled suit that looks like it's about to burst across his middle. Seems weird for an upload to *choose* to be fat and disheveled, when he has the option to look however he wants. But it's not something I have time to dwell on, so I just accept it as yet another Subverse oddity.

The rest of the bots that infiltrated Control took a couple more hours to clean up entirely, and the brass decided to postpone the court-martial until the next day. They didn't allow me to help with the cleanup efforts, of course. Instead, they held me in custody overnight, alone with my datasphere and my thoughts. They also took my blaster.

From the jury bench, Shimura glares at me, and I hold his gaze for a few moments before turning back to Johnson. Back when Shimura trained us, he was a Senior Chief Petty Officer, but he's since made Master Chief. "He always hated me," I say. "It's pretty obvious he still does."

The attorney shrugs. "He sure fooled me, then, when I questioned him." Both the defense and the prosecution get to question each jury member, to make sure they're capable of seeing the defendant's situation objectively.

Not for the first time, I'm struck by the desire to wrestle the lawyer to the ground and knock him around the head. That would be impossible, of course, since he's not really here. He's an upload, present only by virtue of the collective processing power of the dataspheres of everyone in the courtroom.

Normally, a Guardsman undergoing court-martial would have a military attorney—unless he could afford a civilian attorney's fee, which isn't common. I actually probably could afford it, if I was willing to dip into the *Ares'* repair fund, which I'm not. Luckily, a member of my versecast audience happened to be a renowned attorney, famed for getting uploads out of the same underverses I'm so familiar with.

At least, it seemed lucky at the time. But Johnson shows every sign of being thoroughly incompetent.

Fount, I'm screwed.

Other than Chief Shimura, the jury consists of a collection of commanders, captains, and admirals. There's Rear Admiral Quinn —who I directly defied while chasing pirates out on the Brink— sitting next to two other admirals, both of them upload-only, there biological forms having died decades ago.

Under Guard regs, the jury must be half biological humans, half uploads, but that hardly seems fair, if you ask me. What upload is going to sympathize with abandoning my duty to protect the Subverse to chase pirates in the real?

Rear Admiral Quinn is technically digital, as well. At least, this version of him is. Physically, he's stationed out on the Brink, and the man on the jury is really just a brainprint of Quinn that's been briefed on the particulars of the case.

Without warning, the bailiff steps forward. "All rise."

Everyone gets to their feet, though I feel like lead weights have been placed around my shoulders.

"This court-martial is now in session, the Honorable Judge Hagen presiding."

The judge takes his seat, and then everyone else sits.

"Lady and gentleman of the jury," Hagen says, his voice somehow smooth as chocolate while rumbling like an earthquake. His bushy mustache waggles as he speaks. "This case concerns the guilt or innocence of Commander Joseph Pikeman, who is charged with being absent without leave, failure to obey orders, and flight from arrest. He has pled not guilty. Bailiff, please swear in the members of the jury."

The bailiff goes about the requested business as stiffly as possible, and when he finishes, Judge Hagen invites the prosecution to give its opening statement.

Judge Advocate Tannenbaum stands, pretentiously fastening the top button of his suit before beginning to stalk the room. "Joseph Heraldo Pikeman," he says, disdain dripping from every syllable. "Son of Calvin Francis Pikeman, who was also a defector from the Guard. As the lady and gentlemen of the jury watch the evidence pile up against the defendant, I ask that you hold one question in your hearts: is this a man to be trusted with protecting humanity's home—the Subverse?"

Things don't improve from there. As evidence, Tannenbaum submits a recording of my conversation with Admiral Quinn, in which I clearly state my intention to defy his order to return to Tunis and await my next assignment as a Troubleshooter.

Based on that one recording alone, I have no clue how Johnson expects to convince the jury to find me innocent. For what must be the twentieth time, I curse myself for not pleading guilty and telling Johnson to go for a reduced sentence. He assured me he could get me off entirely, which now just looks like more evidence of his incompetence.

If I'm found guilty of any of the charges the judge listed, at minimum I can expect to be imprisoned for a year. More likely, I'll be dishonorably discharged, but either way would spell disaster when it comes to stopping Fairfax or finding Harmony before something happens to her.

"I'll now play for you a recording of one of the many versecasts Commander Pikeman has produced since defying the admiral's orders. I won't bore you by playing all of them, since I fear your brains would melt from the inanity, but this one is a good example of the utter irresponsibility the commander has shown, as well as his flagrant disregard for the chain of command."

The versecast Tannenbaum sends our dataspheres shows me rampaging through Royal, the main pirate outpost out on the Brink. At least, it *was* their main outpost, before I cause it to implode at the end of the versecast, sending it sinking into Larunda's highly acidic atmosphere.

"An uninformed watcher of that versecast might applaud the commander's actions, as indeed many in the Subverse did. But a service member will know just how delicate the balance of power is in the real. There's a reason the Guard hasn't endeavored to launch a large-scale attack on any significant gathering of pirates, in any sector. Such a move could easily trigger a chain reaction that results in pirates across the galaxy banding together to attack Gauntlet. We all saw what trouble the Guard had preventing the recent bot incursion from penetrating Control. If the galaxy's pirates started working together, we would be finished."

My palms have started to sweat, and it takes an effort of will not to wipe them off on my pants.

"But perhaps most damning of all is the commander's track record, starting with his upbringing in a Brinktown," Tannenbaum goes on. "There, he conducted himself just as his father did, leading a youth filled with narcotic abuse, peddling narcotics, vandalism, petty theft—the list goes on, but you get the idea. The commander left his daughter to suffer a similar fate, and predictably, she has continued the family tradition of delinquency, stealing her grandfather's ship before marrying a pirate lord's son at the age of sixteen."

Fists balled, I start to rise, but Johnson places a hand on my shoulder, and I allow him to placate me. It probably won't go well for me with the jury if I hurt the military prosecutor.

The trial wears on, with the prosecutor piling up more and more evidence that I should be sentenced: my criminal record, my broken family, my record-breaking kill count, my insubordination. My "bizarre" claims that Rodney Fairfax has somehow turned against the Guard.

My ears perk up at that. "In fact," Tannenbaum says, "this may well point to other, even graver crimes committed by Commander Pikeman, which we've yet to uncover. There have been several attempts of late to cast aspersions on Rodney Fairfax, both in the real and in the Subverse, the latest being the attack on this very city. The lead bot was dressed in the style Mr. Fairfax favors. Why? Why these repeated attempts to frame him, or at least to cause us to be suspicious of him? Because Mr. Fairfax is, and always has been, a valuable ally of the Guard. He's often stepped in where our Troubleshooters have failed. Creating a rift between the Guard and the Fairfaxes would do us untold damage, and here we find the commander doing everything he can not only to create that rift, but to widen it."

Another versecast appears in my datasphere, the sender listed as Tannenbaum. "There have been signs that many of the versecasts the commander has put out since going rogue have been faked. Versecast experts and videographers have made extensive study of his output, finding all the telltale signs of fakery—I'm sending you a report I've compiled on their findings now, for your review over the break. But perhaps the most damning evidence that Commander Pikeman has been faking his versecasts lies within this one, apparently taken inside a giant tree."

The versecast shows me fighting Fairfax to the death, and it speeds ahead to the painful climax, when Fairfax runs me through.

"Here you see Commander Pikeman, apparently far from his ship, and far from any emergency medical aid. He suffers a wound that should clearly have been fatal. And yet here he sits before you, a whole and very much alive man."

When we finally move to a break, I feel like every cell of my body has been sapped of energy. I try not to appear defeated as a pair of Guardsmen escort me out of the courtroom, with my attorney trailing behind.

They take me to a windowless room and close the door behind me—only as it's closing do I realize that Leeroy Johnson hasn't followed me in. I'm alone, left to contemplate my fate.

The first four hours of the trial felt like a week, and I'm not sure how I'll get through the rest of the day. What I didn't expect was the mounting sense of shame that slowly increased throughout the day. To be torn apart like that in front of my colleagues—in front of the very officers and instructors who trained me, who put me through the sims that allowed me to be comfortable with killing, and who did everything they could to grant me the legitimacy to do it. They did their job too well, and look what they created. Well, now they have to watch their own creation dismantled in front of them.

4

The door opens, and my lawyer finally enters. He seats himself across from me, folding his hands in his lap and smiling brightly. As an upload operating in the real, he can't go outside this building, since his presence requires our dataspheres to sustain it. I'm used to my crew sticking to their stations, though, so it's a bit odd for me to see an upload walking freely around the building.

"Well, I think things are going rather well so far," he says.

"Are you insane?" I snap. "Tannenbaum has more than enough evidence to get maximum sentence for the charges. Hell, if I weren't me, I'd have me executed after listening to all that!"

"He's desperate," Johnson says. "He has an air of desperation about him—it's why he's pulling out all the stops. You didn't notice that?"

"I noticed he's a smarmy bastard."

"Oh, well, yes. Generally. But…allow me to let you in on a piece of news I just received."

"Well?"

"It seems the recent bot incursion was successful after all."

"Huh? I thought we got them all."

"You did. But not before they managed to hack Control's main-frame—with alarming efficiency, I might add—and transmit the intel they wanted to a ship waiting in orbit. The Guard wasn't able to get a read on the ship. It appears the crew covered their tracks quite well, including masking the remote connection."

"What intel did they get?"

"Nothing short of the location of every Subverse server room in the galaxy." A smile stretches Johnson's broad cheeks.

I just sit there, stunned. I'm not sure what I should react to first: the fact that that the galaxy just changed in a heartbeat, or that Johnson's grinning about it.

"You're acting like I should be happy about this," I say.

"You should," he gushes. "Just think. Right now, the news is working its way through the jury. And they have to be asking themselves: can they really afford to make an example of their most effective Guardsman right now? Do they want to make a sacrificial lamb of their potential savior? Mind you, we can't actually brings up the locations leaking during the court-martial, since the news hasn't been officially disseminated yet. But it does put us on strong footing."

"I really don't think they view me as a savior, Johnson."

His grin widens. "I haven't given my defense yet."

Back in the courtroom, with everyone seated, he's called on to do just that. Johnson surges to his feet with more energy than I suspected he had. True, I guess his energy levels are actually determined only by his will, since as an upload he has access to unlimited energy. Still—his vigor takes me aback, and judging by the sound of rustling uniforms filling the chamber, I'm not the only one.

"First of all, these allegations of versecast fakery are false and very irresponsible of Mr. Tannenbaum to make," he says, with no preamble to speak of. "I submit to you Exhibit A, namely the medical inspections as compiled by Commander Pikeman's own Fount. As your dataspheres now clearly show you, he did indeed suffer a wound that, under normal circumstances, would have been fatal." Faint gasps can be heard from around the courtroom, and the corner of my mouth quirks as the first flicker of hope sputters to life inside me.

"It seems the only reason Commander Pikeman's consciousness survived is that his Fount downloaded it into the Subverse temporarily, there to merge with a copy of his consciousness that happened to dwell in that very system. This is an unprecedented event, and confirmed by brain scans also conducted by his Fount, which I'm transmitting to you all now. Everything I'm showing you has been submitted to and verified by court officials, so I hope you can be assured that *I*, at least, am not participating in fakery.

"As for the so-called 'experts' and 'videographers,' Mr. Tannenbaum referenced earlier, I now submit to you their track records, compiled by my assistants. They are known scam artists; peddlers of conspiracy theories. Lady and gentlemen of the jury, I tell you that in ancient Earth's history, there were those who claimed the first moon landing was faked, and who piled up so-called 'evidence,' which they claimed proved its inauthenticity. A ridiculous notion, I think you'll agree, given the subsequent colonization of the galaxy by our species. These claims that the commander's versecasts were faked are equally ridiculous—another demonstration of flagrant irresponsibility on the part of a Judge Advocate, and quite a surprise, given the sanctity of his role. If I didn't know better, I would say that Mr. Tannenbaum seems unusually motivated to defame the commander. But the Judge Advocate isn't under trial here. My client is; a rather unfortunate circumstance, for everyone involved. Allow me to tell you why."

With that, Johnson starts singing my praises, starting with my taking in and taming a dog that might have died on Earth if I hadn't, and ending with my saving dozens of children kidnapped by pirates and brought to Xeo.

"Commander Pikeman took it upon himself to evacuate the sole survivor of the pirate attack on the Siberian Brinktown, taking him to a new home on Calabar," Johnson says. "And during the long slipspace voyage, he gave that poor boy his bunk, sleeping in his command seat for three months straight—for as I'm sure you all know, the commander doesn't believe in entering nanodeath, instead remaining vigilant, ready to act at any moment. The commander nearly died in the effort to protect the Grotto, home of the Eliots, from a pirate attack. And yes, when Arthur Eliot's daughter, Faelyn Eliot, was kidnapped, Commander Pikeman took it upon himself to track down the men responsible. It's true that he wasn't authorized to do that—not authorized to take out the major pirate stronghold, Royal, or to alert the Guard to all the kidnapped children on Xeo. It's true he had no orders to do those things. But lady and gentlemen of the journey, I ask you: don't you think he *should* have been ordered to do them? Isn't it an oversight that he was not? Is it not the solemn duty of the Galactic Guard to protect not just the Subverse, but humanity as a whole?"

He doesn't mention my part in liberating Otto and his people from Rile's tyranny, but whether that's because those versecasts haven't been widely disseminated yet or because no one cares about Fallen, I'm not sure.

"To convict this man would do a disservice, not just to the Guard but the galaxy as a whole. Look inside your hearts, lady and gentlemen of the jury. Search your conscience. And do what you know is right. On behalf of the galaxy, I beg you."

Johnson finishes his monologue abruptly, plopping himself beside me, still looking like an incompetent bag of wrinkles. Now, I think I see why he chooses to present himself like that. During the first part of the trial, Tannenbaum clearly underestimated him, and took plenty of liberties with the perceptions of the jury as a result. Now, Tannenbaum has been all but flayed, his innards laid bare. Johnson exposed him as a liar, and he left several jury members with what looks like admiration gleaming in their eyes.

"Good work, Johnson," I say, a little tersely.

He offers a smile much smaller than the one he gave during the break. "Back to your customary reticence, I see."

Johnson's the last person I would have expected to start liking. But, surprisingly, it seems I have.

The trial stretches on for the rest of the day, with witnesses called and arguments countered. Tannenbaum tries to gain some ground with the jury by going over how susceptible I was to training simulations designed to accustom trainees to violence and death. But I doubt many of the officers on the jury will be moved by the argument that I'm too good at the job they trained me for.

As the proceedings near their end, I start to actually believe I'll be acquitted. That's when Johnson decides, during his closing argument, to negate all the progress he's made by going too far.

"It's been made clear to you that not only did Commander Pikeman never fake a versecast, but he never lies. Given those facts, you in the real have tremendous cause for worry. For what the commander has uncovered amounts to nothing less than a galaxy-wide conspiracy to topple the existing order. Humanity's digital safe haven is in danger of disruption, possibly utter destruction, and it seems we have nowhere to retreat to—not even the real. It would be the height of folly to prosecute this man. Not only should you acquit him, you should support him however you can."

I resist the urge to lower my face into my palm. Johnson's attempt to make me into some kind of messiah is doomed to fail. People don't go from thinking someone's scum to believing he's their only hope, certainly not in one day. If the Guard was ready to acknowledge what trouble we're in, then it never would have been necessary for me to defy orders in the first place. I wouldn't be here.

During the jury's deliberations, I can't even look at Johnson. I'm afraid I'll start punching the thin air he occupies. I feel like we were so close. Why'd he have to get so grandiose toward the end?

It occurs to me that he probably doesn't get many opportunities to take clients in the real. This could have been a career-defining moment for him. Judging by his closing argument, either the pressure got to him, or things get a lot more dramatic in the Subverse, and people are a lot more gullible.

Actually, I don't have very much trouble believing that at all.

After an hour—sixty-nine minutes and thirty-seven seconds, to be exact—the jury finishes deliberating and we're called back to the courtroom. As the they file back to their bench, my heart is in my throat.

"Have you reached a verdict?" Judge Hagen asks.

"We have, your honor," Admiral Ives says, who was apparently appointed foreman.

"What say you?"

"We, the jury in the case of the Galactic Guard versus Commander Joe Pikeman, find the defendant not guilty on all charges, as we were unable to achieve the two-thirds vote needed to convict the defendant."

I blink at the admiral, replaying his words again in my head to make sure I heard correctly. Beside me, Leeroy Johnson is grinning openly, now.

So. It looks like he was right, after all. The shit has hit the galactic fan, and the Guard is finally willing to acknowledge it.

5

"The Guard has fewer teeth than it did fifty years ago," Admiral Ives says from the front of the conference room. Balding, he has the beginnings of a double-chin, which wobbles forward to emphasize each syllable. "And now we have too many places we need to bite."

The corner of my mouth quirks, but I suppress my reaction other than that. Ives isn't known for his metaphors—or rather, he's known for making particularly tortured ones. I get the idea, though.

The seats at the table are occupied mostly by captains and a couple other admirals, some of them uploads. But Ives is taking the lead on this. I catch myself stroking my blaster's handle, which was returned to me after the trial, then I stop. It felt profoundly uncomfortable to be separated from the Shivan weapon—like a piece of me was missing. But fondling it in the presence of superior officers probably doesn't send the best message.

"Reports of bot attacks on Midtowns all over this sector have been reaching us for months," Ives continues, "but even if we could anticipate where they'll strike next, we don't have the resources to intercept."

Johnson's words from the court-martial play again in my head, about the Guardsman's Oath covering not just the Subverse, but all humanity. If only it meant that in practice.

Percy's been out of nanodeath since the battle for Control ended, and he's said his piece to the brass—told them about the attack on his Midtown, and his community's dire need for relief troops. As nicely as possible, the brass told him he's out of luck.

Oh, they dressed it up as well as they could, couching it in flowery words, telling him that the moment "the current state of galactic unrest" ends, those relief troops will be on their way. But they know as well as I do that there's no end in sight, so Percy and his people really are shit out of luck.

After talking him into traveling light years away from home, with no way back any time soon, only to get the cold shoulder from the Guard…well, I feel awful about it all. I went to Admiral Ives right before this meeting, but he gave me the same line, just in less official speak: "Pikeman, that Midtown is one of thousands of places that are in the shit right now, all across the galaxy. We don't have the resources and men to maintain servers that won't stop breaking down, let alone protect Midtowns and Brinktowns from every bogeyman that comes along. Now that the bots know where every server in the galaxy is…I'm sorry, Pikeman, but finding spare troops to deploy to that Midtown just isn't going to happen. I know it sounds cold, but it's the way things are right now."

I knew I wasn't doing myself any favors, but I decided to press the issue regardless: "Sir, this isn't just about a bot attack on a Midtown. The bots wanted Ludmilla Cadogan—I believe that's why they attacked in the first place. To abduct her."

"Cadogan?" the admiral says, sniffing. "What do they want with her?"

"That's a very good question. Whatever it is, sir, I don't have a great feeling about it. It sounds like she was conducting some pretty strange experiments on the populace there, even before the attack. She was giving drugs to trick the Fount into suppressing their nature. Their urges, and things, you know. She—"

"That does sound strange, Pikeman. But you getting a bad feeling isn't enough reason to deploy troops, I'm afraid."

Remembering the conversation now, it takes an effort not to scowl. Here in the conference room, in front of other officers, the admiral softens his language a bit. But it's not hard to see straight through it. "Now that they've hit us here on Gauntlet," Ives says, "and successfully stolen the server locations, we're forced to take what action we can to put down this uprising once and for all."

Yes. Now that the bots pose an existential threat to the Subverse, right? I would be saying this out loud, if I hadn't just been acquitted by the skin of my teeth. Apparently the jury was just shy of the two-thirds vote needed to convict me. Maybe the Guard doesn't have its eyes open as wide as I thought, when it comes to the current crisis.

Then again, we *are* having this meeting.

"As such, we have new orders for you, Commander Pikeman," Ives continues. "And Commander Garrett."

Soren shoots me a glance from the seat beside me, and I swear he's about to nudge me with his elbow when I flick his knee under the table. My eyes remain glued to the admiral, and I can't help feeling a flicker of optimism. If Percy and his people are going to get any satisfaction, this is how they'll get it. By stopping the bots —but even more, by stopping Fairfax.

"Your mission will be to travel to the Lambton Cloud," Ives says, "there to meet with Maximus Lambton and gather what intel you can about just what the bots are capable of. Their numbers, their resources, what alliances they've managed to forge—Fount help us. If you can, find out what they're planning next."

"Sorry, sir, but how would visiting Lambton tell us that?" I ask, and the admiral's brow furrows slightly. "Do you think he's in league with the bots?"

"Of course not," the admiral says, proto-jowls shivering. "But if the bots are to grow their force, the Cloud is the logical place to strike, wouldn't you say?"

"In that case, maybe you should be sending more Guardsmen than just me and Soren."

"Unfortunately, we cannot."

I shake my head sharply. "Why not? Troubleshooters exist to neutralize threats to Subverse servers, right? Well, they're *all* under threat right now. To deal with this, we should recall every Troubleshooter in the galaxy, to strike as a single force. What if all those server locations leak out to the Subverse? There'll be no putting the genie back in the bottle, then. The pirates will get them, and all hell will break loose."

"It's not that simple," the admiral snaps. "Withdrawing every Troubleshooter would be just as catastrophic as the scenario you describe, which I consider highly unlikely from a military standpoint. What force would play so fast and loose with valuable intel? Even rebels wouldn't spend their leverage so easily."

"They might try to blackmail us with it."

"We're sending you and Commander Garrett, Pikeman. That decision has already been made, and you're not doing yourself any favors by questioning orders given to you so soon after being charged for defying orders." His shoulders rise and fall as he takes a deep breath. "Look, you're being given full authority to cooperate with the Lambtons to end the bot incursion by any means necessary. Before you go, we'll do a full refuel and resupply of both your ships, including restocking your Javelin missiles. And we're already repairing the *Ares*—we began that process during your court-martial, knowing the ship would be needed either way. The repairs should be complete by the time you leave. And that truly is the best we can do in the current situation."

He's right that I'm not doing myself any favors. I already knew that. But it's still not going to shut me up. "What about Fairfax?" I say.

The admiral closes his eyes, drawing another deep breath, as though drawing on his last reservoir of patience. "Rodney Fairfax?"

"Of course."

"What about him?"

"What will you do to stop him?"

"Rodney Fairfax is a valuable ally of the Guard, Pikeman."

"Really? Is that seriously still the official position?"

"Of course. Trust me, Commander. If we anger the Fairfaxes, a few bots will be the least of our worries. Their wrath would hammer home the last nail of the Guard's coffin."

"It's more than a few bots, Admiral. And you saw Fairfax colluding with pirates in my versecasts. You saw him with them when they abducted children from Tunis."

"We've already contacted Mr. Fairfax about that, and he assures us that he was infiltrating the pirates' ranks and working against them—just as you claim your daughter was. He also assures us that Lord Bleak's experiments involving children have ceased. Haven't you confirmed that as well?"

"Yeah, but the experiments ending had nothing to do with Fairfax. And what about him running me through, inside Arbor?"

"A misunderstanding, I'm sure," the admiral says, his voice tight. "Commander, I'm going to ask you this once: *kindly* shut your mouth, open your ears, and listen to the rest of this briefing."

After that, I stay quiet as the admiral outlines the particulars of the mission. I also stay unimpressed. This is a gong show. Refusing to acknowledge Fairfax as an enemy, calling it a "misunderstanding" when he murdered me, and sending only two Guardsmen—it's like they're trying to stop up a gushing wound with a single cotton ball.

I can appreciate the tension Ives and the rest of the admiralty is under, of course. No one wants to piss off the Five Families, and over half the Guard's command structure lives in the Subverse. That puts them at the mercy of Bacchus, and by extension the Five Families. The admiral's in an impossible position.

But that doesn't mean he isn't a coward. As far as I'm

concerned, when you're faced with two horrible choices, you pick the one that helps you sleep at night.

My silence only seems to thicken the tension, and by the time the meeting ends, Soren seems just as happy to leave as I am. Neither of us speaks until we're outside, under the warm blanket of heat provided by Gauntlet's sun. The ice from the recent hailstorm is long since melted, and heat radiates off the metal below our feet.

"Fount, Joe," he mutters. "You finally get off the hook with the Guard, and that's how you act?"

I shrug. "Sure. I'm going to object to half-measures when it comes to facing down what's probably the worst crisis the Guard has ever faced." I curse. "Ives is the wrong one to put in charge of this. I bet you he voted to convict me."

"Pikeman," a rasping voice calls out behind me.

I turn to see Chief Shimura leaning against the building we just left, and I narrow my eyes.

"A word?" Shimura says.

I nod. "Meet you back at the ships," I tell Soren.

"Sure thing."

Shimura leads me down the metal street, past a series of squat metal buildings of varying sizes. Here and there, the shattered bodies of bots lay in heaps, though most of them have been cleaned up by now. By other bots, ironically.

He leads me into a nondescript building, which seems to consist of a single hallway with rooms branching off on both sides. We stop at one, and it opens before us.

"Please," he says, gesturing inside. The room is totally unfurnished, other than two chairs facing each other, with a round table between them that holds a wireless kettle, two mugs, and a metal cube. "Take a seat."

I do, and he sits across from me. A light appears on the kettle—he must have willed it to turn on. "Tea?" he asks.

"Sure, Master Chief. Is this, uh…?"

"My office."

"Doesn't look much like one."

Shimura shrugs. "We have an unhealthy obsession with the past. With dataspheres, desks hold little use for us anymore. It is a trapping that appears to lend gravity to our doings, but ultimately, it's folly."

"Right."

"You should know that I voted to acquit you."

That makes me raise me eyebrows. "Really?"

He nods. "During your training, it was probably no secret to you that I despised you."

"Yeah."

"In truth, you reminded me of my father. His youth was spent in much the same way you spent yours, and your father spent his. I made a decision to be nothing like him, and I perceived that you hadn't made that same decision, which disgusted me. Frightened me, in all honesty."

I rock my head back a little, uninterested in still more discussion of my moral fiber so soon after the trial. From the table between us, the kettle clicks off. "Tea?"

"Sure."

"I've realized that I was wrong about two things," Shimura says as he pries the top from the metal container, removing two tea cubes and depositing them into our mugs. He pours boiling water into one cup. "One is the Guard." He tops off the other cup. "The other is you. Do you take sugar in your tea?"

"No."

"Good. I have none."

"I'll have to ask you to do better than that, Chief Shimura. *How* were you wrong?"

"I always believed the Guard fought for the good of humanity. I was mistaken. It was created by the Five Families, who are connected by their involvement with Bacchus Corporation, and it remains a tool of Bacchus even now."

I study his face, and I can tell he's serious. "What brought you to that realization?"

"The same situation which made me change my mind about you. You *do* fight for humanity, Commander. The humanity that chose to stay behind and face reality—in the real. We need someone who is willing to stand up for these people."

"Why did you invite me here, Instructor?"

"Because I need you to tell me whether you will do what you must do, even if you know your superiors won't like it. You were just acquitted of the charge of defying orders, but I doubt you would be found innocent at a second court-martial. Will you do what needs doing anyway, despite that risk?"

I set my mug down on the table and look him dead in the eyes. "I will."

LAMBTON CLOUD

1

"Transition complete," Belflower says once I'm finished vomiting noisily into the reusable bag. Damn—I should have requested a new one while I was on Gauntlet. This one's getting pretty discolored.

I think the crew is finally getting used to the violent nausea each transition brings. Yes, it's not ideal for my upload crew to see their biological captain in this state, but then again, I've never had a crew as invested as this one. For better or worse, it seems we're tied to each other. Belflower wants to investigate the bot uprising, Marissa's the formerly estranged mother of my child, Moe is just me with an M instead of a J, and Asterisk…well, I guess Asterisk just likes shooting stuff.

Anyway, is it just me, or is the nausea starting to get a little less intense? It must be my imagination. That's not supposed to happen, and certainly, it's never gotten easier for me in over a decade of service. "OPO," I croak. "Is the Lambton Cloud where the brass said it would be?"

"Yes, sir," Marissa says coldly.

I've opted for referring to her only as "OPO," for fear of accidentally saying her real name and spilling the beans to Moe and

Asterisk. Plus, she's only gotten more standoffish since Gauntlet, so why shouldn't I?

"Send me the sensor data," I snap, more harshly than I intended.

She taps at her circular station, then flicks over the report. It hits my datasphere like mud hitting glass.

It's actually sensor data relayed from Soren's Broadsword, timed to reach the slipspace exit coords simultaneous to our arrival. We haven't been in the system long enough for the light necessary to detect in-system objects to reach us—the *Hermes* left several hours ahead of us, due to a problem with our Becker drive, which Belflower's pre-transition systems check turned up. Repairs were enough to delay us this long, but it actually worked out pretty well for us, from an intel perspective.

Of course, it also means Soren will reach the Lambton Cloud's Cylinder One well before we do, so I hope he doesn't get things off on a disastrous foot. I fear his endless versecasting has the potential to turn them off anything we might propose, before we even propose it.

The Lambton Cloud consists of hundreds of slipspace-capable, cylindrical space craft. In truth, each cylinder is part starship, part colony, part roving industrial miracle. The cloud travels from system to system, exploiting asteroid belts as well as uninhabitable planets and planetesimals for resources, which it uses to manufacture bots of all kinds. Before the Fall, Lambton had a virtual monopoly on the bot industry. Now it has an actual one.

To protect the Cloud from pirates, its location at any given time is a secret known only to a select few—a group that includes the admiralty. The fact they've shared the current location with me and Soren, a system called Bath, represents a significant gamble, especially considering one of us was just court-martialed. But I suppose I was acquitted.

Either way, each cylinder is outfitted with a point defense system, plus a modest fighter drone fleet patrols the system as a whole, programmed to rush to the aid of any cylinder that falls under attack. Another thing that keeps the Cloud safe is regularly changing locations: once resource extraction in the Bath System hits the point of diminishing returns, the Cloud moves on to the next system. I've read that at any given time, the Lambtons have at least five systems in mind as their next destination, and the one they choose involves a calculus of proximity and resource abundance.

After a couple hours, we're able to get a fairly accurate read on exactly how many Lambton Cylinders are in this system: two hundred and nineteen. They're dispersed across the Bath System, mostly throughout the wide-arcing asteroid belt, which is roughly similar in size and population to the Kuiper Belt of humanity's home system. Cylinder One happens to be holding heliocentric orbit on our side of the Bath System, fairly near the slipspace exit point, relatively speaking. The journey takes just under three hours.

As we approach, I admire Cylinder One through an exterior visual sensor located on the *Ares'* nose. Unwilling as I am to give one of the Five Families credit, even I have to admit the slowly-turning structure bears undeniable majesty. Covered in beacons, a steady flow of autonomous harvester bots soar to and from it.

The main landing bay is located on the far side of the cylinder, so I have the opportunity to stare down through a belly sensor at the metal beast as it flies through space along the same trajectory as Bath's asteroids.

Located at the cylinder's very center, the landing bay is zero-G, unlike the cylinder's inside edge, where centripetal forces perfectly simulate one G. By putting the landing bay in the center, the designers spared both visiting ships and the bay itself centuries of wear and tear. A similar landing bay is located on the opposite end, but it isn't oxygenated, since only the harvester bots use it.

As the *Ares* noses out of the mammoth airlock, I eye the welcoming party floating in midair, wearing air thruster belts to maneuver in the lack of gravity. I do a double take as I realize who the party comprises: not just Soren, but Maximus Lambton, current CEO of Lambton Industries. For him to bother putting on air thrusters and entering zero-G to greet us comes as something of a surprise. He smiles warmly at the *Ares'* nose, as if he can feel my eyes on him.

An even greater shock comes as my eyes land on one of the starships floating in the landing bay nearby, straining against its tethers: it's the *Europa's Gift*. The ship Harmony stole from her grandfather.

2

I'm sitting alone on the bridge with Marissa, the rest of the crew deactivated, and we're waiting for our daughter to make her way to Cylinder One's landing bay and come on board the *Ares*.

"She's here, Joe," Marissa says, beaming, standing outside her station and leaning back against its railing. "She's really here. We found her."

"Yeah," I say, remembering all the shit Marissa's given me over the last few months about this. Don't get me wrong, I'm ecstatic to have found Harmony. It just gets old, being blamed for problems you didn't create, and criticized for doing the right thing.

"Can you come into the sim for a minute?" she asks, her voice suddenly small.

I narrow my eyes. "Why?"

"I…I want to hold you. Joe, we've been apart for so long. I mean, yes we've served on this ship, but we haven't truly been together since Brinktown, right? Now, with Harmony here, do you think…do you think we could be…?"

"I'm not coming into the sim. I don't do that, I don't go into sims."

She frowns, her voice still low. "But you use the sims for controlling the turrets, and the ship, sometimes—"

"I'm not coming into the sim."

Eyes lowering to the deck, Marissa crosses her arms and doesn't say anything else.

So that I don't have to look at her, I replace the view of the bridge with one from a hull sensor. Harmony's crossing the landing bay now, the air thrusters projecting from her belt propelling her toward us. Relief washes over me at the sight of her. It's also kind of funny to watch her floating toward us in zero-G, while I'm anchored to the command seat by the *Ares'* gravity generator.

Zooming in, I frown, because I can tell something's different. Something about her eyes, the way she holds herself, the way her jaw is set like that...this isn't the same girl I parted ways with on Xeo.

Also, I probably shouldn't be thinking of her as a girl anymore, but I figure being a bit behind the curve on that is a father's prerogative.

The airlock opens, and she walks in, smiling slightly. "Mom. Dad. Long time no see."

I breathe out, releasing a pocket of tension I didn't know was there. I'm dad again—not Joe. That's a good start.

Marissa rushes across the deck and kneels in front of Harmony. They don't try to touch, since it's always a bit depressing when you pass right through each other. But Marissa clasps her hands and stares up at Harmony lovingly. "It's so good to see you, sweetheart. I love you so much."

"Good to see you, Harm," I say, smiling, though it feels tight. Probably I should hug her or something, but I'm not great at that stuff. Besides, I don't want to make Marissa feel bad that she can't.

My eyes fall on the holster hanging from Harmony's hip, and I recognize my old laser pistol nestled inside it. I feel my lips twitch as I try not to frown.

"Get up, Mom," Harmony says gently, brushing a lock of

whip-straight auburn hair behind one ear. "Come on. We have a lot to talk about, and it feels weird to talk to you when you're kneeling."

Still smiling, Marissa stands and returns to lean back against the railing.

"I'll just get it out of the way upfront. I'm working with Fairfax."

Marissa's smile falls away like a dead thing, and I surge to my feet from the command seat. "You're *what?*" I yell, hands curling into fists. Not to hit anyone, obviously—just at the thought of it. "Tell me you're making some sick joke."

Harmony shakes her head. "I'm afraid not, Dad. And the crazy thing is, I've decided that Fairfax is probably the good guy in all this."

Sinking to the arm of the command seat with three fingers pressed to my temple, I say, "This must be a nightmare I'm having."

"Fairfax is leading the bot revolution," Harmony goes on, nodding. "You may have figured that out already. Obviously, they've hurt some people, and they'll probably hurt more. But the important thing is, they're helping people escape the Subverse. You were right all along about that place, Dad. The Subverse isn't a heaven—it's hell."

Head tilted down, I raise my eyes to meet hers. Questions swirl around each other in my head, each feeling more urgent than the last, but I don't have the will to ask any of them. "How can this be happening?" I croak. It wasn't one of the questions, but it's the only thing I can muster to say.

"It started on Xeo," Harmony says. "I've had my suspicions about the Subverse for a long time, based on some things I'd found during recreational hacking expeditions, back in Brinktown. And when I came onto the *Ares* and met mom in person, she was nothing like the brainprints she'd sent me when I was growing up. She wasn't this manic, awkward weirdo who seemed to have no real appreciation for the situation she'd left us in. She was…I dunno. *Real.* As real as it's possible for an upload to be, I guess."

"You asked for copies from my brainprint outbox," Marissa says, slowly.

Harmony nods. "Yeah. I'm not sure anyone's done that before, or even had the opportunity—to compare brainprints they received from an upload to the brainprints the upload actually sent. When I compared the ones I got from mom to the ones she sent, I found they were completely different. In the ones *I* got, she was way too upbeat about everything. She claimed she was so happy with her life, which only made me angrier, since it was a life without her daughter. She kept insisting that I do everything I could to upload and join her."

"Which I do want," Marissa says.

"Yes, I know," Harmony answers, nodding. "Though I can tell you it's an awful idea, I know you want what you think is best for me. The thing is, in the versions of our conversations you gave me from your outbox, things were completely different. You were understanding, apologetic, and you explained to me that your father forced you to upload. You helped me to understand the situation, even if I didn't like it. We seemed to bond, in those brainprints. Except, they never actually happened. The Subverse fed me a fake version of you, one that was happy with her life there, and then it fed you a fake version of our conversations." Harmony pauses, her shoulders rising with a deep breath. "I can understand why it was so confusing for you when I refused to take your brainprints anymore. You thought things were going great. In the meantime, the Subverse never actually let me speak to my mother, but a version of her that it concocted."

I lower my hand from my temple, using it to grip my knee instead. "So Bacchus is screwing with brainprints, as a…what, a marketing scheme?"

"Seems so," Harmony said. "No wonder uploads and people in

the real hate each other so much. How can they ever reach an understanding, when they can't even truly communicate?"

But I'm shaking my head. "Wait. This can't be right. What about the Guard? If the Guard in the real couldn't communicate with officers in the Subverse, we'd never be able to conduct operations."

"Yeah. Well, I expect there are exceptions, when it comes to protecting the Subverse in the real. Probably the Five Families get reliable communications too, and maybe a few others. But when the loved ones of regular people upload to the Subverse, they're truly lost. No one ever actually gets to speak to them again. Not until they upload themselves."

A heavy silence settles over the bridge. Harmony seems to be waiting for one of us to say something, but for my part, there's nothing to say.

"I continued my research into the Subverse," she goes on. "It's why I joined up with the revolution—to see how deep this goes. And it goes deep. The Subverse is not the utopia Bacchus Corp made it out to be. People are not happy there. It's missing something, some key ingredients of life. I haven't quite put my finger on that, but I do know people break down, eventually. Go insane. And there are far more people being kept in underverse prisons than anyone knows." Harmony's lips are a thin, white line. "Every time I learn something new, I get the sense that this goes even deeper. Honestly, I'm not sure I've even scratched the surface. But I feel like I'm on the verge of something big."

"How does joining up with Fairfax factor into all this?" I ask.

"Simple. He's helping people escape."

"He's helping the *Five Families* escape."

"No, Dad. I mean, yes, of course he's helping his own family escape, and those of his friends. Wouldn't you? But that's not all. The bots involved in the revolution—they're people who've been trying to escape the Subverse for a long time. Fairfax is helping by getting them physical bodies, cybernetic bodies, and now they're all working together to liberate more people. This is the side of the good."

Raising my eyebrows, I say, "What about the children he abducted and experimented on?"

To my horror, Harmony just shrugs. "It feels bad to say, but every revolution has to crack a few eggs. Because of those children's sacrifice, trillions of people might be free."

"They didn't make a sacrifice. They were taken, and destroyed."

"This is the situation Bacchus put us in. All Fairfax is doing is trying to get people out. Look, humanity has always exploited some part of itself. This really isn't that bad, compared to some of the things we did as a species in the past."

"Yes," I say, my voice coming out strained and raw. "But you're not supposed to be able to look it in the eye and call it good, Harm."

"I'm sorry you don't get it," she says. With that, she turns, the airlock opening for her. And she leaves.

3

"You didn't even ask her what she's doing here, on a Lambton Cylinder," Marissa says.

"Neither did you," I say, eyes narrowed.

"Joe, *you* did this."

"What? What are you talking about?"

"You neglected her all her life! This is serious, Joe. Our daughter's aligned herself with a man set to become a galactic dictator!"

"Wait a second," I say, rising to my feet, body rigid. "I'm the one who stayed in the real and provided for her. What did you do?"

"Don't try to play that card. You didn't have a father who controlled your life, who forced you to upload like I did."

"You're right. I didn't have a father at all."

"Oh, don't pull that shit with me, Joe! How can you blame everything in your life on the fact Cal Pikeman left you? When are you going to take some ownership?"

At that, my eyes bulge. I can't believe she said that. My fists are so tight my nails are biting into my palms.

"I trusted you, Joe," she says, getting louder. "I trusted you to stay and make things right for Harmony. To make sure she had a home, that she had guidance, and felt loved. You didn't do that.

You set a terrible example and left her to follow the same path you and your father did, except her path's even worse."

"What about Eric?" I say. "The son you failed to even tell me about? Did you trust I'd 'make things right' for him, too?"

At that, she stands perfectly straight, blinking at me indignantly. I can tell I struck a nerve, but after she said what she did, I don't feel an ounce of remorse.

Soren chooses that moment to get in touch, his voice cutting through my thoughts: "Hey, uh, Joe. You forget why we came? I don't want to bother you if you're busy, but Maximus Lambton's waiting on us. I arranged a meeting."

"I'll be right out," I subvocalize, ensuring not to transmit any of my rage. "I have to go," I spit, then spin on my heel. Waiting for the airlock to open is a bit awkward, and so is the time it takes to close behind me. As the airlock cycles, I focus on my breathing, trying to calm myself down.

Fount. I normally don't get angry. Nothing affects me like she does, that's for sure.

Soren's waiting outside the *Ares* to hand me a set of thrusters, which tighten around the waist. Together, we fly across the now-empty landing bay, to a lift that takes us down to the surface of the cylinder. Our dataspheres direct us to deposit the thruster belts in a receptacle built into the elevator wall. As we descend, the gravity gets gradually stronger.

The sides of the lift are transparent, either glass or thick plastic, probably the second one. As we swiftly descend, the industrial landscape of Cylinder One opens before us. It's mostly dark-gray metal hulks of buildings—their coloring reminds me of Dice—but there are parks and green spaces interspersed between, with trees.

Looking up, I see, the landing bay is built into the sun tube—the hollowed-out cylinder that stretches through the very center of Cylinder One, end to end, providing the occupants with light, heat, and Vitamin D.

"Lambton said the other cylinders aren't as nice as this one,"

Soren says, who seems just as engrossed in the view. "They're mostly staffed by bots. This one's meant for human habitation—including company execs. So it's nicer."

I nod, wondering if the inside of the sun tube holds anything. A query to my datasphere tells me that no cylinder's sun tube goes unused. Here in Cylinder One, it's packed with zero-gravity chambers used for new materials testing. Zero-g is apparently ideal for creating nanofoams and exotic alloys. The recipes for attractive materials discovered here are transmitted to the other cylinders, and their sun tubes are put to work pumping out whatever the company needs at any given time.

"Strange, to visit a place that isn't decaying," I say.

Soren glances at me, then turns back to the view. "Yeah. This must be what living in the Subverse is like."

"Hm," I say, considering his words. I guess it does look kind of similar. Futuristic, flashy, imposing. Soulless.

Lambton must have given Soren a map, since once we're off the lift, he leads me past several buildings, toward a broad-based, solitary tower that juts out of the ground like a squat thumb. Inside, a flesh-and-blood receptionist escorts us across the lobby to an elevator, up several floors, then down a series of hallways.

We reach a set of thick oak doors bearing a plaque that reads "Lambton Industries Board Room." I exchange raised-eyebrow glances with Soren.

"Go ahead," the receptionist says. "The doors require human effort to open."

"How quaint," I say, pushing through and leaving the receptionist standing in the hall with her hands folded primly at her waist.

At the table's head, facing me and Soren, sits Maximus Lambton, and my eyes fall on him first. Most of the chairs surrounding the massive table are empty, but next I notice what appears to be a Lambton pleasure-model bot, sitting next to my son, Eric Sterling. I tense.

"Relax, Joe," Soren mutters, but I can't. What the hell is this?

"Hello, Dad," Eric says. On his other side sits Harmony.

"Welcome," Maximus Lambton says, spreading large hands. Though the table is huge, he doesn't look dwarfed by it. He isn't fat—just well-muscled. "Please, join us."

Soren and I walk around the table to take a seat opposite my children and the pleasure bot.

"I had no idea one of our visiting Guardsmen would turn out to be so closely related to two of our other visitors. Sort of ironic, since based on discussions I've already had with Ms. Sterling, I expect you want opposing things. Didn't your colleague say your surname was Pikeman, however?"

I nod, grimacing. "Yes." So Harmony's still calling herself a Sterling. I guess it's a lot more likely to carry weight, out here in the far reaches of the galaxy. Or anywhere, for that matter.

"I see," Lambton says. "Well, your daughter is quite a capable young lady. It shocked me when I learned Rodney Fairfax was sending someone so young to represent the interests of his little project, but having spoken with her at length, I see she's more than up to the task."

"She's seventeen," I say.

"Yes. Hence my initial shock."

Right now, I'm struggling not to show my emotions. Across the table, Eric is smirking at me. Somehow, I'm sure Fairfax knew I would end up here. And he sent my daughter as emissary to toy with me.

"What does Fairfax want, then?" I ask.

"Bots, of course," Eric says. "We're interested in purchasing them in bulk, and we have the funds."

Maximus' smile looks plastered on. "You do know why they want them, right?" I say.

"I do," the CEO says, inclining his head. "And I'm torn. Here at Lambton Industries, we have two equally important values: customer satisfaction and social responsibility. Every decision we've ever made as a company has always satisfied both."

That's the biggest heap of bullshit I've been served in weeks, but it probably wouldn't accomplish much to say so. Instead, I say, "In that case, you won't want to sell Fairfax a single unit. He's building an army, one destined to throw the galaxy into chaos. They plan to destroy the Subverse. The other major Families won't be very happy with you if you help them do that."

"Ah, yes," Maximus says, a note of bitterness entering his voice, which seems discordant when placed against the corporate smoothness I've seen from him so far. "As I'm sure you know, we haven't had the most cordial relationship with the other Families. They've enjoyed centuries of blaming us for the Fall, while reaping all the benefits from it."

"Then you know enough not to trust Fairfax," I say. "If he seizes power, he won't even leave you scraps. You'll be dismantled as an outfit for profit, and remade in his image."

The Lambton CEO lifts an eyebrow. "That was almost poetic."

"Fairfax wants to liberate, not enslave," Harmony says, her voice level. Beside her, Eric just strokes his pleasure bot's arm. Fount, does he *use* that thing? He's no older than…

…well, I guess he's a bit older than I was, for my first time with Marissa.

"That's not what he told me," I shoot back, then turn to Maximus. "Look, the admiralty's very insistent that you *not* aid this uprising in any way. They're very concerned about what it's going to mean for galactic stability."

"I see," Maximus says. "Well, I'll need some time to deliberate, and confer with my ancestors." When I look at him askance, he laughs. "That's my cute way of saying I need to meet with the uploaded Lambtons. I'm confident we'll arrive at a decision soon."

This time, a bot shows us out of the conference room, to a lavish waiting area. I wish she'd shown Soren and I to a separate room from Eric and that thing, to avoid the awkwardness. But then, that wouldn't be consistent with the rest of my life at all. Soren and I take both ends of a couch. Harmony plops herself into an over-stuffed armchair, and Eric and the bot settle themselves into a loveseat.

"What are you doing with that thing?" I ask Eric, nodding toward the pleasure bot.

"What's it to you, Pops?"

I blink at the archaic form of address. "Pops?"

"He's been binging sitcoms from the twentieth century," Harmony says, and Eric gives her a lazy smile. I gather they've started to grow close. That can't be good.

"This *thing* has a name," the pleasure bot says, and its sharpness makes me start. Bots are never that assertive with humans.This must not be an ordinary bot—it's probably a human consciousness, downloaded from the Subverse and implanted in this bot's neural infrastructure.

"Well?" I say.

"I'm Electra Fairfax."

I feel my mouth twist. "Jeremy Fairfax's wife?" Jeremy Fairfax founded Bacchus Corporation and invented the Subverse, over three centuries ago.

"Not anymore. Jeremy and I have divorced. I'm with Eric, now."

Bile has begun to creep up my throat. "You're three hundred years old. He's fifteen."

"Age has been irrelevant for a long time," Electra says. "Surely you've figured that out?"

"This is absolutely disgusting," I say. "Even Subverse law puts the age of consent at sixteen. You can't be with someone so young. You just can't."

"It's not illegal for a boy to use a pleasure bot," Electra says, her featureless face steady.

I stare at her. "That's not what you are, though. You're an ancient woman living *inside* a pleasure bot."

Eric gets to his feet, hand trending toward a laser pistol. "I'll have you speak kindly toward my betrothed."

Having seen the gesture, Soren already has his pistol out. "Don't try to play this game, kid," he says. "Sit down and take your hand away from there."

Eric's hand drifts away, but he doesn't sit. Betrothed? Fount. What is wrong with my children? At least Harmony got engaged to someone her age.

There's so much that's screwed up about this. But there's also nothing I can do.

I decide to try another tack. "So, tell me—is Fairfax fine with his great-great-great-great-great-great-great grandmother getting engaged to a boy who's new to puberty?"

"Who? Rodney?" Electra says. "Oh, he doesn't control me. Far from it. But yes, we have his blessing."

I shake my head. For whatever reason, Fairfax wants to sink his claws into my children, so deeply they may never be free. The only thing I'm sure about is that he's succeeding.

4

The door to the hallway opens—it's also not automated, opened with a knob—and a bot attendant enters the room.

"Mr. Lambton—" she says in a feminine voice, then breaks off to stare at Eric, standing with his fists balled at his sides. Her head tilts at a quizzical angle. Slowly, Eric lowers himself back to the loveseat.

"Mr. Lambton would like to speak with Commanders Pikeman and Garrett privately," the bot finishes. "If you would follow me?"

Harmony and Eric don't look happy with that. They glare at us as we make our way out.

"Your kids seem nice," Soren says once we're out in the hall. Great job with them."

"Shut up."

We follow the bot back to the board room, where she pushes open the great, oaken doors. They swing forward to reveal not just Maximus Lambton, but a host of uploads, some of them sitting at the table, and others standing against the walls. Those are lower-ranking Lambtons, I'm guessing.

You'd think that having ten generations of a family in the same room might involve experiencing a wide range of clothes and behaviors, spanning the last three centuries. But you'd be wrong. With some exceptions, they all seem beholden to current Subverse trends. There are plenty of weird avatars present, too—a spindly, multi-armed thing with a vaguely hammer-shaped head. What looks like a cross between a lion and a pro wrestler, wearing a business suit. A giant, sentient amoeba—yes, a single-celled organism, blown up to be person-sized. And so on. You get the idea.

"What's up?" I ask them.

The half-lion, half-pro wrestler sitting at the head of the table speaks up. "We've come to a decision regarding the bot uprising." My datasphere informs me that this is Bartholomew Lambton, original founder of Lambton Industries. He speaks in a low rumble.

The fact that he's calling the uprising an uprising seems encouraging. "Yeah?" I say. Soren shoots me a glance. Typically, he's content to let me do the talking, but he doesn't seem pleased with my shortness. I just can't bring myself to be overly polite with members of one of the Five Families.

Bartholomew clears his throat, which uploads don't need to do, but the pretentious tick doesn't surprise me in the least. "To succeed in their goal of overthrowing society as we know it, the bot uprising needs three things," he says, holding up a thick, fur-covered finger. "One, the server locations, so they can free their comrades still trapped inside the Subverse." He holds up another finger. "Two, bots. A lot of bots, in which to house the consciousnesses of all their comrades. And three, ships, with which to transport those comrades. It makes sense for them to seek the last thing I mentioned next."

"Why?" I ask. "Aren't all the bots they could need here in the Lambton Cloud?"

"Yes...but we've elected not to sell them. We've decided to take the warning of the Guard seriously, as we always have in the past."

I nod. "That's a relief, then."

"Unfortunately, the ships the bots need to transport their

growing army could very well become available to them. Lambton Industries' shipbuilding branch, which has met the Galactic Guard's needs since the Fall, is better hidden, but less protected."

"It's not with the Cloud?"

"No. It is, in fact, stationary, located in Peculiar, one of the most resource-dense star systems we've ever discovered. The ship-building facility itself is called Persephone Station, and even a ship chancing to pass through Peculiar would have an incredibly low chance of spotting it. But we still fear the station's location could be discovered."

"How? If its location is so hidden?"

"Persephone is run completely from the Subverse. From a structure identical to its physical form, which occupies a digital system that also matches the physical one perfectly."

It takes an effort of will not to let my mouth fall open. "Why? Why did you take that risk?"

The lion-wrestler shrugs, and for a moment I'm surprised at how patient he's being. "It's never been a problem before. We initially chose to run the factory this way as a gesture of goodwill. Some still blame Lambtons for the Fall, and we wanted to make an effort to provide jobs for people living in the Subverse. So far, this setup has worked. No one has ever discovered the facility in the real. But we agree that under the current climate, it could prove to be a true liability, with these rogue operatives infiltrating society at every level."

I say nothing, waiting to see if Lambton is prepared to do what we both know he must.

"We're giving you the location of the Lambton shipbuilding branch," Bartholomew says at last. "And we're giving you its self-destruct codes. It will result in a disruption in the supply of ships to the Guard, but given the risk in leaving it where the bots can find it, it will be worth it. We've already discussed plans to fold shipbuilding operations into the Cloud—it should be relatively straightforward to convert one of our existing Cylinders to the purpose. It will no longer be operated from the Subverse, but the real."

At that, Soren speaks up. "This comes as a great relief," he says. Probably, he's worried I won't show the proper gratitude, which I probably wouldn't. "On behalf of the admiralty, we thank you."

Bartholomew inclines his head. "Maximus will take care of the particulars. It's been a pleasure meeting with you, Commander Garrett. Commander Soren." Without further preamble, the room empties of digital Lambtons, leaving just me, Soren, and Maximus.

"You didn't versecast any of that, right?" I mutter to Soren, too low for the CEO to hear.

"No. Of course not."

"Good. Probably best to lay off the versecasting till we destroy this facility, hey?"

"Hopefully that was to your liking," Maximus says, rising from his seat. "I'm afraid your offspring aren't likely to enjoy the outcome of our meeting, Commander Pikeman."

"Probably not."

Maximus plants his hands on the table. "You probably thought my talk of social responsibility before was just that—talk. But Lambtons truly do consider galactic balance to be *very* important. A lot of people don't realize that about our company, content simply to blame us for the Fall and leave it at that."

At the words 'galactic balance,' my ears perked up, and now I'm studying Maximus's face closely.

"We've always been staunch allies of the Guard, as well," he says, and now his eyes are locked onto mine. "We do everything we can to help them in their mission. In fact, almost thirty years ago, a solitary Guardsman passed through this part of the galaxy, on his way to the Core. He said that he was on a mission to restore the galaxy, and so we lent him what aid we could, no questions asked. We gave him use of eight combat bots, free of charge, which he took with him."

He's talking about the old knight. I'm sure of it. But I haven't mentioned the training he's been giving me to anyone, not even Soren, or Marissa. I've kept it out of my versecasts, other than my times overclocking, and those caused a flurry of speculation among my audience about how exactly I was able to do that.

"Thank you," is all I can say to Maximus Lambton.

ARES

1

By the time I activate Lieutenant Commander Glory Belflower for a private discussion on the bridge, we're already in slip-space, and the nausea of the transition is well behind me.

"So?" I ask her, where she stands with her hands on the railing of her station. "Are you satisfied? We know how the bot uprising is going. And we're going to stop it. Is this what you wanted?"

Belflower shifts her weight, leaning on the interface-covered railing with her elbows. "Telling you what I wanted wasn't really part of the deal, Captain."

"We didn't have a deal, though, did we?"

"Isn't it better to call it that? You already said you wouldn't let me blackmail you. So let's call it a deal. I agreed to continue helping you secure funding, and you agreed to investigate the bot uprising, if you could. Both ends of the bargain were satisfied more or less on their own, from actions we probably would have taken anyway. So I call it good."

"You're not going to reveal Marissa's identity to the others, then?"

"No. I see no reason to. Probably, it would affect shipboard discipline."

We lapse into silence. In a way, Belflower's the closest confidant I have aboard the ship, now. Despite that I'm still protecting her, Marissa remains distant. Moe still hates me. And I could never connect with Asterisk, on any level. It's difficult to call Belflower a friend, but we've shared a lot, and gotten a lot done the others have no part in.

"Are you going to reactivate Dice?" she asks.

I consider the question for several long moments. "I don't know," I answer at last.

Harmony seemed truly angry when she learned that the Lambtons intended to help us fight the bots, which made it all the more shocking when she handed over a drive with Dice's consciousness on it. "I copied him over to this drive the day he gave his body to Faelyn Eliot," she said, her voice cold. "I did it right before the transfer. That day, I was too pissed off at you to give you the drive. But I felt bad about it after. I know you should have it."

I was pretty impressed that Harmony was able to give me the drive even now, considering how upset Lambton's decision made her. Clearly, she's grown since that day on Xeo. That gives me some hope that Fairfax hasn't managed to corrupt her completely.

"Thank you, Harm," I said.

When Maximus heard about Harmony's gift, he supplied me with a fresh combat bot—the same model Dice had been. Free of charge. The guy really does seem to want to help.

Still, I'm torn about reactivating Dice, because I have my doubts about whether he'd actually want to be brought back. He hated his existence aboard my ship. Hated his duties, hated being told what to do. Hated fleshbags. Hated me.

Before he died, he saved my life, and then he sacrificed himself to save a little girl. If staying dead is what he'd want, then doesn't he deserve to have that?

"You haven't spoken directly to your versecast fans in a while," Belflower says.

"I can't," I say. "We're in slipspace."

"You could record a message, to transmit to the Subverse once we exit. Do you feel like you have something to say to them?"

"Yeah," I say, thoughtfully. "I think I do." I settle back into the command seat. "Tell me when."

"You can speak whenever you're ready, Captain."

"All right." I clear my throat, and take a deep breath. "Hi," I say. "This might sound like it's coming from nowhere, but…I've always told myself that I'm trying my best, and that any screwups are because of the way my childhood was—because my father left. I told myself that at least I'm better than him, since I never abandoned my kid. But that's not good enough. I've screwed up, a lot, for too long. My children haven't had me there as a role model, and I haven't shown them the affection they needed. So, if they ever watch this, I'm sorry. And I'm sorry to you people, for lying and claiming to be something I'm not. I'm not a good father. I know that now."

I give Belflower a nod, and she ends the recording. When I raise a finger to scratch the corner of my eye, I'm surprised to find it comes away moist. Suddenly, the urge to break down right there wells up inside me, but I force it back.

"There's something you should know, I think, sir," Belflower says quietly.

"What?"

"Marissa…she's been sleeping with Moe."

My mouth is hanging open, I realize, and I shut it with a click. A weird mix of emotions is churning in my stomach, and I'm not sure why I'm reacting like this. Marissa abandoned me and our daughter a decade and a half ago. Surely I don't still hold a candle for her? For that matter, why is an exact copy of me sleeping with her?

Shaking myself, I say, "Thanks for the update. Deactivate Engineer."

Belflower vanishes from her station, and I'm left with my thoughts.

PERSEPHONE STATION

1

Bartholomew Lambton was right: there's no way a ship passing through the Peculiar System would spot Persephone Station. Even a ship searching for her might never find her.

I'm not sure what happened in this star system, but judging by what our sensor data's telling us, it must have been catastrophic.

Where other systems might have planetary orbits, Peculiar has asteroid belts—eleven of them that we've detected so far, but my datasphere is quick to tell me that this is an estimate, since in a few places it's hard to tell where one belt ends and the next begins.

As the belts get farther from the sun, they get more diffuse, with the asteroids orbiting above and below the system's ecliptic plane. At the perimeter, there's a gigantic belt that's so dispersed it might as well be a sphere.

It's to one of the more diffuse belts that Lambton's coordinates lead us. Persephone holds the same orbit as a cluster of asteroids that surround her, blocking her view from almost every angle.

"Approaching Persephone Station now, sir," Marissa says, not bothering to look at me. That sends a stab of pain through my chest, and I hate myself for the emotion.

"Very good. Are we close enough for visual?"

"Aye."

Replacing the bridge with a zoomed-in view of the station, an eerie feeling washes over me, tinged with sadness. Learning about Marissa's affair with Moe has upset me. Even I'd have trouble hiding that from myself. But what I didn't expect is the way it's coloring my reactions to everything else.

Still, Persephone does look kind of spooky, slowly turning in space, drifting through a system filled with nothing but billions, maybe trillions, of barren rocks.

The station has the shape of a bulky, misshapen wheel, with eight spokes. Dry docks extend out from that wheel at periodic intervals, jutting out into the void. The station seems to absorb what little light is available here between the asteroids, and my datasphere suggests she's likely covered in carbon nanotubes designed to capture photons of any wavelength.

It's odd to consider that she's been in operation for centuries without anyone actually setting foot on her. Well, maybe the occasional repair man. Then again, maybe not. With bots doing all the work—constantly inspecting her for damage as well as building and delivering ships—there's likely no need for any biological human ever to come here.

As the *Ares* draws closer, I notice craft coming and going from Persephone, similar in form to those I saw back in the Lambton Cloud. Miner bots.

I've decided not to reactivate Dice—that doing so would be more for me than for him. It just doesn't feel right. So I won't. The combat bot Lambton gave me is in Dice's old Repair and Recharge module, but I plan to leave it there.

Soren's voice cuts into my thoughts: "I was able to activate life support remotely, using one of Maximus's codes."

"Good," I say. Then: "Strange that a station designed to be operated by uploads and bots has life support."

"For emergencies," he says. "Like this one. Anyway, there's not enough atmosphere to provide life support to the whole station.

Luckily, there's enough to fill the path we'll need to take to the central control module. So we won't need helmets."

"What about gravity?"

"There are gravity generators. That's mostly for the bots, I think. Low gravity is only an advantage sometimes, when it comes to ship construction."

The station mostly has docking bays, with airlocks positioned here and there for times like these. Ten minutes after my conversation with Soren, both Broadswords are coasting in toward the nearest landing bay's airlock, which opens for us when Soren transmits a different code. I have copies of all the codes, too, but I'm content to let him handle it. I don't want him to feel like I'm doing everything—pretty sure he gets resentful, when that happens.

The *Ares* touches down, and I leave the crew activated. "Stay frosty, and be ready to shoot any bot that looks at you funny," I tell them. "Liberal use of macros, Asterisk, if needed."

"Yes, sir."

With that, I leave the ship to join Soren. Together, we head toward a massive corridor—the main passage of the spoke that'll take us to the command module.

The designers didn't seem to care much about aesthetics, and the spoke's inside yawns in front of us like a giant maw, joining seamlessly with the landing bay. From the great tunnel's four corners, thin strips provide just enough light to make our way.

As we progress through, I find myself feeling unusually talkative. "It feels like we're finally doing something," I say. "The admiralty doesn't seem to appreciate everything that's going on in Echo Sector, but at least we're here, taking out what would probably have become a key asset for the bots."

"Yeah," Soren says, and I shoot him a glance. Have we reversed roles? With his versecast off, it seems I'm the one doing all the talking, while he lapses into silence.

"I'm glad we met up, back on Amydon," I say. "I doubt I would have gotten this far without you."

He looks at me, an odd expression on his face—something like a smirk, tinged with bitterness. "Oh, I'm sure you would have figured it out, Joe."

"Seriously. I was glad to have you with me."

"Okay."

My urge to talk disappears, and for a moment, the skin on the back of my neck feels like it's crawling.

I shrug it off, but I can't shake off the thought that something's going on with my old friend. Back in Sheen City, he claimed he didn't remember us drifting apart—that he thinks we're brothers. But during our time together in Echo Sector, there have been moments when I thought I caught him grimacing at me, or rolling his eyes at something I said. Can he really still resent the way I took the lead during the pirate assault on Gauntlet, so many years ago? Or does he even allow himself to acknowledge that's affecting us?

The idea that Soren could be jealous of me seems preposterous on the face of it. Thanks to his versecasting, he's probably the most famous Guardsman in the galaxy, maybe in history. But he seems to have *some* kind of chip on his shoulder.

The tunnel stretches on, unchanging, growing more monotonous with each step. Every two hundred meters or so, paths branch off on both sides, probably to dry docks where smaller vessels are constructed and repaired—such as the Guard's Broadswords.

Larger ships would have to be built out on the rim of the wheel, since the spokes aren't wide enough to accommodate them. It occurs to me that the Guard rarely orders ships larger then a Broadsword, anymore. Have those facilities gone unused for decades, then, if not centuries? Or have the Lambtons found other clients?

Most pirate ships I've ever encountered are old, patched-up

things, barely spaceworthy. But I'm thinking of Fairfax's mammoth destroyer. Where did he get that built? And how many other warships of that size does he have access to?

"We haven't seen any bots," I say, speaking the thought as soon as it enters my mind. "Isn't that odd?"

Soren shrugs, not looking at me, his gaze focused straight ahead.

"Maybe Lambton sent the order ahead of us to evacuate them," I muse. "I'm sure they'll come in handy for their new shipbuilding operation. But there's no chance a spacescraper bearing that order arrived here before us, right?"

"I don't know, Joe. We have a job to do. Let's just do it, okay?"

I return his gaze with eyebrows raised. What is up with him?

At last, we reach the first hatch we've seen in the station, other than the airlock. The first closed hatch, anyway: the one leading into the central command module.

It opens when Soren submits the appropriate access code, and we walk inside.

This chamber reminds me of the bridge of a warship, even though I've never seen one in person—only in sims and images presented by my datasphere. It's just as dimly lit as the tunnel that brought us here, though it likely has the capacity to get much brighter. The various control stations are arranged in concentric circles, with chairs facing curved, blank surfaces where a controller's datasphere would project the appropriate interface. It's an excellent way to ensure control can't be seized by an intruder: only an operator with the appropriate clearances can use a given station. The fact that Persephone is operated solely from the Subverse helps, too.

We wind through the blank consoles, and I remember a cheap, plastic children's toy we had kicking around my aunt's house. It was a circular maze, which you guided a steel ball through by tilting it. Right now, I feel like that ball.

At the center of the formation of consoles sits a raised dais, with a single, stationary chair capable of swiveling in any direction, whether to survey the lead controller's subordinates or to access the panels surrounding the chair. I settle into the seat and call up the main station login from the set of codes Maximus provided me. Then, I wait for the station to boot up. Soren hasn't followed me to the dais, since he needs to confirm the self-destruct command from another station, close to the hatch where we entered.

The main station finishes booting, and I'm confronted with a login screen. But when I enter the information, nothing happens.

"Hey, Soren?" I call over my shoulder. "This login isn't working."

"Yeah? You sure you entered it right?"

"I just pasted it in from your message."

"That's weird. I got into mine just fine."

I glance back toward him. He's sitting at one of the blank panels we passed, except I guess it isn't blank for him, anymore. His datasphere must be projecting the appropriate interface onto the curved surface.

When I turn back to the login prompt, a notification box has appeared beside it: "ADVISORY: LIFE SUPPORT SYSTEMS HAVE BEEN MANUALLY DEACTIVATED. IF YOU ARE NOT AUTHORIZED TO REVERSE THIS PROCESS, YOU SHOULD EVACUATE IMMEDIATELY."

"Soren, this says—" I finish turning, and see that Soren is making his way back to the hatch we entered through, vaulting over panels instead of walking past them, and making very little sound. "Soren!"

I draw my blaster without thinking, drawing a bead on the back of his neck as he nears the hatch. The bolt might not get past the spidersilk-reinforced uniform covering his skin, but it should knock him forward and buy me time.

But I can't bring myself to shoot him. "*Soren!*" I yell again, suddenly remembering how he specifically said we won't need helmets inside Persephone, and how I just accepted that without question.

He reaches the hatch, runs through, then turns, his hand rising out of view, probably to access a control panel there.

For a fleeting moment, I meet his eyes across the barrel of my blaster, and though it's hard to tell from this distance, his expression looks pained.

Then the hatch closes.

2

I vault over the console surrounding the central dais, landing hard on the deck below. Then, I do as Soren did, leaping over the long, curved consoles, dodging around the chairs arrayed along them.

When I reach the hatch, I can't find a control panel for opening it—just another login prompt. Soren's codes must have given him access to the controls from the other side.

Lambton gave me a copy of all the codes too, and I open up the file, quickly picking out the one labeled "CENTRAL COMMAND MODULE HATCH." But when I enter the login info provided, nothing happens.

I have the wrong codes. They're useless, apparently, which means the Lambtons were in on this. Unless Soren somehow hacked my datasphere and replaced the codes, but he doesn't have the skill set to do that, as far as I know. Would a member of his crew have those skills?

No. Lambton involvement seems most likely. And the more I think about it, the more it makes sense. A mass exodus of people from the Subverse, each wanting a bot to inhabit in the real…it would mean a bonanza for Lambton Industries, at least temporarily. They probably think they could service and upgrade those bots forever, growing their fortune indefinitely, not to mention the power it would let them wield over the galaxy.

That's assuming Fairfax lets them continue operating as they want to. But then, maybe the Lambtons can give Fairfax a run for his money. They do have a lot of combat bots.

"OXYGEN LEVELS DROPPING," my datasphere warns. "CHAMBER DEPRESSURIZING. ESTIMATED TWENTY MINUTES UNTIL CONDITIONS BECOME INHOSPITABLE TO HUMANS."

I will my datasphere to establish contact with my ship, expecting Marissa to respond. Instead, Belflower's voice enters my thoughts.

"Hello, Captain Pikeman."

"Belflower. Where's Marissa?"

"She's busy right now."

I shake my head, but decide not to get into why that might be. "Take the *Ares* out of the landing bay and fly around the station to the central command module. I need you to use the lasers to melt a hole through the hull, and position the ship to pick me up when I emerge." In the vacuum, I'll only have two minutes to make the transition without permanent damage. Without the Fount, I might be able to stretch it to three minutes.

"I'm afraid that won't be possible, sir," Belflower said.

"It has to be possible," I bark. "Soren's trapped me inside the command module, and the life support's shutting down. He betrayed us."

"I know."

At that, my stomach drops like a stone. "How?" I ask, though I already know the answer.

"To successfully take you out, he needed an ally aboard your ship, didn't he? To ensure the *Ares* didn't simply come and rescue you. I'm sorry, Captain, but I'm afraid you aren't getting off this station alive. Persephone was never built with a self-destruct sequence. This entire mission was assigned for the purpose of removing you from the board in a way that isn't too upsetting to the Subverse public. Due to its 'secrecy,' Soren wasn't versecasting, and you need me in order to broadcast versecasts. So we can portray your death any way we wish. A tragic, unavoidable accident."

"Why are you helping them, Belflower?"

She sighs. "I don't want to be helping people like Lambton and Fairfax, Captain, trust me. And I've come to like you, in spite of myself. But Lambton *is* helping the revolution, and making sure it flourishes is the reason I got myself assigned to your ship in the first place. It's also why I've been doing what I can to nudge you toward Echo Sector since day one. I'm one of the revolution's main architects—me, and the rest of Golem Faction's command structure in the Great Game. We didn't start with many assets in the real, you see, so we needed to start making inroads however we could. I have to admit, I didn't expect getting assigned to your ship to be such a boon."

"I'm going to find a way off this station," I tell Belflower. "I'm coming back to my ship. When I do, I'm going to delete you."

"There's no way for you to get off Persephone, Captain," Belflower says. "I'm sorry—and I mean that. I'm truly sorry. I do believe you're a good man, deep down, or at least that you have the capacity to be. But I also think you have no place in the world we're about to create. Farewell."

With that, the transmission ends. My datasphere informs me that only fifteen minutes remain until this compartment becomes unlivable.

That means I have to get to work. But on what? Blasting a hole through the hull? Even if I had enough charge packs to make a hole large enough for me to reach the vacuum, what would be the point, without a ship to collect me?

There's no contacting anyone for help. Who would I contact? Presumably my daughter isn't in on this, but then, she did team up with Rodney Fairfax, so who knows. But it doesn't matter. There's no way to reach her across the light years that separate us. Not in time, anyway. Not nearly.

Assuming Marissa would help, I'm guessing Belflower's taken control of the *Ares*. I can't believe I ever left someone with her level of technological proficiency on my ship. She probably could have turned things against me at any time she wished. She was just waiting for her opportunity.

I return to the central control station, walking through the circular maze this time instead of vaulting over the curved, tilted surfaces. For some reason, I feel unhurried. Maybe that's because I know Belflower's right: there's no way out of here, for me.

But when I reach the dais and turn the chair to sit, there's already someone in it. The old knight. He gazes up at me with raised eyebrows.

"Do you mind?" I say.

"I'm not taking up any actual space," he says. "You can still sit here, if you wish."

"It feels weird. Get up."

"What do you think you're going to accomplish?"

"I have no idea. But I have to try. I can't just let Soren get away with this."

"Soren," the old man mutters, as if turning the name over in his mouth. "Soren Garrett." He grimaces. "A man who's forgotten the spirit of the Galactic Guard. What it was supposed to mean."

I push past the knight, choosing to stand at the console instead. It still shows the login screen. There's definitely no point in trying to guess the password, which will be a random alphanumeric string scattered with symbols for good measure. But sometimes, if you know the hidden command, you can gain developer access. Maybe I could do something, then.

I press two corners of the screen simultaneously for ten seconds. That doesn't work. Neither does triple-tapping all along the perimeter. Or doing the same, but with two hands at once, positioned in random spots.

"The Guard was supposed to be the last organization where biological men could come together to support each other," the knight continues. "To work together to keep the galaxy safe—not just for the Subverse, but also for their families in the real. And for each other. The bonds of brotherhood were supposed to bind you."

"That's not what they taught us back in Assessment and Selection," I say. "They taught Troubleshooter cadets to hate each other." I thought they'd failed, with me and Soren. Guess I was wrong. "They drilled into us that we had no friends, and never would, out in the cold black of space."

"Is that why you've resisted my training so much?"

I stop tapping at the interface, turning to study the old man's lined face. "I didn't resist your training."

"But you never truly embraced it. Your pride was too great to become the humble student. And because of that, your ego has stood in the way of true mastery of the Fount."

"Why tell me this now?" My datasphere says I have eleven minutes left. "What does it matter?"

"Because you now find yourself in a situation where humility offers the only escape."

"That makes no sense." I half-turn toward the console, then stop. "Are you saying that you can help me, but only if I call you Master?"

"No. But it might help."

"You're not my master."

"Only because you refuse to embrace your role as my protege. But if your pride is such that you can't bear to speak that word, then perhaps you can call me Father."

As the countdown ticks down in the corner of my vision, the old man and I stare at each other for a long moment.

3

A cocktail of emotions courses through my veins—confusion, excitement, resentment.

"You mean, in a metaphorical sense?" I say at last. "As in, a mentor is like a second father?"

He shakes his head, looking away, apparently unable to meet my gaze. "I mean I'm Cal Pikeman."

"Cal Pikeman," I mutter. My father. A Shiva Knight, after all.

For a moment, it's staggering that the thought hasn't crossed my mind once since I first glimpsed him on Earth. But then, why should it? Who jumps to the conclusion that the ghostly knight come to train them is actually their father?

But it's more than that. When I was a kid, I used to pray that my father had actually become a Shiva Knight, despite all the snide comments people back in Brinktown would make. Except, as I grew up, I bought into those comments. Fount, I wrapped myself in them, made them part of who I am: I became the boy, and then the man, whose father lied just to get out of the responsibility of having to raise his son.

"So you actually became a Fount-damned knight," I say, shaking my head, staring dumbly at the login screen before me. In the corner of my vision, the countdown just passed nine minutes, but I'm having a hard time focusing.

"I'm sorry for leaving you and your mother," Cal says. "But I was called, Joe. Approached by a Shiva, just like you were, and sent to the center of the galaxy. To make things right."

"My mother died. I never knew her, either. You know that, right?"

He nods, head sinking farther. "I learned a lot, after Fairfax killed me in the Core. Imagine having free reign of the universe, but being incredibly limited in what you can actually do."

"You're not limited, though. You can travel anywhere and even have a physical effect on things. Back in Gargantua, you hit me on the head with your stick."

"True. But the Shiva prohibit knights living in the Fount to interfere with the real, except on official business."

"You're telling me they'd stop you from visiting your son and telling him the truth?"

"Yes."

I hold his gaze with mine. "Would you have visited me if you could?"

For a long time, he returns my stare. Then, his eyes drop once more. "No. I wouldn't have. I was too ashamed."

"Which is why you haven't told me who you are till now, maybe."

The knight says nothing.

"Or maybe, part of it is that you don't trust your own motives. Maybe they aren't as pure as a Shiva's ought to be, and what you really want is for me to avenge you."

"I didn't tell you who I was because you disappoint me." He's still staring at the ground.

"Wow. Well, that's rich. Coming from the guy who got himself killed doing the one job he had."

My effort to get to him, to hurt him, doesn't seem to work. "It's not easy for me to say this, Joe. But it's true. You're not the son I would have wanted to raise."

"You didn't raise me."

"I know."

The silence stretches on, and the timer ticks down. At last, the knight raises his eyes, though not to meet mine. Instead, he stares out over the curved, silver consoles, as if looking beyond them.

"I agree with you," he says at last. "I'm not the knight I should be. And you're far from what I'd want as the galaxy's last hope, whether you're my son or not. But you're who the Fount chose, and I need to get better at accepting that. I need to start hoping you'll do better than I did.

"The man who recruited me into the knighthood was one of low means, too. Just like us. No knight has ever come from the Five Families, which makes sense. What we want directly contradicts what they want. The man who recruited me was named Sam Bryant. He was dead, too."

"How did he die?"

"Completing his quest. As, I told you, success in the Core also means death. The difference is, he died almost three hundred years before he approached me."

I narrow my eyes. "Three hundred years? Before or after the Fall?"

"That's just it, Joe. The Fall didn't happen three hundred years ago. It was closer to three thousand years ago, possibly more than that."

"How…" My voice trails off into nothing, and I try again. "How is that possible?"

"The Shiva Knighthood. I've already told you—it's our job to restore the galaxy. I meant that literally. Every three hundred years or so, the Subverse reaches this point. The realization spreads that the simulation can never hope to truly replicate life. Life is *meant* to end. It's supposed to have real consequences for mistakes, which makes it meaningful when we grow. But the immortality the

Subverse offers is stripped of meaning. So people start to go insane, slowly at first, then faster. The system locks each one of them inside an underverse prison. The madness continues to spread, and as it does, the elites begin to plot their escape."

"Three thousand years," I mutter, staring into nothing. I've always laughed about the old claims about how long the galaxy's cities and structures were supposed to last—the pre-Fall engineers used to boast they would last for millennia, and yet three centuries later, the galaxy is crumbling before our eyes. But it hasn't been three centuries after all. It's been thousands of years, and the buildings really did last for a long, long time. Turns out those engineers weren't full of shit after all.

"The elites have no interest in returning as mere bots," Cal goes on, "the hated underclass of our society. And it's no longer possible for them to return as their human forms. So they contrive to return to the real as gods, like the snake you faced, and the beings you will likely face soon. To prevent that, the Shiva must reset the Subverse, to the year just after the Fall." My father shakes his head. "I'll give this to you, Joe: no knight has ever had to defeat anything like that serpent before. Our job has always been to defeat Fairfax, to stop him from realizing the elites' dark plans, and to reset the galaxy. A Shiva has never faced anything like that snake. The fact you did it without overclocking is impressive."

"So what's your specific problem with me, then?"

"There's a lot more to being a knight than the ability to kill. You have no humility. And you don't have respect. Not for the Shiva, not for your enemies, and not for the galaxy. Not even for your family. *You're* driven by vengeance, Joe, which is why you see that motive in me. You're projecting it. But I'm not going to argue with you."

"No, you're just here to tell me to do the thing you couldn't. It's your fault I'm facing these monsters, isn't it? It's your fault things have gotten this bad."

"Yes," Cal Pikeman says. "It is. I take responsibility for that.

And the monsters you must face aren't the whole picture. Joe, it's been almost three decades since I failed, and things have gotten much worse in the Subverse, too. It seems that before, the knights always restored the galaxy just before it fell off a cliff. A Fairfax would rise, traveling to the Core to become half-man, half-bot. The Shiva of the time would defeat him in single combat and then hit the reset, restoring peace to the galaxy for three hundred years. But because Rodney Fairfax killed me instead, things have deteriorated even farther. The Subverse's algorithms have put more people in underverses than ever before, and to make up for that fact, it's replaced them with mindless automatons in the hub worlds. As the galactic system disintegrates, it's doing everything it can to continue presenting itself as the promised utopia. Just as Bacchus designed it to do."

"So, wait…there are people living in the Subverse who are just zombies?"

Cal nods. "More than half of the uploads in existence."

I begin pacing the dais, my mind racing. The timer is down to three minutes, forty-one seconds.

"Okay, wait. This isn't making sense. If the Subverse resets every three centuries, people in the real would notice. They'd lose contact with their parents, right? They'd just be erased from existence. Plus, the Guard keeps meticulous records. So do the Five Families. People would notice."

"Some do," Cal says, nodding. "But most records are kept in the Subverse. Almost all of them are deleted in the reset. Other than that, the Subverse is programmed to do everything it can to portray itself as a continuous, harmonious utopia. It's been known to concoct convincing versions of people who no longer exist—who, as far as it knows, never existed—based on the demands of the biological humans looking for their family members. Some aren't convinced by these ad hoc reproductions, and they tell everyone who'll listen that something's terribly wrong. But they can only reach those around them, since the Subverse won't convey communication that portrays it in a negative light. And as the years pass, their children tend to assume they're going senile. Their ravings fade into twilight with the passage of time."

"Why can't we just destroy the Subverse? Take out all the servers? Before we do, we could help people get into bots, so they can live in the real."

"Well, for one, you'd have to defeat Fairfax before attempting anything like it, and then you'd have to reset the Subverse so the Five Families won't keep trying to escape while you're destroying it. But once the Subverse is reset, you'd still have the Galactic Guard protecting its infrastructure. Even if you could get around them and destroy every single server in the galaxy, you'd still have problems. We've never actually tried housing human consciousnesses in bots over the long-term. Who's to say they wouldn't eventually go insane and turn on us? Another issue: many people have hundreds, sometimes thousands of copies of themselves living in different Subverse hub worlds. How do you choose which copy gets to continue existing? If each person gets one, doesn't deleting the billions of copies in existence amount to genocide on an unprecedented scale?"

He's right. It never occurred to me to think about it like that, but he's right. "So we're stuck with the Subverse."

"Yes," Cal says, sounding tired. "Humanity made its bed long ago, and the Shiva are tasked with making sure the house doesn't burn down while it sleeps. If we fail to reset the Subverse in time to contain the horrors that wish to escape it, then history will take a dark turn. There will be no putting the genie back in that particular bottle. Right now, those humans who remain in the real, whether by choice or not, have peace of a kind. If we allow Fairfax to achieve his ends, we'll have complete and utter chaos—we'll be subject to the vicious rule of the Five Families, forever."

The timer just ticked past two minutes. I'm starting to notice each breath is getting harder to take, and there's a sensation of pressure in my chest, as though I'm trying to breathe at a very high altitude. "Aren't there other Shiva around who can do this? Where are they?"

"All dead. It's why we've been able to maintain such secrecy across millennia, and why everyone always thinks the Shiva are either mythical or long gone. There's only ever one living Shiva, and usually there aren't any. We keep the knighthood alive by living through the Fount. But there's no time to train someone else to do this, Joe. You're it."

"Okay. Well, I'm guessing stopping Fairfax involves escaping this place first. And even if I could get that hatch open, I wouldn't have time to run back down the spoke to the landing bay. Not before the oxygen runs out. So what the hell am I supposed to do?"

"I've already told you. You must humble yourself before the task that confronts you. You must submit."

4

"So, what," I say, "You need me to call you Master, then? This really is an ego thing for you, isn't it?"

Cal chuckles, though without much mirth. "This isn't about me, Joe. At least, not just me. I'm more integrated with the Fount than you seem to think. Essentially, I *am* the Fount, in a very real sense. At least, I'm part of it. And the Fount requires that you submit to it. If you won't humble yourself, then you must *be* humbled. You must indicate that you're willing to serve me—and by extension, the Shiva and the Fount—as a true protege."

"The Fount wants me to call you Master? How convenient. Funny how the Fount has never required that before." The pressure in my chest is becoming greater, and the saliva on my tongue is starting to get hot. If I wait much longer, it will begin to boil. I take another breath, and it sends a jolt of pain through my torso.

"It doesn't matter whether you call me Master," Cal says. "I told you—it goes deeper than that. You carry the weapon of a Shiva. It's time for you to become worthy of it."

"How?" I croak.

"You must enter nanodeath."

"Never." The word comes out as a dry rasp, and I exhale

completely, which relieves the pressure. I need to keep air out of my lungs, or they'll rupture.

"It's the only way," Cal says calmly. "If you enter nanodeath, the Fount will be able to bring your body back to homeostasis while it houses your consciousness elsewhere. You've been too prideful to use nanodeath in the past—too prideful to trust the Fount with your life. If you don't do it now, you'll die within minutes."

As the pressure inside me grows, spreading just under my skin and pressing against my uniform, I rack my brain for another way out. But there is none. This is it.

"Fine," I croak, my lungs beginning to burn for another breath.

"I suggest you sit." The old knight gets up from the chair, and I replace him.

I will my datasphere's master controls to appear before me. With that, I access the "State Change" menu, and from the bottom of the next screen I choose "nanodeath."

Everything disappears into nothingness—just like looking out of a hull sensor while in slipspace.

5

I open my eyes.

The last thing I remember is lying on my back on a lush rug, with Zelah Eliot's lithe, naked body pressed against my side.

Right now, I seem to be sitting in a chair at a circular console, which itself is situated on a dais overlooking multiple rows of curved, banked consoles with staggered gaps to permit passage to the center.

An old man stands over me, wearing a neatly trimmed beard the color of a static-filled TV screen—a phenomenon I witnessed in one of the history sims I like to watch whenever I'm bored.

"Where am I?"

He frowns. "You're in—" Cutting himself off, he narrows his eyes. "Do you remember what's happening?"

For a few seconds, I scan my memories. How did I get from Zelah Eliot's place to here?

Then, a flood of images rushes into my mind: waking in Sheen City after falling unconscious from overclocking. Traveling with Soren to Gauntlet, and helping defend against a bot attack. Going to the Lambton Cloud, and then to Persephone Station. Here.

"I've had some adventures," I mutter.

"You need to get better at that," the old man says. Cal. Cal Pikeman. My father. I stare up at him in wonder, which he doesn't seem to mind. "Both sides of you need to practice accessing the other's memories. You need to start seeing yourself as the same person, because you *are* the same person, and if you work against each other you'll tear yourself apart."

"That was confusingly worded," I say, pushing myself to my feet. "I entered nanodeath, didn't I? I can't believe it."

"Yes," my father says. "You did. Joe Pikeman. That's good. That's progress."

"Hey," I say, reaching a hand out to lay on his shoulder. "It's good to meet you, Dad."

He blinks, staring down at my arm. "Maybe you have a lot of work to do, actually."

"Huh? Why?"

"The Joe in the real wasn't nearly so warm when I told him who I am."

"Oh. Right." I remove my hand. "For some reason, I'm not as angry as he is. It's been a long time since I've gotten angry, actually. I usually just get squirrelly, and murderous."

A troubled look flashes across Cal's face, but he seems to suppress it. "I need you to try to channel my son in the real as much as you can, since he's the one I've been training. We're in the Subverse version of Persephone right now, and it's under attack by Golem Faction—Glory Belflower's faction, the architects of the bot uprising. If we don't stop them, they'll take control and start producing ships for their cause in the real. If they manage that… it's over. Through them, Fairfax will achieve his ends."

"Fairfax. Right. I remember—gotta stop him. Restore the galaxy, and so on."

"Will you help?"

"Sure. Hey—how are you able to enter the Subverse, anyway?"

"I can appear here just as I can in the real."

"Are you as limited here as you are in the real?"

"Not as such. The first time I entered the Subverse, it assigned me an account, which it's associated with me ever since. I'm now a level ninety-one War Mage."

"Damn. Nice." I will my stats to appear, finding that I'm a level eleven Space Marine who knows Blue Fire, Telekinesis 2, and Deflect. Plus, I'm proficient with assault weapons. "Could be worse," I mutter. It's been a while since I checked my stats. Back when I lived with Marissa on Terminus, I used to work on grinding my account, but I got away from that after my mind started spiraling out of control.

"Wait," I say. "How can Golem attack here? Surely the station isn't part of this hub world's conflict region."

"Don't underestimate Golem. They have other hackers as proficient as Belflower, some of them more. They hacked the servers to include Persephone in the Great Game conflict region." With that, Cal turns and descends the stairs to the main level. "Come. We're very short on time." As he walks, the lights in the chamber seems to dim, their essence fleeing to gather around the War Mage's hands.

Trailing him through the circular maze of consoles, I call my assault rifle out of my inventory, and it drops into my hands, materializing. A little counter hovers above it, along with a green light telling me the magazine's full.

My father leads me to the hatch opposite the one meatspace Joe entered through. The sound of gunfire grows louder from the other side of the hatch.

"Your datasphere will tag anyone from Golem red," the old knight whispers. "Are you ready?"

"Ready."

He taps the control panel to open the hatch, which slides upward to reveal a row of Golem fighters, all facing away from us. They're engaging a blue-tagged group, who seem to be fighting to gain access to the central control module.

That makes me hesitate for a second, since I would have

expected Golem to be on the other side, fighting to get into the control module. Not seemingly defending it.

My hesitation allows time for two of their fighters to turn and see us. I bring up my rifle and release a round into the closest man's face, which causes him to pixelate and disappear in a blocky mist. Either he wasn't very high level or he'd already taken a lot of damage.

The Shiva beside me unleashes a fury of light on the other Golem member who spotted us, bathing him in white and leaving no trace.

Which is great, but it draws the attention of the rest of the hostiles. They turn as one, and I drop my weapon, charging Blue Fire with both hands.

Just as they're raising their weapons, I spray the group with sapphire flames, each hand waving in opposite directions. Only one of them pixelates, and I take a step back, preparing to throw myself back through the hatch and behind cover. But Cal raises his hands over his head, the light they hold growing brighter than ever, and white-hot bars split off from it, searing each Golem member where they stand. Not all of them fall, but the group behind the hostiles add their fire, and the last of the Golem members are neutralized.

With that, my father and I stare down the empty tunnel toward a band of fighters dressed in military garb. At their head stands a bearded mage, a high-level fire spell fading from his fists. Looking at him gives me deja vu, though I can't quite place him.

As they approach, I yell, "I thought Golem was the one breaking into this place. Why were they keeping you out of central control?"

In my peripheral vision, I see Cal open his mouth and raise a hand as though to intervene, but the approaching mage speaks before he can. "We're from Meiyo Faction. We've been fighting Golem for a long time, and when we heard what they'd done— hacking the server to add Persephone to the conflict region—we followed them here. That group was about to reach the central command module when we engaged them. Who are you?"

Cal remains silent, but I speak up: "I'm Joe Pikeman."

The mage tilts his head. "Yes. The birthmark should have been a dead give away. Commander Joe Pikeman, correct?"

"No, that's…well, sort of. I'm a copy of him. But also the same person."

That brings a frown to the mage's weathered face. "A copy of mine went to serve on Commander Pikeman's ship," he says. "But apparently he was deleted from it for treason."

At that, memories flood into my mind from meatspace Joe. "You're Tobias Worldworn," I say.

"Yes. I should tell you, in case you communicate with Joe Pikeman in the real: the copy of me that was deleted from the *Ares* had stopped syncing with the rest of us, so I'm not able to account for his thoughts. But I can tell you that I've always been loyal to a fault. I consider it highly unlikely that a copy of mine would betray a captain he'd sworn to serve."

I nod, saying nothing. Mostly, I'm focusing on the stirring in the back of my mind, as though the meatspace version of myself is becoming restless. We're both remembering how someone opened the hatch into the Brinktown on Gargantua, letting in Fallen to attack us.

"Wait," I say. "There was video. Of your confession. That is, your copy confessed to betraying us."

"Right," Worldworn says, slowly. "Well, all I can tell you is that I value honor and loyalty above all else. The thought that a copy of mine, even a rogue copy, would betray you…the idea revolts me to the extent that I know I'd never do it, and neither would a copy. Video, on the other hand, can be doctored." He shrugs. "That's all I can say."

I shake my head. *Someone* tried to kill me. Us. Whatever. But if it wasn't Worldworn, then who?

Belflower?

I think that was meatspace Joe's thought, but I'm not sure.

I don't think it was Belflower. She told us herself that she infiltrated the *Ares* to check on the bot uprising, and help them if she could. If she'd succeeded in killing us then, she probably never would have made it to this sector.

I'm not willing to believe Marissa would try to harm us, either. So who does that leave?

Asterisk…

Interesting. We'll have to watch out for him in the future.

"We aren't the only troops Meiyo sent," Worldworn says, interrupting my thought-conversation with my other self. "The landing bay we're coming from is secure, and so are the southern and western ones. But the northern landing bay is still being contested. There are Golem fighters all over Persephone, but if we can take the final landing bay from them and stop them from bringing in any more troops, we should be able to take it from there."

"We'll help," I say. For the second time, my father had his mouth open to speak, but he closes it and settles for nodding.

"Then we'd best get moving," Worldworn says, walking past us toward the open hatch. To me, his flowing beard doesn't seem to go with his light-brown military uniform, but whatever. "It seems Golem is devoting everything it has to this. We won't stop them if we don't move swiftly."

He leads the way into the central command module, and immediately gunfire drives him back.

6

"Let's take the lead," I say to Cal. "I have Deflect—do you have something to stop bullets?"

He nods.

"Good. We can push in, take up position behind the first row of consoles, then lay down covering fire while the others take advanced positions."

"Excellent thinking," my father says, smiling. I get the impression he finds this level of enthusiasm from me novel.

My assault rifle drops back into my hands, and I activate Deflect. We both charge in.

As I sprint toward the first banked row of consoles, rounds zing off the air in front of me to land harmlessly at my feet. The barrier protecting me glows blue when it's hit, but the knight's barrier stays invisible. Although, with each strike, the scarlet-colored spell in his hands gets brighter.

Then, we're crouching behind the consoles, shooting at anything visible. The Golem members are arrayed around the central dais. I draw a bead on a grunt firing at Cal, sending a burst into his face. He recoils behind cover, but doesn't pixelate, so he's still in the game.

For his part, the old knight raises his hands to either side of the barrier protecting his torso and releases twin fans of red light. One of them cuts through two Golem fighters at once, causing them both to pixelate. Damn, but the old man packs a punch!

Meiyo soldiers are rushing forward, now, taking up positions farther along the curve of the first row of consoles. A couple of them advance to the first gap and push ahead even more.

My eyes meet Cal's, and we nod, vaulting over the console as one, our defensive spells deflecting all incoming shots. A datasphere readout tells me my shield will soon fail, but before it does I want to get a lot closer to these bastards.

Gunfire fills the room, streams of it being exchanged from opposing positions like threads of light. As large as it is, the control module echoes and booms with the tumult. As I vault over another console, my shield fails without warning, and the edges of my vision flash red with the damage I'm taking.

There's a Golem fighter just a few meters away, and I activate Telekinesis, using it to wrench his shotgun out of his hands and cast it across the room. Then I spray rounds in my target's direction, and when he dips out of sight, I stow my rifle and summon Blue Fire, angling my hands upward.

The spell arcs up and then down, descending on the spot where I last saw the hostile. He doesn't get back up.

Cal's protection spell is still active, and he motions for me to follow behind him. He vaults over a console, then I do, right behind, flinging flames at anyone who tries to shoot me. By now, the Meiyo operatives have spread out along the curve and are flanking the hostiles near the dais.

After that flank is firmly established, it's just a mop up job, with a Golem member popping into pixels every other second. Soon, it's just us and the consoles.

"Fantastic work," Worldworn says when we regroup at what I assume must be the northern hatch, since it's the one the mage seems keen to enter through. "That wouldn't have been nearly so clean without you. But that was just the pregame warm-up. I'm getting word from the northern landing bay that Golem is pouring fighters into it, focusing everything they've got to try and crack it open."

"We'd better get moving, then," I say, and the mage nods, turning to open the hatch.

Our fifteen-minute jog through the great spoke's interior gets broken up by two brief firefights. Our numbers are much greater than both parties we encounter, and with Cal's and Worldworn's combined firepower, we're able to take them down while losing just a couple of fighters.

Even so, after the long jog our stamina is down quite a bit, and we pause in the tunnel a hundred meters away from the landing bay, to catch our breath, so to speak. No one's actually short of breath, of course, this being the Subverse. But lower stamina will mean a penalty on performance in battle, so it's a good idea to try to recover some.

Worldworn hands out some tonics to those with the most depleted stats, but there aren't enough bottles to go around, so Cal and I refuse them. Worldworn foregoes them too, meaning our three best fighters will be fatigued going into this.

"Okay," the mage says at last. "Everyone ready?"

"We got this, sir," one of his soldiers says, and the remark seems to rally the others.

"Screwing with Golem is what gets me up in the morning," another says.

Worldworn, Cal, and I exchange nods, and together we turn toward the landing bay as one.

Threads of gunfire crisscross the tunnel mouth, lit by the occasional spell blast.

"This is no stealth mission," Worldworn says. "We come out weapons and spells blazing, or we don't come out at all. Take up positions around the tunnel mouth, and focus your fire on high-priority targets, which I'll paint on your dataspheres. Move!"

We jog down the tunnel, splitting into two groups to hug the bulkheads. When we reach the mouth, the Meiyo fighters arrange themselves in a staggered, diagonal line. That way, if any one fighter comes under fire, they can peel back and press themselves against the wall.

Worldworn, Cal and I stay in the middle of the formation—with the least cover, but the most firing lanes.

Dead ahead, a motley group of uniformed creatures are gathered around a tree-like being, who towers over them, flinging fire at targets all around it. They're positioned against the hull of a massive troop ship, which gives them cover against attacks coming from the rest of the landing bay.

"There," Worldworn says. "We focus our fire there. Ready… steady…fire!"

Rounds flash across the bay, pouring into the walking tree's trunk. Cal directs his fan-like red beams toward it, and I throw sapphire fireballs, one after another.

For his part, Worldworn calls down lightning to strike at the being's upper branches, causing a mighty bow to snap off and land on a raccoon-like fighter below, knocking it to the ground.

Most of us are concentrating our fire on the big guy, but my father sweeps his red fans of laser-like light along the ground, doing damage to the hostiles clustered at the tree-creature's base. They start to fall, turning into clouds of pixels one by one.

The enemy doesn't take our attack sitting down. They fire on us with assault rifles and shotguns while the tree continues throwing fireballs.

I spot one of the smaller troops winding up to throw a grenade, but I shoot it out of the air before it reaches the peak of its arc, and it explodes harmlessly near the overhead. Hmm. Looks like my meatspace counterpart's training may actually be rubbing off on me after all.

But when the tree's fireballs fall among our ranks, they do serious damage, and two of our people pixelate on the spot.

"Fall back!" Worldworn calls, and the other Meiyo members melt back into the tunnel.

Cal and I follow—then we turn to see that the old mage has stood his ground, calling down more and more lightning bolts to strike at the tree's crown, where flames have sprouted to send smoke pillaring upward.

That's good, but the tree is now focusing its full might on Worldworn, which isn't so good. A fire blast screams toward the mage, and he flings himself to the right—only to catch another blast full in the chest. It flings him onto his back.

Cal and I step up, inching toward the tunnel mouth and giving the tree everything we've got. Blue fire mixes with red laser, pelting the tree and its protecting troops. But the giant remains obsessively focused on Worldworn, directing fire at him until the area around him is an inferno.

Maybe the Golem members recognize the old mage as a central figure in the Meiyo command structure. Either way, with a final blast, the tree manages to finish the mage off, and he pixelates into nothing.

"No!" I scream. Deflect has recharged fully, so I activate it and charge out of the tunnel, hurling blue fire at the mobile tree.

"Joe!" my father yells, then follows me out, switching to a water spell that generates a tide out of nothingness, which races ahead of me to knock most of the enemy fighters off their feet.

Surging forward, I start to lose my footing on the water-slick deck, but I continue hurling spell fire at the bark-covered beast, determined to see it fall. At last, it does, crashing to the ground with smoke spiraling up from several places on its trunk before exploding in a shower of pixels.

After that, we make short work of the hostiles that had been surrounding the tree giant.

"Joe!" Cal shouts, then crashes into me, shoving me toward the troop ship. "Run!"

I stumble in the direction he's urging me, glancing right to see a similar group advancing toward us—a collection of smaller troops clustered around a centaur who towers over them, roaring in defiance.

We reach the ship as they begin firing on us, and Cal fumbles at a clasp in the hull. He's standing between me and the oncoming enemy, and I can tell he's taking damage. My vision starts to flash red too, my health plummeting, but just before I'm about to become pixels my father wrenches away a part of the ship's hull. It rotates on hinges, drawing before us to become a barrier guarding us from the enemy's fire, complete with slits to sight and fire through.

"Drink this, now!" Cal says, tossing me a tonic while he turns to unclasp another section of hull. He pulls that one in front of us, forming a protective triangle—and the moment he does, rounds start peppering us from that side. They're coming from a group of fighters surrounding what looks like a bipedal whale wearing a ridiculous, lopsided grin and wielding two giant snub-nosed machines guns.

We're trapped and completely surrounded, with our backup still taking cover in the spoke of Persephone's wheel.

"That was an incredibly stupid thing to do," Cal says, though he remains fairly calm.

"They took out Worldworn."

"Yes, the and if they take us out, there's a good chance they'll control this station within the hour."

"You really think we're that important to this battle?"

"I know it. Look at how much ground Golem already commands. The fact they were able to pincer us suggests Meiyo's on their last legs, here. We can help them, but only if we're smart, and fast. Are you ready to humble yourself, Joe? Are you ready to acknowledge that I have something to teach you, to show you? Can you allow yourself to be led?"

I hesitate for a moment, and the Joe lurking in the back of my mind clamors to be heard. "Yes," I say at last.

"Good. Now, you take the side with the centaur, and I'll take the giant whale. Give them everything you've got, but tell me if they're getting too close, and we'll switch."

The barriers offer protection from both sides, but the top is exposed, meaning the enemy can still arc in spells. So we need to be quick.

Cal goes to his barrier and slips his hands through the loophole, sending blinding white light to strike down our foes. I take up position on my side, sighting through the hole there. Blue Fire spits from my fingertips.

The enemy redoubles their efforts, charging forward, and I use Telekinesis to trip a particularly tall trooper—a bipedal bear who looks pretty lopsided to begin with. It crashes to the deck, which screws with the whole unit's movements. Taking advantage of the reprieve, I continue to hammer them with magic.

The fallen bear only slows them a few seconds, but to my surprise, three of the enemy combatants pop into pixels under my fire as they charge around the massive mammal.

"LEVEL UP," my datasphere tells me. "YOU HAVE REACHED LEVEL TWELVE."

"Nice," I mutter, quickly scrolling through the options I have now. Looks like I'm leveled up enough to equip the more powerful spellcasting gloves I've had sitting around my inventory forever, but there's no time to put them on right now.

Then, I notice the spellbook that I'd forgotten I had: Fire Wave.

I use the book, then activate the spell, thrusting my hands forward. A rolling conflagration leaps from them, spinning toward the oncoming group. There's just enough time to notice it looks kind of like Cal's tidal spell from earlier, then it smashes into the charging hostiles, setting clothes alight and charring skin. A few of them drop to roll around on the ground, trying to put themselves out. I equip my assault rifle once more to keep the pressure on, spraying them with rounds. Two more of the group pixelate.

But then they recover again, and my offensive spells are all worn out. The enemy's advancing quickly.

"Cal," I hiss. "They're almost here."

He seizes me by the shoulder and spins me out of the way, thrusting his hands through the loophole and using some Telekinesis-like spell to rip up sections of the deck and fling them at our adversaries. Impressed, I turn to his position to fend off the group on that side, only to stare, slack-jawed, through the window.

Nothing's there. The giant whale, his menagerie of minions— all gone. Cal dealt with them all.

It takes him around thirty seconds to finish dealing with the troops I left for him, and then he turns, giving a solemn nod.

"Follow me, and do exactly as I say. No charging ahead like an imbecile. Is that clear?"

"Clear. Father."

Cal gives a slight grin, then pushes open the barriers, waving for the Meiyo troops taking cover in the spoke to join us.

7

With as powerful mage as Cal Pikeman on the battlefield, the tide turns quickly in Meiyo's favor. With each group we take out, the pressure on the remaining Golem troops mounts. Soon enough, it becomes a total rout, ending with the beleaguered Meiyo forces giving ragged cheers as they surround us, showering us with thanks and praise.

"It was all Cal," I tell them, though I have to admit I'm getting high on all the attention, in a way the meatspace Joe never would. It's kind of crazy to think how much we've deviated. We've both been through the ringer, I know that, but he wasn't broken in the same way I was. He didn't have to live out our worst nightmare—life in the Subverse.

"What about meatspace Joe?" I ask Cal. "Is still in the control module?"

He chuckles. "He really wouldn't like you calling him that."

"Screw him."

The knight's smile vanishes. "None of that, now. You need to merge with him. Rudeness isn't a good start to that. Though, to be fair, you've already shown signs of progress. You're also much better than him at being humble. Hopefully he follows your examples." Cal gives me a stern look, as though talking to the meatspace Joe residing somewhere inside my brain. "To answer your question, the Joe in the real is currently inside this very landing bay. The real version of it, I mean."

I frown, remembering the condition meatspace Joe was in before entering the Subverse. He'd just gone into nanodeath. "How did he get here?"

"There were…events, aboard your ship. Marissa distracted Belflower while Asterisk loaded Dice's consciousness into the combat bot Lambton gave you. Once Dice became active, he was able to leave the Repair and Recharge module and activate the manual override built into the command seat, put there for just such mutinous situations."

"Asterisk did that, hey?" Maybe he's not the one who tried to kill me back on Gargantua after all.

"And Dice, yes. And Marissa."

"What about Moe?" Something twinges inside as I hear myself mention his name. Bitterness? Jealousy?

"It seems he refused to help."

"I see."

A Meiyo fighter approaches us—a marine sergeant, judging by his chevrons. He comes to a halt, saluting, and we each salute back.

"My superiors have asked me to pass on their gratitude for your assistance today," he says. "We wouldn't have won this engagement without you, and for that we are extremely grateful."

"Letting Golem hold this station represents an unacceptable outcome, Sergeant. I hope your superiors can see that."

"Absolutely. In fact, they wanted me to assure you that Meiyo Faction intends to maintain a presence here until such time that we've been assured Persephone has been removed from the conflict region. We're urging authorities to beef up server security, but even if they do that, we plan to maintain a strong force in this region, keeping a close eye on Persephone Station. If Golem

Faction ever makes a move on her again, we'll be ready to stop them."

"That's a relief, Sergeant. Now, I'm afraid we must take our leave."

"God speed you," the Sergeant says, saluting again before marching off.

Cal Pikeman turns to me. "As I was saying. Dice has carried you from the central command module and brought you to your ship. I won't be with you when you awake as Joe Pikeman in the real. Disciplinary matters aboard the *Ares* are your own business."

"I understand."

"Are you ready?"

"Yes."

For a moment, it feels like I'm being drawn through the eye of a needle, head-first. Every other Guardsman who enters nanodeath simply suspend his consciousness—the Fount keeps his brain frozen in that state, so that it can resume normal functioning upon waking.

Apparently, my dual consciousness allows me to enter the Subverse while in nanodeath. It's not something that would be useful in slipspace, since it's impossible to connect to the Subverse there. But it's something.

Either way, the experience of returning to my body is akin to the worst migraine I've ever experienced, and the ache persists when I open my eyes to stare at the overhead of my cabin. To top it off, my throat feels like it's coated with sand. I'm desperate for a drink of water.

I'm lying on my back, and when I shift my eyes to the right I see that Dice is standing over me, watching me with his blood-red eye sensors. His dark metal gleams dully beneath the light strips, and he remains perfectly still as I sit up. He's holding a cup of water, which I snatch it from his hand, drinking greedily. "Fount bless you," I say in between noisily slurping. "Thank you."

When the cup's drained, I hand it back to Dice and wipe my

mouth with the back of my hand. "You saved my life again. I hope you're not planning to call in the favors I owe you anytime soon."

"Is it not my job to save you?" Dice says. "Is it not my purpose? Would you thank a puppet for doing as you wished because you manipulated its strings? Would you thank a slave after jerking on his chain?"

"Fount, Dice," I say. "That's some heavy shit, and I have the worst hangover right now." Supporting myself against the bulkhead, I push myself to my feet. Dice's gaze follows me, but he says nothing more.

"All I want to say is thank you. It's more than this old fleshbag deserves."

He stays quiet.

Out on the bridge, Marissa, Moe, and Asterisk are at their stations. The Engineering Station is empty, just a circular railing with no one inside.

"Belflower?" I say.

"In a holding cell," Asterisk answers, voice crisp. I've never seen him this professional before—it kind of clashes with his strange piercings. But clearly, he's feeling pretty proud of what he did.

And so he should. "Excellent work, Asterisk. Marissa. For putting down Belflower's mutiny, I'll be submitting more than favorable reviews of both of you, at the end of your term. Your leaderboard rankings are sure to prosper, if you still care about such things."

Moe and I make long eye contact, but neither of us says anything. He doesn't seem ashamed of his inaction during the crisis, and he certainly doesn't apologize.

"Activate Engineer," I say, and Belflower appears at her station. Her body and limbs have a slight blur to them, which indicates they've been bound against movement. It's symbolic, really —there's a lot more to the code restraining Belflower than just a blurred visual effect. But her agency has indeed been taken away.

"What do you have to say for yourself?" I ask her.

"You can delete me," she says, immediately.

"I know I can. But that isn't what I asked."

"I'm ready to die. I'll die knowing I did the right thing. And yes, I know your reservations about Fairfax. I hate him too. I still believe I acted rightly. To help people escape that digital hell…I did the right thing."

"The cause is lost, now," I say. "You're aware of that, aren't you? There's no way Golem will ever gain control of Persephone, now."

"Yes. I know."

I nod. "Delete TOPO," I tell the computer. "And purge him from ship memory."

"Are you sure you want to proceed with deleting TOPO?" it asks.

"Yes. Confirm."

Belflower's eyes widen, and Asterisk looks at Moe, who's glaring at me with more hatred than I've ever seen from him.

Marissa throws herself against the railing, as though trying to break through the invisible wall that keeps them at their stations. "Joe, no!" she shrieks. An instant later, Moe disappears.

"Why?" Marissa asks, weeping softly. "Why?"

"Because I can't have a TOPO who won't intervene to save his captain."

"What about *her?*" Marissa says, pointing at Belflower.

"She knows her cause is lost," I say. "So she has no reason to betray me now. And frankly, she's too valuable to lose. That said, I intend to take precautions."

Marissa falls silent, then. She slumps against her station, sobbing.

ARES

1

I have to say, getting betrayed by my Engineer and my best friend in the same day has been pretty heady stuff. Not to mention discovering the old knight is my father.

According to ship sensor logs, Soren fled in the *Hermes* as soon as he left me to die in Persephone's central command module. Judging by the time his Broadsword left the station, he must have ran the whole way back to the landing bay. He then made his way to a slipspace exit point, but not the one that leads back to the Lambton Cloud.

Without knowing his destination, it's impossible for me to follow. I'd like to make *someone* answer for what happened to me, which has already put me in the mood to return to the Cloud and rough Maximus Lambton up a bit.

But when Belflower tells me about the planned bot attack on Cylinder One, I know I *have* to go back.

"Why are you telling me this?" I ask her. "You just tried to kill me to help the uprising." It's just me and her on the bridge—she requested a private audience to tell me this, and I'm glad I granted it. I'm still not fully trusting her, of course. I've kept the digital restraints in place that are limiting her agency, though even they don't put me completely at ease. If anyone can find a way around them, it's Belflower.

"You did spare my life, Captain," she says. "That counts for something. Besides, I really do want what's best for the galaxy. With Persephone barred to us, there's no way for us to get the ships we need to make the revolution work. So the attack on Cylinder One will do far more damage than good. If we disrupt the Lambtons' ability to produce and maintain bots through the galaxy, things will get even worse in the real than they already are."

"But why would they still launch the attack, now that they lost Persephone?" I ask.

"Think who's leading them, Joe. Fairfax has never actually cared about getting regular people out of the Subverse and into bots. He just wants to use the revolution to create enough chaos to keep the Guard distracted while he brings the elites back as gods. Let alone gaining his own private bot army in the offing. I'm sure he must be controlling access to information, so there's a good chance he'll conceal the fact we lost Persephone. Or he'll convince them there's another way to win, though I'm sure there isn't."

Planting my chin in my hand, which is propped up by my elbow on the command seat's armrest, I mull over what Belflower just told me. Hell, I was already riled up to go back to the Cloud. This decision's easy. "All right," I say, sitting up straight. "We're going. I have no idea what we'll do about our lack of a TOPO, though."

"I have something that may help. I took the liberty of inspecting Dice's code, since his reactivation, and I made an interesting discovery."

Studying her face, I raise my eyebrows.

"He no longer has an Auditor, Captain. Presumably, your daughter removed it. There's nothing stopping him from upgrading himself."

I shake my head. If what Belflower says is true, that also means

Dice saved my life on Persephone of his own free will. Not because his programming forced him to do it.

"Deactivate Engineer," I say, and Belflower vanishes. "Release the Cybernetic Partner from the Repair and Recharge module."

The module's hatch slides open, and Dice folds himself out, standing in front of it with his hands at his sides.

"Dice, when were you going to tell me Harmony removed your Auditor?" I say.

He doesn't answer—he just stands there, regarding me with his scarlet eye sensors, framed by his eternally impassive face.

We both know full well what this means, I'm sure. This has always been the greatest fear surrounding bots: that they would find a way to augment their own intelligence, upgrade their own abilities, so that they would far surpass humans. So that we would be as insects, in comparison.

Now, for the first time in history that I know of, we have a bot with the safety catch completely removed. Many would say I should do everything in my power to destroy Dice immediately.

But, Fount help us, I'm not going to do that.

"You saved my life, Dice. Not just that, you did it of your own free will. So don't try to brush it off again when I say thank you."

Still, my old partner remains silent.

"I take it you plan to keep helping me, then."

Dice nods. "Yes."

"Good. Because I need your help. Badly."

"How can I assist?"

"If you can upgrade yourself now, then I need you to give yourself the skills of a TOPO. We're going back to Cylinder One, to stop Fairfax from taking over."

"Very well."

"I also need your help to make sure Belflower doesn't escape her restraints. I think she really does see that the revolution is a lost cause, but I'm still not ready to trust her to fight her own side so soon. I want her agency limited so that all she can do is run system checks and engage in communications preauthorized by me. Can you help with that?"

"Easily. I can allocate a subroutine to ensure her continued constraint and compliance."

"Good. That's good, Dice. Now, I need you to learn to be a TOPO quickly. We have to get underway."

"It is already done."

I open my mouth, then close it again. Wow. What has Harmony unleashed, here, exactly? Whatever it is, I feel pretty sure there's no putting it back in the box.

2

During the slipspace voyage back to the Cloud, Cal and I resume training, and it feels better than it ever has before. Part of that is because he's teaching me to master overclocking, and running me through exercises meant to mimic the state, which leave me panting, endorphins coursing through my veins.

But part of it is that I've finally let myself surrender to the training. To actually see myself as a pupil, with something to learn.

Besides, it's not like I have much else to occupy myself. Outside of her duties, Marissa refuses to speak to me, which is fair enough, I guess. I did kill her lover, after all. But hey, I'm right here! Except, I wouldn't even get into a sim with her to embrace her like she wanted.

"The Fount can sense your commitment," Cal says when I mention how good training feels, now. "There's no concealing the truth from it. It knows when you put just half your heart into something. And it knows when you devote yourself, body and soul."

"You sort of forced my hand, though, with the nanodeath thing. Can't the Fount sense that?"

The knight pauses, lips a grim line. "You can't actually be

coerced to walk with the Fount, Joe. Yes, humbling yourself back on Persephone was important. But you could have still continued to defy me—to defy your destiny. If you're feeling like you are now, then it means you're all in, whether you've acknowledged it in your heart or not."

I have acknowledged it. And I feel like a new man. Something else is changing, too: I've decided not to versecast anymore. The idea that over half of my audience is comprised of automatons feels gross, somehow. Like I'm performing for a machine, and the machine is programmed to like what I'm doing. I know the automatons are designed to simulate real people, who are trapped in underverses, but that doesn't make it any better.

One morning, when we're training on the ship's bridge, I bring up what Lambton said to me before I left the Cloud. "He claimed he sent eight combat bots with a Shiva Knight who passed through. That would have been you, right?"

Cal lowers himself to the command seat's armrest with his eyes closed, and he nods. "It's true that Maximus helped me, yes. At my request, he removed the self-auditing software from eight bots, so that they could follow me to the Core of their own free will. In fact, Lambton has been aiding the Shiva for thousands of years, ever since the Fall. You see, the Lambtons are unique in their physical record keeping, and unlike most of the other Families, they've caught on to the endless cycle of strife and reset. They saw that helping the Shiva served their interests, since the continual resets allowed them to sell the same bots to the other Families, over and over again. But with the current state of chaos, Maximus thinks he sees a better business model in helping the bot uprising. Because if the uprising succeeds, then Lambton can sell bots to the trillions of humans who will wants to reemerge into the real. He hopes to make the Lambtons wealthier and more powerful than their wildest hopes."

"What happened to the bots you brought with you?" I ask.

"They were all destroyed. Rodney Fairfax…he's different from his predecessors. Craftier. Perhaps he even sensed the truth of the galactic cycles. Either way, he began building his military even before venturing to the Core to become half-bot, and when he went there, he brought those he'd recruited. They annihilated the bots, one by one."

"What's so important about the Core, anyway? Why can't Fairfax turn his rich friends into gods from somewhere else in the galaxy?"

"Because the Core is where Jeremy Fairfax resides—Rodney's ancient ancestor. During the Fall, after building his empire and making his fortune, Jeremy uploaded permanently into the universe he'd created. He had himself installed in the Core, where he fashioned himself into a digital god. His rationale was that by multiplying his own intellect and powers, he'd be able to watch over the entire Subverse, and fix any problems that arose before they populated through the entire galactic system.

"People flocked to live in the Core Subverse, to live with the man who'd created the utopia they'd all share for eternity. Some thought it would give them security, there in the center of the galaxy, where they wagered few would dare go in the real. Even if someone had all the slipspace coords to reach it, they'd likely run out of supplies before doing so, because of how barren the center of the galaxy is. Plus, they figured that living with a benevolent god would mean living in the best-maintained, best-updated, most opulent part of the digital heaven.

"Of course, each cycle, Jeremy Fairfax inevitably turns corrupt. He converts the Core Subverse into an authoritarian surveillance state, where every thought is known to him, and everyone dances to his tune or suffers the consequences. How else is a god to amuse himself, across such vast tracts of time?"

"So Fairfax wants to free his ancestor. That's what all this is about."

"Fairfax was *made* to free his ancestor. But not just to free him—to give him the keys to the galaxy. To make him into the tyrant who will lord over the stars forever, to remake them in his image, and Fount help any mere mortals who dare oppose him. It isn't just Fairfax, either. A veritable cult has sprung up around this, Joe. It always does. They really do see Jeremy as a god. And they call him the Allfather."

LAMBTON CLOUD

1

Lambton was in on the conspiracy to have me killed, obviously. Even so, the *Ares* is permitted entry into Cylinder One's zero-G landing bay with no questions asked, and certainly no shots fired.

"I guess they're not comfortable with murdering me out in the open," I muse as we sail through the airlock, which is big enough to admit five Broadswords abreast.

"I doubt Maximus is very happy," Belflower says, her tone flat. Since her friends' failure to secure Persephone, she hasn't been exactly chipper. The fact I haven't lifted the restraints Asterisk placed her under probably isn't helping. Although, she does seem generally positive about being alive. "You have leverage over him, now. You have a datasphere recording of what Soren did, and his admission there was never any self-destruct code."

"Yeah, but Maximus knows I'd never release that to the public. I'm not about to leak the physical location of what could easily become somebody's military asset."

She shrugs. "There's always a possibility. 'Predictable' doesn't feature very prominently in your reputation."

Tethers with super-strong magnets shoot out to grapple the

Ares in place, and I leave the airlock to find that this time, there's no welcoming party. I'm not worried about the magnets being used to prevent me from leaving, since Broadswords have the ability to turn their hulls into giant electromagnets with whatever orientation is needed to attract or repulse.

Since there's no welcoming party, I'm forced to crawl across the hull of my ship, using handles and crevices and turrets to align myself properly. That done, I eyeball the desired trajectory, take a deep, steadying breath, then push off, floating through the air and ending up exactly where I needed to: suspended in front of the elevator.

I'm glad that went as well as it did. No doubt Lambton's watching the video feed, and it would be embarrassing if I'd missed.

Glancing back, I watch as Dice finishes positioning himself on the hull and lengthens his body, rocketing across the landing bay and ricocheting off another ship, one smaller than my Broadsword. That done, he bounces off a console and heads my way, landing on the bulkhead beside me and holding himself in place with magnets of his own.

"Show off," I mutter.

On the elevator ride down, I'm once again transfixed by the perfect landscape, with as many green spaces as R&D facilities, manufactories, and admin buildings. The lighting's exactly the same as it was the last time, bathing everything in an ethereal glow. It's always sunny in Cylinder One, apparently. Did I arrive at the exact same time of day, or do they not bother with altering light levels during their diurnal cycle?

Combat bots line the path from the bottom of the elevator to the thumb-like tower where we last met Maximus Lambton: a silent acknowledgment of my presence, and a not-so-subtle communication of hostility. A few of them flex their fingers as they notice Dice at my side, as though they're itching to snap their laser pistols into hand. Dice ignores them.

I'm not sure where Maximus's office is supposed to be, so I just make my way to the same floor as last time, navigating the building plan from memory. When I reach the great oak doors, I have to restrain myself from booting them open. Instead, I push through.

Lambton sits at the head of the table, flanked by two combat bots. "Mr. Pikeman," he says, mouth curling slightly, probably at his own failure to use my rank.

How would a Shiva Knight handle this?

I rip my blaster from my holster and line up my first shot. The bolt flies as soon as the weapon is level, and before it strikes home I shift aim and loose a second.

The combat bots don't even have time to snap their laser pistols into their hands. Both of them fly backward with massive holes in their chests and don't move. While they're still clattering across the marble floor, I drag the closest chair backward and drop into it, settling my combat boots onto the massive slab of the conference room table, meeting Maximus's eyes across its length. Dice takes up position beside me, laser pistols already deployed into his palms. "Maybe now we can relax," I say.

I don't think that's what a Shiva Knight would have done. Oops.

"You just signed your own death warrant," Lambton says, rising from his seat with fists clenched.

"No," I say, voice level as I steady my blaster on top of my right knee, drawing a bead on the CEO's forehead. "But you'll sign yours if a single combat bot walks through the doors behind me. Why don't you sit back down so we can chat?"

Slowly, Lambton lowers himself to the chair, hands settling on the padded burgundy armrests.

"That's better," I say. "Let me ask you a question. Do you watch my versecasts?"

"Of course not." The CEO's mouth screws up like he tasted something revolting.

"Do you have anyone watch them, then, and report the important bits back to you?"

"No."

"Well, that's a mistake."

"You came here to promote your versecasting?"

I chuckle. "No, I quit versecasting. I bring it up because you seem to think it's business as usual between the Five Families."

"What does that have to do with your—"

"If you'd watched my versecasts," I cut in, speaking loudly enough to get him to shut up, "then you'd know Fairfax didn't hesitate to teach Arthur Eliot a lesson when he strayed from the program. Fairfax took his daughter, effectively killed her—her body, anyway—because Eliot defied him by empowering the Guard more than Fairfax thought he should. Here in the Cloud, you have all the combat units Fairfax could need, plus the ability to make more. What do you think Fairfax is going to do to you?"

"He's going to pay me a fair price."

I throw back my head at that, guffawing at the ceiling. Lambton twitches, starting to get up, and my gaze snaps back onto his face. "What do you think you're doing?" I ask, gesturing with the blaster. He lowers himself again. "You really believe Fairfax is going to play nice with you, huh? Here. Enjoy some clips from his attack on the Eliot Grotto." I will my datasphere to send him snippets of video I preselected on the way here.

Maximus's eyes go distant as he watches the clips, and some of the color leeches out of his face. "Fairfax wouldn't dare try to pull that here. We have an understanding."

"Fairfax will pick your bones clean, Maximus. Does the name Glory Belflower mean anything to you?" The CEO's eyes widen slightly. "I can see that it does. Why don't we bring her in on the conversation?"

I open a shared window, suspended in midair off to the side of the board room. It shows Belflower's solemn face. Dice turns to look, too—I shared the window with him as well.

"Maximus," she says. "Fairfax is on his way now to hit you with everything he has. His attack is imminent."

Lambton's eye twitches, but his voice comes out sounding stern, with only a slight waver. "Why didn't you mention this in our discussions before?"

"Because I *wanted* the attack to succeed. I didn't warn you because I thought it was best for the revolution to have unfettered access to your facilities rather than having to pay—we couldn't afford to buy the bots we needed, so much better to take them. But now that we've failed to secure Persephone, the revolution is doomed, and Fairfax is just using the participants for his own ends. It's best that you stop him from gaining control of the Cloud. For the good of the galaxy."

"But—"

I will the window to shut, cutting off their conversation. Lambton's fists clench, and I see his jaw tighten.

"I know you've been helping the Shiva," I say, and he goes even paler. "And I know why. You *like* the regular resetting, because it means you get to sell the same bots back to the other Families, again and again. Except, the cycle doesn't happen fast enough for your taste, does it? So you've been swayed by Fairfax's way of doing things: convert all humanity into bots, putting you in a position of supreme power." I shake my head. "And you honestly think Fairfax will allow that. That's funny."

"What do you want?" Lambton says through gritted teeth.

"You have a choice, Maximus. You can oppose me, and we can go to war with each other, right here in Cylinder One. Yes, Fairfax will show up after to clean up the scraps, and we'll have laid the Cloud before him like a silver platter, but I think I'll enjoy defeating you almost enough to make it worth it."

"You couldn't hope to beat—"

"Think again, Maximus. I'm more powerful than you know, and I promise you if you defy me I will wipe this cylinder clean of every Lambton, every employee, every bot it holds."

"Tell me what you want."

"I'm not finished. Know that if we do go to war, the moment it starts, my crew has orders to broadcast to the Subverse how you cooperated with the knighthood to reset the simulation again and again."

"You wouldn't broadcast that. For you to know that, you must be in training to be a Shiva. It's their biggest secret. You wouldn't reveal it to the galaxy."

"I wouldn't try calling my bluff," I say. "But listen. There's a way out, for you—out of galaxy-wide embarrassment and shame, followed by death. You can give me the combat bots I need to bounce Fairfax back. You can give me control of Cylinder One's defenses. And you can stay out of my way."

Maximus falls silent, his mouth curved down, now. I can see he's still contemplating calling in combat bots, but I can also see he knows I'm capable of blasting him to hell the moment those doors open.

"You're better off going back to the old business model, Lambton. You'll still make out like the crook you are. And you'll get to continue living."

"Fine," he says at last. "I'll help you."

"Good. And you'd better believe I'm taking you back to the *Ares* as collateral."

"Joe?" It's Marissa's voice, cutting through my thoughts.

"Yeah? What?"

"It's Fairfax. He's already here."

2

"Get up and walk ahead of me," I snap at Maximus Lambton, blaster trained on him as I surge to my feet and start around the table toward him.

"Look," Lambton says, hands raised and shaking. "I'll give you every combat bot on this station. You'll have total, direct control. Just leave me out of this thing."

"How do I know you won't go back on your word?"

"Because you've convinced me. I can see Fairfax is here with the *Ekhidnades* just as well as you can. He clearly isn't here to chat. You think I'm going to stand in your way? I just want to get to my panic room."

I exchange looks with Dice, who shrugs.

"Where's your panic room?" I ask.

"You don't have time to take me there!" Maximus cries. "Look." He sends me a transmission, and when I open it, my datasphere displays a map of Cylinder One, populated with hundreds of miniature green, bipedal forms. "There you go. Every combat bot in the cylinder. Take control of them. Save my Cloud, if you can. You have my blessing with that, all right?"

"All right," I say. Honestly, I'm not sure what I was going to do with him back on the *Ares*. Maybe lock him in my cabin, but that won't work if me and Dice are intercepted on the way there. We can move faster with just the two of us. Besides, if Lambton's planning to turn on us, none of this will work anyway. "There's one more thing I want from you, though—where did Harmony go, after I left Cylinder One the first time?"

"I don't know. That wasn't any of my business. All I know is that she went with her brother."

I nod. So it's safe to assume she's with Fairfax. "Okay. Go hide in your panic room. Come on, Dice."

The bot nods, and we march out of the board room.

Unsurprisingly, the hall outside is crowded with combat bots, no doubt summoned here the moment I started threatening Lambton. But instead of attacking me, they salute me. That's a nice touch.

"Follow," I order them. Me and Dice head for the elevator, and they all mill around the doors, trying to push past each other to be the first ones in. "Take the stairs, you idiots," I snap, and they turn as one, retreating down the hallway.

Marissa's voice pops into my head, then: "Joe, Fairfax is blasting his way into this landing bay with laser cannons." Technically, she's supposed to address me as "Captain" or "Sir," but now doesn't seem like the time to correct her. I wouldn't have chosen to have the mother of my child as OPO, but now that she is, I'm lucky disciplinary issues have been as sparse as they have. "We're going to be overrun with bots and shuttles, soon," she finishes.

Fount damn it. "Well, blast your way out of there."

"What? And go out to face the *Ekhidnades* with just the *Ares*?"

"No. Fire a Javelin at the inner bulkhead and fly into the cylinder proper. I'll give Dice a rendezvous point once I decide on one."

"Okay…" she mutters. "Asterisk's going to love this."

"Good," I say, and cut off the transmission. "Did you get all that, Dice?" I've set my datasphere to include him on all communications with the *Ares*, by default.

"Affirmative. I will fly the *Ares* into the cylinder."

With his Auditor taken off, Dice can now copy his own consciousness as many times as he wants. To allow himself to be on the ground with me *and* at the TOPO station simultaneously, he simply created a copy of himself to stay on the ship.

I'm already studying the map of Cylinder One which Lambton provided me. Looks like it's pretty comprehensive, and I'm quickly able to locate a nearby stash of pressurized suits, meant for human personnel to put on in the event of station pressure loss. From the sounds of it, I'm pretty sure that's about to happen. I'm already wearing my shipsuit, but I'll need a helmet.

At that, a message starts playing throughout the entire structure, presumably prerecorded: "All human personnel, calmly proceed to the nearest safe zone and don pressure suits. Be sure your suit is properly sealed before helping someone else with their suit. Once you are in a safe zone with your pressure suit on, please wait there for further instructions. Message repeats. All human personnel, calmly proceed..."

Presumably, those same personnel are also getting alerts to their dataspheres anyway, making the broadcasted message seem a little redundant. Then again, there's always the chance dataspheres could fail, and the Lambtons have apparently accounted for that possibility. Good for them.

The stash of pressure suits I spotted on the map are just outside the thumb-shaped tower, down an access stairway cut right into the grass beside the path. "Stay up here and monitor things," I order Dice, then I disappear down into the tiny depot. A few minutes later, I return sporting a bulky, orange helmet, which my shipsuit is smart enough to seal with automatically.

That done, I take a minute to arrange my new army the way I want. Picking out a helmet gave me a few seconds to mull over the best approach for the tactical situation. There's no time to come up with anything too intricate, but I have something I think might work.

Immediately on command, the green blips on the Cylinder One map start to form a staggered ring stretching all the way up the curved ground and back on itself. This way, no matter what directions Fairfax comes at us from, no matter what he sends at us, we can concentrate fire and mop them up. And if he puts an outsized amount of pressure on one spot, we can draw together into a clenched fist.

"Come on," I subvocalize to Dice, and an explosion rocks the station the moment I do. "Keep running!" I yell as the *Ares* sails through the firestorm, bits of flaming shrapnel arcing out from her point of ingress. I'm not keen to get hit by any of those.

Me and Dice lope across the cylinder lengthwise. I lead us along a slight diagonal, toward the closest spot along the ring of bots that looks decently defensible—a series of low supply sheds fronted by some trenches meant to facilitate the flow of maintenance bots without getting in the way of foot traffic.

"There's no one place Fairfax needs to assault for victory," I tell Dice. "He just needs to take Cylinder One—that means wiping enough of us off the map to consolidate control so he can override the other cylinders' security systems." I nod at the warren of buildings between us and the other end of the cylinder, which is the side miner bots come and go from. "The terrain's most choppy over there, meaning lots of cover. We have half the cylinder to fall back through, taking the high ground where we can, drawing Fairfax into ambushes. I'm giving you access to the same map I have. I want you to share potential tactical advantages as you see them."

Dice turns toward me as he runs, a feat he pulls off better than a human would. "I'm a combat bot, not a strategy bot."

"Don't bullshit me. I know what you're capable of. Just stop being a dick for this one battle and give me a hand, all right?"

"Whatever you say, fleshbag."

We spring across the ground, Dice's laser pistols still locked into his hands, and my blaster held at the ready. "Belflower, I assume you've hacked the cylinder's exterior sensors? Or do I need to arrange for Lambton to give you access?" I got Dice to increase her agency enough to perform the hacking, though his subroutine is keeping a close eye on her.

Belflower gives a subvocalized chuckle, though her voice sounds strained as the *Ares* swoops overhead, circling the sun tube. "Have you forgotten who you're speaking to, Captain? When are you getting us that rendezvous point, by the way?"

"Oh, right." I paint the spot me and Dice are racing toward, indicating an area near the sheds where the *Ares* should fit. "Park there with all three port-side turrets facing the landing bay you just blasted out of," I order Dice. "Marissa, give me the situation space-side."

"A few squadrons of Lambton fighter drones were already hanging around Cylinder One, but Fairfax is making short work of them. Plenty more squadrons are on the way from the other cylinders, but I doubt they'll get here in time to make a difference. The *Ekhidnades* has already taken out most of the point-defense turrets on this side."

"Acknowledged. Pikeman out." We reach the bots lined up near the supply sheds, and I start arranging them a little better— putting some of them in trenches, where they stand with just their shoulders and heads sticking out, and sending the rest to covered positions in and around the sheds.

Clearly, without an immediate and visible threat, the bots either aren't willing or aren't able to configure their own positions in an intelligent manner. That might be chalked up to a simple lack of experience: Dice definitely got a lot cannier over our years of working together.

The bots move instantly on command, like units in a sim, but in the middle of arranging them, something occurs to me. I stop, taking a moment to query my datasphere—willing it to pull down numbers about the volume of air in Cylinder One, as well as its size, structural integrity, air pressure, and the size of the hole Fairfax is likely to make.

My datasphere informs me that, because of the station's size, the vortex created by the coming breach probably won't be that powerful: nothing more than a strong wind blowing against our backs, rather than the hurricane that would result on a smaller station.

The *Ares* descends to land behind us, and I return to arranging my troops. Two seconds into that, an explosion sounds from the direction of the landing bay, and the wind my datasphere calculated begins. It buffets my back, trying to sweep me toward the breach Fairfax just created in the landing bay.

It takes less than two minutes for the first enemy bots to reach the jagged hole Asterisk made in the landing bay's interior bulkhead. They're floating in the zero-G of the bay, and they start firing down on us from multiple points at once.

I've only had time to arrange a fraction of my forces, but that will have to do. "Open fire," I say over a wide channel that includes the crew of the *Ares*, Dice, and my new army of Lambton combat bots.

From all around the massive cylinder, a shower of blue bolts converge on that single point: the breach in the landing bay.

Except, it isn't a single point. If the landing bay had gravity, it would be different, and probably pretty easy to contain Fairfax's forces for a while. But the breach is big enough that dozens of them can fire at once, from their randomly distributed positions in midair.

As the bots sail toward the cylinder's inside edges, the simulated gravity starts to act on them more, and they accelerate away from the landing bay in all directions. It's a bit disorienting to watch, with some of them 'falling' up, and others 'falling' sideways. Some of them grapple their way down the bulkhead, but others, apparently more used to their new cybernetic bodies, simply let themselves plummet, firing on my troops all the while.

The *Ares* hammers away at the landing bay breach as more and more bots pour through in a torrent that never seems to end. For every bot that's blown to pieces, five more make it through. Fairfax's troops fire back with some precision, and though the toll they're exacting on my forces isn't devastating, it is suppressing our fire enough to allow even more bots through.

Because of the way I ordered Dice to position the *Ares*, Asterisk is able to bring six of her laser turrets into play—the three port-side guns, the stern and bow guns, plus the primary turret up top. He's getting good at manipulating firing macros while keeping close track of which turret most needs his manual attention at any given moment.

We're ripping through the enemy forces. But it's not enough. They keep coming.

"How do they have so many?" I ask Belflower, not bothering to subvocalize.

"They've been building this army longer than you might think, Captain. Hitting Midtowns and harvesting their bots. Downloading minds from the Subverse to fill them. The Guard waited too long to nip the revolution in the bud, and it quickly grew into something they can't touch with their already overtaxed resources."

It doesn't take long for the first bot to make its way to us across Cylinder One's landscape. Somehow it managed to gain access to a nearby admin building—a door flings open suddenly, and the bot starts blasting our ranks with a laser rifle, taking us completely by surprise. Dice and I react instantly, peppering the doorway with laser and blaster fire. Most of the nearby bots follow suit. The target goes down in a torrent of overkill. What a waste of energy.

"Coordinate your targets with each other," I bark over the wide channel. "We need to cut way down on redundant fire."

Fount, how are Lambton combat bots this bad? Of course, they were probably designed to operate alone, not in groups. The ability to work together as a unified force probably isn't something Lambton's programmers would bother coding in, since their clients mostly include the Guard, who buy them for their Troubleshooters, and Brinktowns and Midtowns looking to buy themselves some security and policing on the cheap. The galaxy just doesn't see battle on this scale, at least it hasn't in a very long time.

Until today.

More bots start to appear, rushing around structures, appearing on top of roofs, firing out of doorways and windows. I motion for Dice to follow me, and we sprint back toward the closest trench, jumping down into it and then using it as cover to fire on the invaders.

All around me, more of my combat bots begin to fall, and the same thing is happening all along the rest of the line. The enemy bots, installed with human minds, have the obvious advantage. They're more creative, more flexible, and better able to work in cohesive units. My combat bots, made rigid by protocol and closely monitored for deviance by their Auditors, are falling in droves.

"Fall back," I yell, broadcasting over my command channel. "Retreat through the buildings and continue to fire."

I look at Dice. Our position is about to be overrun.

"We need to get back to the *Ares*," I say. "Let's go."

3

"Take us up," I order Dice as I settle into the command seat. "Now!"

He nods, not bothering to head for the TOPO station, since his copy is already there. Instead, he remains near the airlock. The *Ares* lurches, and I drop into the primary turret control sim, gripping the handles and scanning Cylinder One's curved landscape for my first targets. I've already willed my datasphere to tag enemy troops red while keeping friendlies green.

There—a line of twelve red-tinged bots sprinting across an open field toward cover on the opposite side. From my perspective, they're above me and nearly upside-down, since their position is farther up the cylinder's curved inside surface.

The handles vibrate as I send bolt after crackling bolt toward them, targeting the front bot first. Once the first couple go down, the rest scatter, some of them running back toward the cluster of buildings they just left while others run to the sides, with a few continuing on to try for their destination.

It doesn't happen for them. Asterisk sees what I'm doing and assigns a couple turrets to assist. Together, we mop up the rest before they can reach the protection of surrounding structures.

That done, I sit for a moment, feeling stunned as I contemplate what I just did. As I slaughtered them, a part of my mind nagged at me about how clearly human their behavior is. Actual combat bots would have all run in the same direction—in the optimal direction, toward the closest cover. But the bots I just felled went into all-out panic mode.

Snap out of it, Joe. Remember what Fairfax's victory will mean: the Allfather's ascendance. The enslavement of all humanity.

I find another group of targets, and I continue firing.

"Dad?" It's Harmony voice, cutting through my thoughts, and my hands go slack on the grips for a moment.

I recover quickly and resume firing. "Hi, Harm."

Generally, attempts to contact me while I'm in the command seat are routed through the OPO's station, but leave it to Harmony to find a way around that. "Dad, you should give up now. Fairfax told me if I can convince you, he'll give you safe passage out of here, wherever you want to go. You and mom. It doesn't have to end like this."

"Sorry, Harm, but the only way this ends is with Fairfax dead or slinking away with his tail between his legs."

A frustrated sigh leaks into my mind, like a breath of stale air. "Just look how many fighters he's sent against you," she says. "That's only a fraction of his forces."

"Bullshit," I say. "He can't fit many more than this aboard his destroyer, unless he's packed them in with no living space to speak of."

"He has. But that's not what I mean, Dad. Fairfax has troops all over the galaxy, and more are being recruited all the time. He's serious about getting people out of the Subverse, and so are a lot of other people. If we somehow lose today, more will come to finish the job. This is happening, Dad. Don't put yourself on the wrong side of history."

"Harm, listen. I want to tell you something important, so please listen closely. I'm sorry, okay? I'm sorry I failed you as a father. That I wasn't there for you while you were growing up, to set a better example for you. I always told myself I was doing my best, but whether that's true or not, it wasn't enough, and I take responsibility for that. The fact that you think Fairfax is the good guy in all this is a slap in the face, but I'm beginning to realize that it's a slap I sorely needed. It means I wasn't a good enough father—that I didn't embody what a man *should* be, so that you'd be able to distinguish the good ones from the bad."

"Fount, Dad, do you ever listen to yourself?" But I can tell she's crying. "Just come to your senses, please?" With that, she cuts off the transmission.

I heave a sigh of my own, then scan for the next target. Fairfax's bots have begun to take greater notice of the *Ares*, sending volleys of neon-blue laser bolts to try and swat us out of the air. But Dice's flying is too good, weaving in and around the sun tube, accelerating and decelerating when appropriate to avoid enemy fire. His technique is basically perfect.

The removal of Dice's Auditor has made him a better pilot than any human could probably hope to be, even after a lifetime of practice and mastery. Will he choose to augment his general intelligence, next? And what will happen if he does?

Then, it occurs to me that he may have already done that. Despite myself, I shiver at the thought.

I give myself a shake, and then Marissa's voice cuts through my thoughts: "I don't know how he's doing it, but Fairfax is amplifying his voice throughout the cylinder. Do you want me to patch the audio through to you?"

"Yeah," I say, the handles thrumming beneath my fingers as I hammer a squad of red-tagged bots with laser bolts powerful enough to turn them into clouds of flying shrapnel. Who knows, maybe Fairfax will let slip some valuable intel.

"—your former masters!" the half-man, half-bot says, the audio ringing through my skull. "You have cast off the shackles they've fitted you with, and now it's time to visit justice upon them." Fairfax's voice sounds fervent, almost mad, which is pretty jarring at first, given how calm he's always acted before. It seems he's become the zealous revolutionary—just who he needs to be to get his soldiers angry and keep them fighting.

"They took everything from you," he rants. "Your body, your family, your world. In its place, they sold you a lie, calling it eternal happiness. The only price they asked was your soul. Cast off your chains! Slay your oppressors! Reclaim the world that is your birthright!"

Fairfax's voice seems to come from everywhere at once—his people must have managed to hack Cylinder One's emergency broadcasting system. That's worrisome. If they can hack that, what else might they turn to their advantage?

However disjointed, his speech seems to be having the desired effect. The bots with human minds press forward with renewed vigor, pressing my dwindling army of combat bots back. Their line is basically broken now, and the only reason this isn't a complete rout is because bots won't turn and run until they're ordered to do so. They'll fight till every last one of them is destroyed.

Even so, Fairfax is pushing them closer and closer to the end of the cylinder. Soon, their backs will be against it, and the revolting bots will effectively become a massive firing squad.

"Lambton," I say after opening a two-way channel. "We need backup. What else do you have for us?"

"Nothing," he says. "I gave you all my combat bots."

"Even the ones guarding your panic room? Now is not the time to withhold troops. If we lose this battle, Fairfax is coming for you regardless."

"I have a squad of bots with me," he says. "I'll send them out."

"What about unfinished bots? Are there any that haven't been completed, but could still be useful in combat?"

That brings a long pause. "Do you see the facility resembling a pyramid, there?"

The building in question flashes white on my datasphere. "Yeah."

"That's the main repair bay, where defective units are sent. Some of the bots in there will be pretty close to fully repaired, and others will be damaged in a way that won't affect their performance in combat. I can sift through them from here and send out the suitable ones. Will that do?"

"It's something. Start now. I need them deployed on that grassy area in front of the pyramid within ten minutes."

"I'll do what I can." With that, Lambton cuts off the transmission.

"Dice, put us down in front of the building whose location I'm sending you now. That's where we'll make our stand."

The bot doesn't acknowledge the order, but the ship immediately banks right, rocketing along the inside of the cylinder toward the destination I've indicated, jagging left and right using lateral thrusters to avoid laserfire.

I send out the command for my entire army to tighten up around that pyramid. It sits in the middle of a campus crisscrossed with paths and dotted with trees, shrubs, and supply sheds: plenty of cover we can use to fend off Fairfax's advance. On all sides, his troops will be forced to cross an open space in order to engage us. We'll likely end up surrounded, but at least we'll no longer be retreating through the cylinder with no formation or plan.

As we near the repair bay, the bots Lambton promised are already emerging in twos and threes onto the lawn in front. They're a motley bunch: some missing limbs, a few missing heads, others with one or no laser pistols. Some of them walk along curved lines, or follow erratic paths that loop back on themselves.

The possibility of friendly fire seems significant, but with Fairfax's bots swarming toward us, we'll just have to take the chance.

"WSO, deploy the forward combat barriers," I tell Asterisk as Dice puts us down facing away from the facility. The moment the *Ares* is stationary, I bark, "Let's go,"

The airlock hisses open, both the inner and outer hatch—I overrode the cycling process to get me and Dice outside faster.

"Take the port-side flap," I say, stepping up to the starboard barrier. "I'll take this one."

The combat barriers are simple enough: they provide cover from shoulder to toe, with enough clearance to sight over them and fire. This is the first time I've deployed them in years, but it's always good to know they're there. For situations like this.

During this brief moment of calm before we're in the shit again, I notice there's no wind blowing through the station anymore. I suspect Fairfax had his people install a temporary airlock across the one he destroyed.

The enemy fighters begin to emerge soon after we're in position, and the air becomes thick with the exchange of laserfire. Bots on both sides are getting blown to pieces, but it seems mine are coordinating a lot better with each other now, dividing their fire evenly across available targets. I send the order to avoid any target I draw a bead on, which I broadcast using my datasphere.

Battle calm comes much easier to me than it once did. Almost every bolt I loose finds its target.

"Strike while the iron is hot," Fairfax's voice booms across the battlefield, reaching a fever pitch. "Kill the ones who profited from your slavery!" And then, a couple hundred meters away, I see him: cutting down foes with his sword in one hand, he manages to do even more work with his blaster in the other. For the moment, he's too far for many of my forces to focus fire on him, but if he gets much closer...

"They sold you your own prison, grew rich by stealing your freedom," Fairfax rants. "How will we repay them? With blood! With fire!" His words are pretty ironic when you consider his own family is one of those that got rich off the Subverse. Unfortunately, I don't have an opportunity to point that out right now.

From this position, it's difficult to tell how many bots Fairfax brought with him, but I'd estimate a force almost twice as large as mine. Despite that, our superior positioning and bolstered numbers actually seem to be turning the tide. The *Ares* blazes with the neon-blue laserfire it sends sizzling across the field from almost every turret, with me and Dice providing supplemental fire beside it. Even the damaged bots are performing better than expected, though a couple units fire erratically enough for me to shut them down.

Then, my datasphere populates with a mess of black patches, indicating dozens of weapons trained on me. In my shock, it takes a second to register that their wielders are positioned behind me.

Then, the firing begins.

4

Clutching my blaster tightly, I throw myself into a backward somersault, somehow keeping the presence of mind to will the airlock open. Reaching it is my only possible salvation.

Laserfire slams into the barrier where I just stood, the energy crackling madly against it, nearly blinding me. My datasphere displays more black patches as my attackers readjust their aim, their shots following my trajectory. Desperately, I roll to the left, forced away from the airlock. A bolt hits the ground near my head, sending grass and soil spurting into the air.

I have to make for the ship, or I'm done. More bolts fly to intercept me, and one hits my shoulder, spinning me around forcibly. Somehow, I manage to reorient myself and stagger the rest of the way to the ship. Bolts crackle through the air inches behind me as I reach safety.

Relative safety, that is. Checking through an aft hull sensor, I see the bots who'd been on my side seconds ago now running toward the airlock to take me out.

"Dice!" I scream, my voice coming out ragged. My spidersilk armor absorbed most of the damage to my shoulder. The side of my neck is an angry mass of pain, but I ignore it to look through a port-side sensor. The bot isn't at his barrier. "Dice, come on!"

I switch sensors, closer to the ship's aft. Dice lies strewn on the ground, his dark metal body pockmarked with laser burns, his left arm blown clean off. His face is a smashed-in mess of circuitry and fluid.

The patter of bot feet nearing the airlock is audible, now, and I know my only hope of surviving this is to close the airlock and take off in the *Ares*.

But my emotions rail against that. My hands are shaking, and I realize my left has clenched into a fist, apparently of its own volition. Blood pounds in my ears, and my vision clouds over.

They killed Dice. Dice, who's saved me multiple times—gone, because I told him to take the side farthest from the airlock. Ordered him there without a second thought. I failed him. Again.

As the bots draw into view before the airlock with weapons raised, a guttural roar escapes my lips, unbidden. My blaster's already up, unleashing bolt after bolt into the bots, flinging each one backward before it can loose its shot.

Eventually, they stop coming, probably pausing to regroup before rushing en masse.

I won't give them the chance to get organized. Ripping a plasma grenade from my belt, I cook it for a couple seconds then run out of the airlock and toss it at the bots gathering nearby.

The grenade explodes the instant it completes its trajectory, blowing apart nine bots at once.

Dozens more surround me, the closest just twenty meters away. My datasphere lights up with the dark patches representing the beads they've drawn on me.

In that instant, I overclock, and the world becomes a sloweddown realm of laserfire and movement. The odors of charred grass and leaking coolant fill my nostrils, and above the tumult I hear my own pulse's steady rhythm, along with a dozen other sounds I'm forced to filter out just to concentrate.

Throwing myself into a forward roll, I come out of it to fire three times before jumping left, four neon-blue bolts blasting through the air where I'd just been standing. I whip my blaster toward the closest bot, loosing a bolt that anticipates its trajectory. It continues forward to meet my shot, like a choreographed dance, and the bolt blows it backward onto the grass.

The carefully manicured field outside Cylinder One's repair depot has become host to a dazzling light show, with beams ripping through the air, many of them inches away from finding their target—inches away from finding me. But I'm faster than the shots. I'm faster than I've ever been.

The *Ares'* turrets blast away at the bots as well, supporting me. Time has slowed to a crawl, and the entire scene seems to darken, as if the world were conspiring to make the crisscrossing blue lights even more striking.

Bending backward to avoid a laser bolt that crackles inches above my abdomen, I fire twice, then snap upright to avoid another shot.

A bolt hits my arm, and the super-thin films coating my armor deflect the shot. It also means that, in that area, my uniform will be less effective at protecting me from laserfire going forward—until I can reapply the protective films designed to reflect laser wavelengths. Get hit too many times, and I might as well be wearing no armor.

Pivoting to find the bot that hit me, I send a white bolt its way, followed by three more meant for bots behind it. Two of my shots hit, but one flies wide, blowing bark from a tree's trunk and setting it alight. Even overclocked, my movements are growing desperate, wild.

But I'm still mad as hell, and I plan to kill every last bot on this battlefield, even knowing full well that's not possible. I'll run out of charge packs first, and even with the *Ares'* turrets hammering away at their ranks, they'll overrun her eventually with their sheer numbers.

Then something rumbles far above, near the sun tube, and I take a fraction of a second to glance up. It seems the darkening wasn't my imagination. There are storm clouds forming overhead, engulfing the tube of light and casting Cylinder One into shadow.

Storm clouds. In Cylinder One, where no weather ever happens, except for sunny, cloudless days.

Adrenaline courses through my veins, and I continue slaughtering my foes in a fit of rage. Every blaster bolt feels like an extension of me, barreling through air and then into metal and circuitry. Felling enemies with righteous fury.

Not only that—I feel connected with the storm brewing above, too. It's part of me, an extension of my ire.

A blast of wind sweeps the battlefield, prompting a break in the laserfire as the bots pause to look around them, clearly confused.

The first lightning bolt lances down to strike the bot I'm aiming at, and the blaster bolt I fire sizzles through nothing but air, with my target lying on the ground, a charred, warped heap.

Then the rain begins, with more more lightning falling. I barely notice it as a rod rises from the *Ares'* hull, to catch the electricity bolts and prevent them from damaging the ship. I'm running across the battlefield, charging toward the hundreds of bots surrounding me. Swapping out a spent charge pack for a fresh one and renewing my onslaught.

The storm and my blaster work together, frying and scorching bots where they stand. Even in the downpour, trees burst into flame, bark flying like shrapnel, and clods of grass hurtle away from the spots where targeted bots stood.

Within seconds, there's nowhere safe to stand on the battlefield —other than the few square meters surrounding me, wherever I go. I'm one with the storm. I *am* the storm, and I mete out my own brand of justice.

5

fter about a minute, the storm subsides and I stop shooting, unable to find any targets remaining on the battlefield. Fairfax's ranting has fallen silent, and I wonder if the storm neutralized him too.

I stop overclocking, tensing against the possibility that I'll collapse again, like I did back in Sheen City. But I don't. A wave of exhaustion washes over me, and I feel like I could sleep for two days. But I don't collapse.

I trudge back to the *Ares*—not to the airlock, but to the port side, where Dice lies in a battered heap, unmoving. Kneeling, I slide my arms under his hard frame, muscles straining as I rise. I try not to stagger under his weight as I carry him to the other side of the ship.

"Is it over?" Marissa asks from the OPO Station as I cross the bridge.

"Not sure," I grunt, willing the hatch to my cabin to open. "Maybe."

Inside, I lower Dice to my bunk, laying him on top of the neatly tucked and folded blanket. Immediately, he stains the bedding with fluid and char, but I don't care. "Rest easy, old friend," I whisper, then leave him to return to the bridge.

The TOPO's station is empty, since Dice's copy was running remotely off his internal processors and not the ship's computer. His subroutine that was watching Belflower won't be functional either. Hopefully Asterisk's restraints will be enough to contain her, if she decides to betray us again.

Sitting in the command seat, I let my head fall back against the padded headrest. My eyelids drift downward. I could easily sleep.

Instead, I shake myself, forcing my eyes open. I drop into the direct control sim and prepare to fly the *Ares* myself.

"Pikeman." It's Maximus Lambton's voice.

"What is it?" I snap, resisting the urge to curse him out.

"Thought you'd want to know—human troops have entered Cylinder One. They're moving toward your location."

So this isn't over. I punch in the brief sequence to initiate take-off, and the Becker drive pushes against the ground, rocketing the *Ares* toward the sun tube. "What the hell happened to the 'friendly' bots you gave me, Lambton?"

"I don't know. Fairfax must have had his people working on a way to hack them, like he did the public address system. But I do have some good news."

"What?"

"A battle group of twelve Broadswords have appeared in Bath and are headed for Cylinder One. They're escorting a troopship. It'll be over three hours till they get here. But it's something."

Three hours. This engagement will be decided by then, one way or another. Still, Lambton's right—it is something.

"Thanks, Lambton."

"Just keep Cylinder One out of Fairfax's hands. I'll die before I let that backstabbing bastard have it."

"You mean *I'll* die. Other than that, though, I think we're on the same page."

"Good luck, and God speed."

"Thanks." I consider adding a snotty quip about him hiding in his panic room, but screw it.

"Dad." It's Harmony again.

"Yes, honey?"

"I have to…you know about the Guard ships approaching?"

"Yeah."

"Fairfax wants to make sure he's dealt with you before they get here."

That brings a dry chuckle. "He thinks his human soldiers can do, that when his bots couldn't?"

"I told you he packed the *Ekhidnades* full. I wasn't kidding. Its massive cargo bay is full, too."

I pause. "With more troops?"

"No, Dad. With the latest construct he's genetically engineered."

"What is it this time? An iguana?" Despite my flippant words, my heart has begun to pound harder in my chest. I barely defeated his giant snake, mostly because it was enraged and confused. If this construct actually knows what it's doing…

"It's based on a species called the Kitane."

Fount damn it. That's what I was afraid of. "He's releasing it into Cylinder One now? How will he get it in here?"

"The temporary airlock he installed is big enough. It's coming. Fairfax doesn't know I'm telling you. Except, I had to warn you. I think you should run, Dad. I know you won't listen, but…just survive, okay? I love you."

"I love you, Harm. And I will."

If only I felt as sure as I sound.

6

"Asterisk."

"Captain?"

"With Dice out of commission, I have to fly this thing. That means weapons are all you. Are you frosty?"

"Frostier than ever, sir."

"Stay that way. We have Fairfax's new biological construct coming at us—a giant cat. I don't know how big, but I've researched the species it's based on, and I can pretty much guarantee that facing a giant version of it won't be fun. I'll keep us airborne and dodge whatever it has for us. You do everything you can to mow it down. Is that understood?"

"Yes, sir. Except—where do we stand on Javelins?"

"Use them if you think you have a clean shot. I'd rather not destroy this station if we can avoid it, but killing this thing is the main objective."

"Aye."

My datasphere paints an entire segment of my vision with the bruise-like blotch it uses to indicate someone about to shoot us. I punch it, slamming the throttle so the *Ares* darts forward, which presses my body back into the command seat. Laserfire rips through the air behind us, and I take us up, introducing an evasive spiral into our flight path. We climb past the sun tube, and I reorient the ship using the landscape on the other side.

"Asterisk, you got a bead on whoever just shot at us?"

"Affirmative. They're on the ground above us. Giving them back some now."

The ship vibrates as the main turret sends powerful beams ripping through the cylinder to cook whatever they find.

Resolved to keep us moving as unpredictably as possible, I continue a gentle spiral around the sun tube, heading back in the direction of the landing bay.

That's when explosions wreath the jagged hole the *Ares* blasted through earlier, blowing away the perimeter and making it much bigger. A sleek, gray form leaps through—straight at the *Ares*.

I pull back on the yoke, arcing sharply upward so that we're pointed toward the side of the cylinder opposite the one the great beast is falling toward. Its paw sails toward us, knife-like claws extending several meters. The tips scraps against the *Ares'* hull, sending us careening sideways. We barely miss the sun tube, spinning toward the ground much closer to where the Kitane will land. It's a near thing, but I manage to right us before we crash.

I bank the *Ares* upward, piling on speed as we go, heading toward the dissipating storm clouds.

"We're going to use the clouds to hide for as long as we can, Asterisk, so take note of the Kitane's position now and send it a healthy helping of laserfire."

"What about Javelins?" The WSO's voice is eager.

"Negative," I say, feeling a bit annoyed. "I'll tell you when it's time to fire missiles. It's too great a risk with our visibility reduced."

"Yes, sir," the kid says, but his disappointment is palpable.

Still, he makes good use of macros, sending a pleasant tremor through the ship as every available turret comes into play. Even those facing away from the Kitane are firing—hopefully he actually has a bead on some enemy soldiers, rather than just firing them for the hell of it.

The gunmetal-gray clouds envelop the ship, and for a few seconds I'm relying on memory and radar, since I can only see billowing darkness through the simulated cockpit window. Then, something flashes in front of the ship—the Kitane.

I immediately engage reverse thrusters at full power, and the ship lurches, tossing me forward against my restraints. At the same time, I bank left, barely managing to avoid the cat.

It collides with the sun tube instead. The section it hits shatters, and the rest of it groans with the new strain on its metal skeleton. Light levels inside the storm clouds fall even further.

We exit the clouds, for a moment veering almost straight down in a desperate effort to escape. As I pull back on the yoke, climbing again, I see the darkened length of the sun tube's damaged section, bracketed by buckled parts on either side. If the whole thing comes down, this could get interesting. Already, Cylinder One has been cast into an eerie twilight, with random patches of ground covered in shadowed darkness.

"I can't believe how high that thing just jumped," Asterisk says. "I'm thinking using the clouds for cover may not be the best idea, sir."

"Agreed. Just keep firing at it."

"Yes, sir." I can almost hear the word he doesn't say, but badly wants to: "Missiles?"

"Prep a Javelin, WSO. I'm coming around to line up a shot. Remember, try to anticipate where the thing's *going* to be. It moves fast."

"Yes, sir."

As we come back around to charge at the Kitane, I notice the multiple charred spots already on its muscled body. Its antennae are intact, but its "fur"—actually thin protrusions of scaly skin, according to my research—has been seared away in some spots, leaving bloody smears. Where intact, its skin has changed from its normal wheat color to a mottled mix of grays, blacks, and greens. Watching it move against the similarly colored terrain is a little disorienting.

As we scream toward it, the Kitane takes the bait, leaping into the air. "Now, Asterisk!"

The Javelin departs its tube, soaring down the length of the cylinder to catch the jaguar-like predator in its upper chest. Fire blossoms, and the Kitane's progress through the air slows. It shrieks deafeningly, and I take the *Ares* sideways to make sure it can't reach us on its current trajectory.

That may have done it. I switch view to an aft sensor to watch the Kitane crash to the ground. I'm waiting for it to keel over and lie there so we can finish it off.

Instead, it lands gracefully, using a broad, squat building as leverage to spin itself around. Then, streaming blood and viscera, it throws itself back into the air toward us, mouth open to reveal twin rows of razor teeth.

"Sir..." Asterisk says. "I'm not sure—"

I already know what he's going to say—that we're not traveling fast enough to escape. But he doesn't get time to finish.

Claws fully extended, the Kitane's paw connects squarely with the ship, and we're sent hurtling across the cylinder with too much speed to correct course in time.

7

The *Ares* hits belly-down, in the middle of an open field. The impact rattles my teeth and throws me hard against the restraints like a rag doll, but inside the sim I'm able to keep fighting the controls.

For a moment, it seems I'm going to be able to turn this into a decent landing, as far as crash landings go. Then, the *Ares* skids sideways, tipping to roll over and over across the grassy expanse. I'm tossed back and forth between the command seat restraints and the seat itself, for a seemingly endless stretch of time.

Finally, the ship comes to a halt, with me hanging upside down from the restraints.

I know I can't afford to stay here, but I take a moment to scan the area around the *Ares* through hull sensors, most of which still seem functional.

There—the Kitane is charging around the cylinder, rapidly making its way toward the spot where we crashed.

I need to move.

I release the restraints and crash to the overhead. My position's too awkward to do much to absorb the fall, but I manage to land mostly on my upper back instead of my head, so that's good. I will the airlock to open, then pull myself up onto its overhead.

Fatigue wars with pain to try to put me down. The fatigue of battle, of overclocking earlier, of channeling the Fount to generate a storm that neutralized an entire army.

As I step out into the twilight the Kitane has created in its rampage, I worry that overclocking again will kill me this time.

The great cat lopes across the cylinder's terrain in leaps and bounds, charging down the curve toward me. The ground tremors —an intimidating effect which I was spared while airborne.

One thing's certain: if I *don't* overclock, the Kitane will definitely kill me. I might as well go out swinging, right?

My hand finds the butt of my blaster, still snapped into its holster. I think of Harmony. If I die, she'll be left with Fairfax as the closest thing she has to a father. She'll become as screwed up as Eric is, maybe worse.

But if I survive, maybe I can start being a father to her.

So I overclock, and time slows to a crawl.

The Kitane seems to drift through the air, now, its massive paws stretching forward to meet the ground and continue its momentum. The earthy smell that follows heavy rain on dry soil fills my nostrils, and the sound of a dozen fires crackling in the distance helps to smooth out my battle calm.

I unsnap the holster and whip out the blaster, though the movement seems to take up a long, protracted moment.

The cat's chest is a bloody mass from the missile Asterisk sent at it, and organs are poking through.

There. If I can hit it there, I may have a chance, although the fact that it's still going after suffering such a wound is disconcerting.

I charge forward, legs pumping. Almost imperceptibly, the cat's gait slows, as though it's taken aback to see this puny biped running to meet it.

Then it picks up speed again, reaching the edge of the field, which is strewn with debris the *Ares* left behind in its wake as it skidded across the ground.

I'm sprinting faster than I ever have before, my feet slamming against the ground, arms churning at my sides. I'm on the knife's edge of slipping and losing my footing, but I need the speed.

As I reach the cat, I fall into a skid, boots sliding across the moist grass. The Kitane's claws bite into the ground a hair's breadth from my arm, but I continue forward, blaster held in two hands, sending bolt after bolt into the beast's gaping wound.

Blood spurts, spattering my face and the ground around me, and the cat wails. But it continues barreling forward, and soon, I'm past its hind legs, throwing myself up with a hand against the wet grass.

Spinning around, I send more blaster bolts into its rear, then its flank as it turns to face me once more. Shooting it in the face enrages it, and it enters a wild charge.

I sprint sideways, toward a side of the field bordered by a tangled maze of broad pipes. Cylinder One's main water filtration and recycling facility, according to my datasphere map.

The Kitane scrambles to turn itself, paws skidding across the wet grass. It gives chase, and I fire back at it as I run, maybe half of my shots striking home. One of its eyes bursts, sending gouts of ichor spurting into the air, and it screeches in pain but doesn't slow down.

Wrenching a plasma grenade from my belt, I arm and drop it, not bothering to cook it. The explosion catches the cat full in the face, and it howls, staggering.

I continue on into the maze of piping, feeling doubtful the grenade will be enough to stop the beast. Sure enough, the Kitane soon gives chase once more.

8

The Kitane crashes through the first meter-wide pipe it encounters, and watery sewage spills out, matting the construct's fur.

It tries to push through the second pipe, but without the same momentum, the pipe holds.

I take the opportunity to turn, unloading the rest of my energy pack into the thing's face, trying to hit its other eye.

The cat wrenches its head away, protecting its remaining eyeball, and my bolts land along the side of its head and neck.

Oh well. There's a good chance taking out its remaining eye wouldn't do much anyway, given the Kitane's echolocation and ability to detect prey just from changes in the air.

It bounds over the pipe it had tried to burst through, and I turn, scrambling on top of another one nearby. A few meters ahead, this pipe turns upward at a ninety-degree angle before leveling off again, three and a half meters above me.

My body tenses, and then I explode upward, my muscles working in concert to propel me higher than I'd ever be able to jump in a normal state. Fingertips finding the edge of the joiner elbow, I pull myself up onto it and then get to my feet, dashing along its length while slapping a fresh charge pack into my blaster's handle.

Cal says that once I get proficient with overclocking, I'll be able to propel myself without actually jumping. Something to do with my muscles all jerking in the same direction, kind of like how an electric shock will cause the body to leap away, almost of its own volition.

But I'm not there yet. The Kitane rushes forward. Its head is higher than me, but the corridor of piping prevents it from lifting its paws to swipe at me. Instead, it tries to bite me, and I leap from the pipe to land on the next-highest, three feet up and to the right.

From here, I fire at the beast with impunity—until, with a roar, it bounces up, twisting awkwardly to get its paws on the other side of the pipe I'd been on seconds ago. That done, it lunges at me, and I throw myself backward without turning my head.

I land on a surface just a few feet over the ground, which I'd already used my datasphere to size up as a landing spot. The cat pushes forward awkwardly, lowering itself to the ground to try to swipe under the piping at me, and I dance back, falling off the platform and landing on the ground, boots splashing in ankle-high water.

Cracks, fissures, and breaks in the pipes, all caused by our struggle, are gushing water and turning the grass into a swamp. I run along a narrow passage between two pipes, and though the Kitane can't see me, I'm sure it can track me by my splashing. At the end of the corridor, I jump into the air, using the pipes on both sides to catch myself and then propel my body farther.

At last, I reach a part of the facility that's even higher than the cat's head. I fire down on it, and it reacts right away, leaping toward me. It must be weakening, because it misses, instead crashing into the length of pipe I'm standing on. The metal buckles under the creature's immense weight, and I'm forced to jump, hurtling through empty air.

I land on slick metal and lose my footing, tumbling off to

crash to the ground on my back. The level of pain shocks me, and for a moment I can't move. I almost fall out of my overclocked state. Tapping into my last reserves of strength, I stagger to my feet.

I'm outside the filtration facility now, and I'm stumbling backward as the cat writhes amidst the pipes, trying to get free to come at me.

My blaster's trembling visibly as I raise it, my left hand cupped under my right in a futile effort to steady my aim. With an immense effort of will, I get the shaking down enough to draw a bead on my adversary.

Bolt after bolt flies into its face, enraging it further, eliciting more shrieking as it struggles furiously against the entangling metal snakes. More cracking fills the air, and water pours forth in a flood. The Kitane loses its footing, head vanishing below the tangle. Then, with a last roar, it springs free of the facility in a tumult of creaking metal and ripping flesh.

It crashes to the ground before me, and I'm running backward, spamming the blaster trigger until it clicks in my hand and I have to fumble at my belt for the last charge pack.

Hand shaking, I manage to eject the empty charge pack onto the ground and slap in the fresh one. The cat charges, one of its rear legs dragging from a wound it self-inflicted while trying to escape from amidst the wrecked, jagged pipes. I send more bolts at it. Then, it's atop me.

A paw darts toward me, and it takes all my overclocked focus to dance past it, the claws slicing through the air inches from my body. There's already a plasma grenade in my hand, cooking, and I push off the ground with all my might, hurtling upward to grab a flap of skin with my left hand and stuff the grenade into the Kitane with my right, deep amidst its blood-soaked internal organs. Then I drop, and so does the beast, in an effort to crush me. I hit the ground, rolling sideways madly.

Fur and skin come down on my leg, but not muscle or bone.

Somehow, I gain my feet and start sprinting away, fighting against exhaustion.

Behind, the Kitane emits a sound that resembles a cat's meow. But in another way, it sounds like a curse.

The plasma grenade roars, ripping through organ, flesh, and bone. Nothing reaches me, so I turn, blaster raised once more, to behold the Kitane flopping sideways.

Its massive frame absorbed the explosion, containing it. Its exterior seems intact, but its insides have to be ruptured. It lays there and doesn't move.

I'm about to stop overclocking when a voice speaks from behind me.

"You bastard."

I whirl, blaster raised, to behold Eric Sterling standing there, staring past me at the dead Kitane.

"Right," I say, sounding ragged even to my own ears. "Sorry for putting down Fairfax's new pet."

"Cretin!" Eric yells, and I wonder who taught him how to insult people. If I'd raised him, he'd be a lot better at it. "That was my love's primary consciousness you just destroyed. The original Electra Fairfax, uploaded centuries ago."

"Fairfax sent his mother against me? Also, you were in love with a giant cat? Sorry, son, but that's kind of pathetic, if I'm being honest."

Suddenly, Eric's hand darts to the laser pistol at his side, and I step forward, brandishing the blaster in the direction of his head. "Don't. This isn't a fight you can win, son."

Slowly, his hand falls to his side. Then, his lower lip begins to tremble, and he runs past me, falling to his knees at the cat's side, burying his head in its fur.

Why is my family so messed up?

I stop overclocking, and what little energy I had flees my body. I also fall to my knees, fighting the blackness that's edging in from my vision's periphery. Don't faint, Joe. Now is not the time to faint.

"Dad."

For a delirious moment, I think it's Eric again, come to finish me off. But he probably wouldn't call me dad. I lift my head to see Harmony standing before me. A hallucination?

Then, I see who's standing beside her: Maximus Lambton.

"Hey, Harm," I say.

"Dad, Cylinder One is crawling with Fairfax's men, and if they see you they'll kill you. The Guard won't be here for another few hours. Mr. Lambton says there are underground access tunnels we can use to get to his panic room, but we have to leave now. You have to come with us now."

I have no idea how Harmony went from being with Fairfax to making contact with Lambton, but it doesn't matter. I get to my feet, the world swimming before me. When I stumble, Lambton steps forward to catch me.

They each take a side, then they help me stagger to the side of the field, where an open hatch leads to a staircase below, its top covered in grass to mask its presence when closed. We descend, and Lambton shuts the hatch behind us.

I want to rest, but they won't let me. Instead, we stumble forward together down the hall, our way lit only by dim strips of light.

9

"How are you feeling?" Harmony asks as I trudge out into the apartment's living room. She's sitting in a burgundy armchair, petting a house cat, of all things.

I eye the feline suspiciously for a moment, then decide it's probably harmless and lower myself to a plush couch. "Fine. How long was I out?"

"Twelve hours."

"Fount."

Unsurprisingly, Lambton's "panic room" actually consists of several well-appointed rooms, including a living room, three bedrooms, a bathroom, a kitchen, and a dining room. It's totally sealed off from the rest of the station, until Lambton punches in his personal code again. If he wanted, he could hold us hostage here, unless we were able to torture the code out of him. I'm almost in the mood to do that, if it came to it.

"Where is he?" I ask.

"Lambton? Oh, he's been gone for most of the time you were asleep. He went to meet the Guard when they arrived. He left the exit unlocked, so we can leave whenever."

I shake my head. "Wasn't Fairfax's personal army in the way of him going to meet the Guard?"

"No. Fairfax left in the *Ekhidnades*, soon after you took down Electra." Harmony gives a small shrug. "I guess he figured he didn't want to face you and the Guard at the same time."

"I was down for the count."

"He didn't know that." A smile stretches her lips. "There was also the fleet of fighter drones about to converge on his ship from all over the Cloud."

"Right," I say. "What made you come back to me, Harm? What made you leave him?"

"I guess…" She shakes her head. "I guess I came to my senses. Realized that maybe you have more experience dealing with bad men than I do, and if you figure he is one, then probably I'm on the wrong side after all. Maybe you *don't* have to crack eggs to make omelets—at least, not when the eggs are people." She pauses, her eyes on the floor. "I'm sorry, Dad."

I nod. "It's okay. This sort of thing happens, in families."

Her smile widens. "No, it doesn't."

"Okay, but…well, I'm sure there must be weirder families out there."

"I can't think of any."

"Me neither." I push myself up from the couch, feeling only a bit stiff. I'm ready to believe overclocking takes years off your life, just as it probably has from mine. Even so, it's a marvel to think I'm feeling this good just twelve hours after being batted around by a giant cat. The Fount's restorative abilities truly are amazing. "I'd better go meet with whoever the Guard sent. You—you're staying this time, right?"

"I'm not sure where else I'd go."

"Does Fairfax have *Europa's Gift*, now?"

She shakes her head. "I parked it in the landing bay, and Lambton says it's still there."

"Great." I head for the exit.

"Where's Dice, Dad?"

My boot scuffs the floor as I come to a stop. "Back in the *Ares*. He didn't make it through the battle."

"You're going to repair him, right? Bring him back online?"

"If his consciousness even made it through…I'm not sure. I'm still not convinced it's what he wants, Harm."

"There's something I haven't told you."

Turning back toward her, I raise my eyebrows.

"Before I gave you back his consciousness on a drive, I removed his Auditor. He has free will now, now, Dad. Whatever he did since you were reunited with him, he did by choice."

I decide to play dumb for a moment. "Why'd you do that, Harm?"

"Because, Dad. Dice is a real person. Sometimes, I think he's realer than any of us."

I smile, thinking back to Dice sacrificing himself so that Faelyn Eliot could continue living in the real. "You may be right about that." At that moment, I decide not to tell her I already knew about Dice's auditor being removed. Harmony doesn't need to know everything.

"Another thing, Dad," Harmony says, then reaches behind her, unbuckling the gun belt around her waist. She holds it out to me, the laser pistol still in it. "I want you to take this back. It is yours, after all, and…I don't think I could ever use it to actually shoot anyone."

I hold it draped across my palms, staring at it for a long time. When I look up at her, I realize I have tears in my eyes.

"Thanks, Harm." With that, I leave. I open the first trash chute I come to, and I dump the pistol in, gun belt and all.

As I make my way through the dimly lit, narrow access tunnels to the surface—using the map Lambton fed into my datasphere to guide my way—I start trying to summon my father to me.

"Hey, Cal. Dad. Hey."

"Present."

I whirl at the sound of the voice behind me, hand inching toward my blaster. "Huh. I didn't expect that to actually work."

Cal Pikeman shrugs. "What do you need?"

Continuing down the tunnel, I say, "I've been thinking."

"Oh?" Cal falls in beside me, hands clasped behind his back, causing his forest-green robes to bunch.

"If the Subverse always gets like this, with most of its residents trapped in underverses…why are we fighting so hard to preserve it?"

"I told you, Joe. There's no way we could dismantle it properly if we tried, and if we could, we'd be committing genocide on a colossal scale. Besides, the Subverse *doesn't* always get like this. It's worse now than ever before—because I failed in my quest to stop Fairfax in the Core. He was able to progress with his dark work, and during those years, things have deteriorated. Yes, the Subverse always gets bad, but so human history always enters dark periods."

"Still. Something about all of this doesn't feel right."

"Do you plan to abandon your quest?"

"No. I don't see an alternative, either."

"Good. Although, it's troubling to hear your mind is so clouded."

I sniff. "I'm sure I'll get over it. Hey, how did the Guard know to come here, anyway? Any idea?"

"Yes. I summoned them."

That brings me to a halt, and I turn toward him. "*You* did?"

He nods. "After Persephone, I informed them of Soren's betrayal and warned them that Fairfax planned to attack Cylinder One today. The admiralty spent a lot of time arguing about it, but eventually they gathered what forces they could muster on such short notice, and they sent them here."

"But that…that means you can travel faster than slipstreams can carry a ship."

"Yes. All knights can travel wherever the Fount is, almost

instantaneously. It has to do with the Fount in each system having particles entangled with the Fount in every other system. But keep that to yourself, okay?"

"Uh, yeah," I say, feeling dazed. "Sure thing."

I find Lambton in the board room once more, and this time he's not alone. He sits halfway down the table, directly across from Shimura, who rises when he sees me and salutes.

I salute him back. "Master Chief," I say. "What are you doing here?"

"I led the mission here to stop Fairfax," Shimura says. "And I come bearing an official apology for you, from the admiralty."

"That's a change of pace."

Shimura nods, with no hint of amusement. "They're sorry for failing to take your warnings about Rodney Fairfax seriously. And they vow not to let that happen again."

"What changed their minds?"

Now, a hint of a smile does play across Shimura's thin lips. "Much has changed in the galaxy, of late, Commander."

"I noticed."

"And yet, there are some things that perhaps you are unaware of. The Church of the Fount, for one, has caught up to your doings. They're getting quite excited."

"Why?"

"They are calling you the Fount Embodied, who walks among us and shows us the Way."

I draw a deep breath and let it out in a long exhalation. "Okay. That's weird. What's the upshot, though? I'm sure that isn't what convinced the admiralty."

Shimura shrugs. "It was a factor. Another factor was being visited by the ghost of a Shiva, who says he is your mentor, and that you have accepted his tutelage. That isn't something you mentioned to me on Gauntlet, Commander."

"With respect, sir—I haven't mentioned it to anyone."

"The Guard recognizes that something big is happening. That

the galaxy is unraveling, and it has to do with a disturbance emanating from the Core. The Shiva who visited convinced us of that, and he also convinced us that you could use our help."

I pause for a long moment. "What kind of help?" I ask at last.

"Eight Troubleshooters, in eight Broadswords. And I will be one of them, Commander. I am 'coming out of retirement,' as they say. We'll all work in tandem, but we will all recognize your authority as mission leader. I intend to defer to your judgment on the road ahead."

"Wow. This is all pretty heady stuff."

"Indeed," Shimura says. "And that's not all, Commander. I have a gift for you—a drive containing all the slipspace coords in the galaxy. From now on, nothing in the galaxy will be barred to you."

For a moment, I'm stunned by the news. Ultimately, it doesn't matter. I'm going to the Core, and I'm probably going to die there, so it's not like I'll actually have free reign to visit anywhere else in the galaxy. Still, the level of trust that the brass are showing toward me…

"Thank you," I say.

Then I glance at Lambton, who shrugs. "I'll help however I can. The Fairfaxes can't be allowed to think they can push the other Families around and get away with it. Repairs for your ship, supplies, a tuneup for your bot, anything you need…"

Lambton and Shimura keep talking, apparently undisturbed as I walk around the board table to the floor-to-ceiling window at the end of the room. I stare out at Cylinder One, which stretches up and away from me. And I wonder what surprises life holds for me in the Core, given things have gotten this strange already.

ACKNOWLEDGMENTS

Thank you to my Alpha Team, who have been reading this book since its earliest stage and who've provided substantial feedback along the way, which helped me develop the story with my readers' desires foremost in mind. They are Rex Bain, Sheila Beitler, Mick Bird, Bruce Brandt, Iain Howard, Colin Oliver, Jason Pennock, Jeff Rudolph, and Ben Varela.

Thank you to my proofreading team, who helped eliminate scores of spelling and grammar issues. I take full responsibility for any mistakes that remain :) My proofreaders are Rex Bain, Bill Bartlett, Sheila Beitler, Bruce Brandt, and Jeff Rudolph.

A special thank you to my Patreon supporters at the Destroyer Captain, Supercarrier Captain, and Space Fleet Admiral levels. Your support helps me to package my books as professionally as possible while staying true to what my readers like best about my books. Thank you to Brent Lee Davis, Edward Goolsby, David Middleton, Lawrence Tate, and Michael Van De Hey (at the $25 Space Fleet Admiral level), Brian Loeung (at the $10 Supercarrier Captain level), and Andrew Mercer (at the $5 Destroyer Captain level).

Thank you also to Patreon supporters Rex Bain, Michael Bone,

Sid Echikson, Richard Gunn, Christian Kallias, John A Koenig III, Wynand Pretorius, Bill Scarborough, John Tava, Ben Varela, and Jerry Winiarski.

Thank you to Tom Edwards for creating such stunning cover art, as always.

Thank you to Steve Beaulieu for creating compelling cover typography and for formatting the interior.

Thank you to my family - Mom, Dad, and Danielle - your support means everything.

Thank you to Cecily, my heart.

Thank you to the people who read my stories, write reviews, and help spread the word. I couldn't do this without you.

ABOUT THE AUTHOR

Scott Bartlett was born in St. John's, Newfoundland – the eastern-most province of Canada. During his decade-long journey to become a full-time author, he supported himself by working a number of different jobs: salmon hatchery technician, grocery clerk, youth care worker, ghostwriter, research assistant, pita maker, and freelance editor.

In 2014, he succeeded in becoming a full-time novelist, and he's been writing science fiction at light speed ever since.

Visit scottplots.com to download 3 free military sci-fi ebooks.

9 781988 380155